A Love to Call Mine

Front Porch Promises

Book 3

I0652842

Merrillee Whren

Merrillee Whren
www.merrilleewhren.com

Publisher's Note: This is a work of fiction. Names, characters, places, and incidents are a product of the author's imagination. Locales and public names are sometimes used for atmospheric purposes. Any resemblance to actual people, living or dead, or to businesses, companies, events, institutions, or locales is completely coincidental.

[Scripture quotations are from] THE HOLY BIBLE, NEW INTERNATIONAL VERSION®, NIV® Copyright © 1973, 1978, 1984, 2011 by Biblica, Inc.® Used by permission. All rights reserved worldwide.

Book Layout © 2014
BookDesignTemplates.com

A Love to Call Mine/Merrillee Whren -- 1st ed.
ISBN   978-1-944773-01-4

This book is dedicated to friends and family who have battled cancer.

My help comes from the Lord, the Maker of heaven and earth.

— Psalm 121:2 NIV

CHAPTER ONE

"**D**o I have a terrible disease?" The words tumbled from Max Reynolds's mouth as he sat alone in the exam room and stared at the pale-yellow walls. Even the supposedly cheerful color failed to cheer him today. Instead, the hue sent up a caution signal. What would the doctor have to say?

Bad news?

It had to be bad, or the office coordinator wouldn't have called him to come in immediately after the doctor received the results of Max's recent medical tests.

For months he'd been dealing with a series of maladies, including rashes, night sweats, and a cough. All previous appointments with doctors had resulted in a diagnosis followed by a prescription that cleared up each problem temporarily. He hadn't been concerned until he'd unexpectedly lost ten pounds in the last two months and a painful cough had reoccurred.

This time—no prescription, only tests followed by an urgent phone call. He took a deep breath, then let it out in a harsh rush of air. He hated the uncertainty. He hated the vulnerability. Most of all, he hated the waiting. Why were they making him wait when they had insisted he come in right away?

Maybe he should leave. He'd been to enough

doctors—doctors who had done little for him. Why should this doctor be any different? Max stood, but as he took a step, he heard a muffled conversation outside the door. He returned to his seat as the doctor walked into the room, a stethoscope dangling around his neck.

Dr. Vargas immediately pulled up a chair and sat facing Max. "I have bad news. Your test results show that you have lymphoma. Hodgkin lymphoma."

The word lymphoma sliced through Max's mind. He couldn't speak while a sinking sensation filled his gut. He swallowed hard.

Cancer.

How could he have cancer? At twenty-seven, he was too young...but that wasn't true. Cancer was no respecter of age. He'd spent the last four years working in labs and looking at other people's cancer cells through a microscope—people of all ages and occupations. Cancer could change a person's life in an instant.

His moment had come.

The young physician's face blurred. His black hair seemed to float above his head like a wig. Max tried to focus, but everything remained distorted as the doctor talked. Max heard "cancer" again, but everything else buzzed in his head like static on a radio dial.

"I'm not an oncologist, but I'll get you an appointment with one. We'll do whatever it takes to fight this thing." The doctor's last sentence penetrated

Max's foggy mind.

Max nodded, still unable to speak. His mouth felt as though he'd poked it full of the cotton balls that sat in a jar on the nearby counter.

"I know it must be a shock to learn of this diagnosis, but like I said, we'll get you through this." His dark eyes filled with concern, Dr. Vargas touched Max's arm. "Max, do you understand what I've told you?"

Max shook his head as much to clear it as to answer the doctor's question. "I'm a research scientist in the oncology field. I know about cancer, but I'm not familiar with all therapies."

"Where do you work?"

Max swallowed another lump in his throat. "I work in the cancer research department of Oakton General Hospital in conjunction with their clinical trials."

"Then you aren't a complete stranger to the process that goes with cancer treatments."

"I don't know much about lymphoma."

"Let's get you an appointment with someone who's an expert." Dr. Vargas stood. "Come with me to my office."

Max followed the doctor down a hallway with doors on either side, until they reached the one at the end of the hall. Dr. Vargas opened it and motioned for Max to take the chair next to the desk. The doctor used his desk phone to make the call.

With a hand to his forehead, Max slouched in the chair. He'd only moved to Massachusetts a few months ago. All his previous appointments had been with doctors in Montana or Washington. Most of his time in Massachusetts had been spent at work, and he'd made few attempts to forge friendships in his new location. He rented a studio apartment in a house not too far from work so he could walk. On a couple of occasions he'd gone out to eat with some of his coworkers, but most of them had families—spouses and kids. He didn't have much in common with them except work.

Alone. That's what he was. Here alone to face this terrible disease.

His mother and his adopted father lived clear across the country near Spokane, Washington. Another problem. How was he going to break the news to his mom? How would she take it? Bad news shouldn't have to come over the phone, but there was no other way.

"You've got an appointment on Monday with Dr. Joseph Duffey, who is a lymphoma specialist." Dr. Vargas pushed a card across the desk. "Here's his information—time of the appointment and address of the clinic."

The doctor's statement shook Max from his troubling thoughts. "Thanks. I appreciate finding out what's actually wrong with me."

Dr. Vargas nodded. "I'll monitor your progress through Dr. Duffey's office. I know you can beat this."

Trying to smile, Max stood despite the great

weight that seemed to press down on him. He shook the physician's hand. "I hope you're right."

"I have great confidence in Dr. Duffey. He's an excellent doctor."

"Good to know." Max turned toward the door but stopped before he went out. "Thanks again."

Shrugging into his jacket, Max rushed out of the office as if he could distance himself from the disturbing diagnosis. Once outside, he stopped and closed his eyes, wanting it to be a bad dream. But making impossible wishes wasn't going to change the truth of his circumstances.

When he opened his eyes, he glimpsed his reflection in the window of the nearby building. He stared at it for a moment.

A healthy-looking young man gazed back at him, but the image lied.

He ran a hand through his hair. He'd been intending to get it cut. The treatment for his cancer would mean the loss of his hair. No need to worry about a haircut now.

What would become of his reason for moving to Massachusetts? He'd come here to find his father's family—the father he'd never known. Would the treatments render him too tired to pursue that goal? He hoped not.

As he walked toward his car, Max tried to take a deep breath, but the pressure in his chest didn't subside. Half of this attitude was probably psychological. He hadn't come into the doctor's office with that feeling. Worry, yes. A depressing burden, no.

Now he had both.

***

"Hey, Heather, hubby and I are going out to dinner on Friday. How would you like to double with us? I can fix you up with the guy that works with my husband. I know he'd be perfect for you." Emma Butler joined Heather Watson at the table in their favorite fast-food lunch spot.

Heather grimaced as she picked up her sandwich and took a bite, hoping to avoid talking about her friend's insistence on setting up blind dates.

"Well, what do you say?" Emma's blue eyes brimmed with expectation.

Heather frowned at Emma. "Will you quit trying to find dates for me? So far you've convinced me to go out with your mechanic, your hairdresser's brother, and the guy who lives down the street. None of them were perfect for me."

"But this guy's different." Emma bobbed her head, her shoulder-length blond hair swishing around her shoulders.

Heather shook her head. "I think that's what you said when you fixed me up with your neighbor, and you know how that worked out."

Emma grinned sheepishly. "Yeah. That was a mistake. I didn't know he was such a jerk."

"I'd say a big jerk." Heather reached into her purse and rummaged through it until she held up a piece of paper in triumph. "Just for you. This might help you avoid future mistakes."

"What's this?" Emma took the paper and studied it, then looked up at Heather. "You can't be serious."

"I'm very serious."

Emma waved the paper in the air. "A list of qualifications for the perfect man? You'll never find him."

"Good. Then maybe you'll quit trying to fix me up." Heather took another bite of her sandwich.

"This piece of paper isn't going to stop me from trying to find you a man."

"And why would I need one of those?"

"Because I want you to be as happy as Ryan and me."

"Did you ever think I might be happy just the way I am? Single."

Emma blew out a harsh breath and frowned. "Haven't you ever heard the expression, 'two is better than one'?"

"Debatable, but if you happen to find someone who meets all the qualifications on my list, I'll be happy to meet him."

Why did all of her coworkers insist on trying to find her dates? Did she look desperate? Did they feel sorry for her because she sat home alone on Saturday nights watching rented movies and eating microwave popcorn?

Emma finished the last of her fries, then grinned. "I'll be sure to work on it. You've given me a challenge I can't resist."

Heather refused to comment. Her efforts to change Emma's mind were a failure. Head down, Heather decided she should eat and say nothing.

"Over six feet tall?"

Heather glanced up. "Yeah, since I'm five feet ten, I'd like for the guy to be at least a couple of inches taller than me."

"Dark-brown eyes and hair?"

"Yeah. What about it?" Heather wrinkled her brow.

Emma continued to study the paper. "Interesting that you're looking for a guy with the same color eyes and hair as you."

"Quit reading the list." Heather wadded up the wrapper that had come on her sandwich and dumped it on the tray with the discarded napkins and paper cup.

"You gave it to me, and I want to know exactly what I'm looking for."

"As you said, you'll never find him, so why bother?" Heather stood and grabbed her jacket from the back of the chair. "We'd better get back to work. Lots of patients to see this afternoon."

"Trying to avoid discussing your list?" Emma gathered her things and followed Heather to the trash bin by the door.

"I am. I wish I'd never shown it to you. So let's drop it."

"Okay." Emma pushed open the door and patted her purse. "I won't talk about it now, but I've got it right here for reference."

Heather squinted against the sun and wished again that she'd never mentioned the list. She hurried down the sidewalk as if walking fast could put some distance between her and that silly thing. Time for a change of subject. "I've got a challenge for you."

"And that is…" Emma looked at Heather expectantly.

"Join me in training for the Pan-Massachusetts Challenge. Come be part of our team."

Emma wrinkled her brow. "How do you expect me to join the team when you've been training for weeks and I haven't?"

"You could always ride in the car on the first day and join us on your bike during the last day. We have a fun time, especially on Saturday evening when we're camping out."

"Camping? Not for me." Emma shook her head. "Besides, what good would my being part of the team do?"

"You'd be raising money for cancer research."

Emma slowed her pace. "Even if I don't do the whole ride?"

"Yeah. I'd love to have you on the team. We're all riding to support Hailey, our Pedal Partner." The image of the cute little seven-year-old popped into Heather's mind. "And many of us are riding in memory of someone we've lost to cancer."

Emma sighed. "I do want to support Hailey. She's the sweetest little girl and a real inspiration—always happy, even when you know she's hurting."

"And you can reach a circle of family and friends that the rest of us can't. That's what's so great about our team. Our outreach is tremendous. I have family and friends in Montana, and you have family and friends in Ohio and Indiana."

"You're right, but I'll have to think about it." Emma skewed up her face. "After all, I'm not very athletic, and you are. But maybe all that bicycling will take off some of these extra pounds."

Heather didn't want to make Emma feel bad by agreeing with her about the extra weight she carried. What could she say that wouldn't hurt her friend's feelings? "Why don't you recruit Ryan for the team, too? Then we can all get fit together."

Emma appeared thoughtful, then smiled as they reached the clinic. "You've almost convinced me. I'll talk to Ryan tonight."

"Fantastic." Heather held open the door for Emma as they went inside. "I want to surpass the amount of money we raised last year."

"A worthy goal, but what about the project to create housing for the families of cancer patients? Aren't you trying to raise funds for that, too? I would think you're spreading yourself too thin."

"I've been doing the PMC for several years. I don't want to stop now just because I have another project. I'm determined to make this the best year ever for both the PMC team and the housing project."

Emma shook her head. "I don't know. It sounds like you're taking on too much to me. I wish I had your energy."

"I have lots of helpers. We've almost raised enough funds to buy the property, but someone else has put in an offer that's better than ours. So we have to match it, or we lose."

"Do you have a deadline?"

"Ninety days."

"Do you think you can do it by then?"

"I've got lots of people working to make it happen."

"Sure hope you reach your goal."

"Me, too." Heather stopped at the nurses' station and gathered her paperwork. "Is Mr. Murray coming in today? I love his crazy jokes."

Emma nodded. "He is. I wonder what gems he'll have for us today."

"I wish all the patients could have his outlook."

"I know, but cancer is a hard disease to deal with. I hate that the treatments often make people feel worse." Emma sighed. "Sometimes I question why I work as an oncology nurse."

"I try to remember the good results and not the bad."

"Do you ever think about changing jobs?"

Heather frowned. "Why? Are you considering getting a different one?"

Emma shrugged. "Ryan hates to see me down, and

you know I get down when we lose a patient."

"But doctors and nurses have to deal with life and death." Heather remembered sitting by her beloved grandfather's bedside while he battled kidney cancer. She'd become an oncology nurse because of him.

"I know, but I've been thinking I should get a job at a doctor's office—"

"You wouldn't like it. Besides, we need you at the clinic." Heather patted Emma's shoulder.

Emma smiled. "Thanks for saying that. I guess I'm a little down after sweet Audrey Lipscomb died."

Heather nodded. "That was sad, but let's hope Mr. Murray has some really funny jokes that will cheer us up today."

"Okay."

Heather waved a hand toward the window that looked out on the town square. "We can't be sad on such a glorious spring day. A perfect New England day—not a cloud in the sky and blossoms everywhere."

"You're right. I should look at the good things around me."

"Besides, since you're going to join our PMC team, you can ride in memory of Audrey."

"You're making it really hard for me to say no."

"That was my intention." Heather chuckled. "Now back to work. I've got a full load this afternoon and a new patient."

"New patients always make the day interesting." Emma led the way down the hall and stopped in front of one of the exam rooms. "Good luck with your new patient."

"Thanks." Heather continued walking as she gazed at the new patient's file. The name at the top made her stop midstep.

Maxwell Reynolds. Age twenty-seven.

Heather stared at the closed door in front of her. The name had to be a coincidence. The Max Reynolds she knew lived in Montana, and she didn't even know whether his full name was Maxwell.

No. She shook her head. Couldn't be.

Only one way to find out. Heather knocked.

"Come in." The male voice on the other side of the door didn't sound familiar. Or did it?

Heather turned the knob and let the door swing open. Her mouth went dry. Max Reynolds—Max Reynolds from Montana—sat on the exam table.

Pale, thin, and frowning, he stared at her. "What are you doing here?"

Heather didn't miss the annoyed surprise in his tone. While his brown eyes, filled with worry, continued to gaze at her, Heather couldn't help remembering Emma's reaction to the eye and hair color on "the list." Max had dark-brown hair, too.

She had to quit thinking about the ridiculous itemization of traits for the perfect man. As Emma pointed out, he didn't exist. And despite Max's physical appearance, nothing else about him fit Heather's wish list.

Other than being thinner, he appeared much the

same as he had when he'd been dating her former roommate. He was still a handsome man. Max and Brittany had broken up just weeks before Heather had moved to Massachusetts. He'd been a lousy boyfriend for her friend. He'd make a dreadful boyfriend for anyone. But she couldn't dwell on that. She was here to help him through this difficult diagnosis, and she would do her best.

Finally, she managed a smile. "I'm going to be your nurse."

***

"Isn't that just wonderful!" Anger bubbled up inside of Max. How was he going to deal with Heather Watson? What was God trying to tell him? First the cancer. Now a nightmare of a nurse. His own "Nurse Ratched," wearing a blue smock.

Heather was the last person he'd expected to see here. The last person he wanted to be around while he battled cancer. The last person he wanted to help him through this troubled time. Could he request another nurse?

"I'm glad you feel that way. This is a surprise."

"Yeah. Not exactly how I would choose to meet again." Max had never dreamed of seeing her another time. He couldn't help noticing the way her mouth quivered a little while she tried to ignore his sarcasm. Maybe he wouldn't have to request a new nurse after all. Maybe she would take herself off his case.

"Well, here we are. Renewing old acquaintances." Her back to him as she spoke, she set a folder on the nearby counter. "We have some catching up to do."

Was she serious? When she turned to look at him, she smiled again. Maybe she was serious, but he didn't want to catch up with her for any reason. "I suppose."

Heather busied herself with a computer-like instrument sitting on a cart next to the exam table. "But that's not why you're here."

That was an understatement. Was she trying to make him feel at ease, or was he just edgy about everything right now?

He had to get a better attitude. She was here to help him. How ironic. In his mind, she'd been his adversary. He'd always put most of the blame for the demise of his relationship with Brittany squarely in Heather's lap. She'd made it abundantly clear to him that she thought he was inconsiderate, self-centered, and a loser. She'd convinced Brittany that she would be better off without him.

Guess Heather was right. Brittany had married someone else. That someone else just happened to be Heather's uncle. She'd wasted no time introducing them after Brittany had broken up with him.

How was he going to look at Heather without thinking of Brittany? Lowering his head, he closed his eyes and took a deep breath. Wishing Brittany was back in his life would do him no good. He had to move on, but he'd been trying to do that for over two years. He hadn't been very successful.

"Are you okay?"

Max looked up. "Yeah, just thinking about what lies ahead."

"Well, I'm here to help you deal with all of this. Now I have a few preliminary things to go over before Dr. Duffey joins us."

"Sure. What's on the agenda?"

"First, I'm going to get all your vital signs."

Max remained stoic while Heather performed all the necessary tests—the same things he'd gone through every time he'd stepped into a doctor's office in recent months. But this time, he knew what was wrong. Knowing was part relief and part anxiety.

When Heather finished, she logged information into the computer, then turned to him. "I'll be back in a few minutes with Dr. Duffey."

"Okay." Max watched Heather exit the room, her dark-brown hair swinging just above her shoulders. She was wearing it longer these days. He liked it a lot better than that short spiky hairdo she used to have. He shook his head. Why was he even thinking about it?

He had more important things to consider. He still hadn't talked to his mother. He'd used the excuse that he wanted to get this appointment behind him so he'd know what lay ahead. Then he could tell her about the planned treatments. Would that ease her mind? He doubted it. How could he ease her mind when he couldn't ease his own?

A knock on the door interrupted Max's deliberations. "Come in."

Heather entered, followed by a tall, broad-shouldered man with thick gray hair and a comforting smile. The man extended his hand. "Hello. I'm Dr. Duffey, and I'll be monitoring your treatment."

While the doctor and Heather went over his treatment options, projected timeline and preliminary tests, Max tried to put aside his worry and focus on what they were telling him. Did all cancer patients have this panic build up inside of them?

When they finished, the doctor turned to Heather. "Ms. Watson will be your advocate throughout this process. You're in good hands. She'll take excellent care of you. After we get back the preliminary tests, we'll have a better idea about your treatment."

Max nodded, but he really wanted to stand up and shout. *How can she take good care of me when she doesn't even like me?* But he sat there with his mouth clamped shut. This wasn't the time to get emotional and lose his composure. He'd already spent the days, between his appointment with Dr. Vargas and today's appointment, letting the anxiety build until he thought he might lash out at someone—anyone who was nearby. So far he'd managed to keep things under control.

"We're all a team, and we're going to help you beat this cancer." Dr. Duffey shook Max's hand again. "Ms. Watson will finish giving you more information and help you find the support groups you need."

The doctor left, and Max wished he could leave, too. He wasn't sure he was ready to grapple with this disease or his discomfort with Heather. Did he dare mention the old animosity? He had to do it. There was no other way.

But Heather didn't wait for Max to speak. "Okay, we have a lot of things to talk about. First—"

"First, let's clear up the past."

"The past?"

"Yeah, the way you came between Brittany and me."

Heather sighed, but still looked him right in the eye. "Max, would you prefer that another nurse be assigned to your case? If so, I'm sure we can make a switch."

There it was. She was handing him the chance to get rid of her—his nemesis. So why did he hesitate? Was he crazy, or only mixed up because of his fear? "You don't have to do that, but I didn't want our bad history to sit there like the so-called elephant in the room. I don't want another nurse."

Had he just said that? Had he passed up the option to switch nurses? Cancer must already be affecting his thought processes, because there shouldn't be anything comforting about Heather's presence. But despite his ill feelings toward her, she was someone familiar—someone who shared part of his past in this strange place. He needed some familiarity. Oddly enough, he needed her.

CHAPTER TWO

"Okay, if that's what you'd prefer." Heather's stomach sank. Over two years later, was Max still carrying a grudge? This couldn't be good. Brittany had found someone else. Why couldn't he accept that?

Heather waited for him to say something, but he sat there mute. "You're sure you don't want another nurse to take my place? Maybe that would be easier."

"No, it wouldn't." Shaking his head, he fell silent again.

"You seem to be torturing yourself over this. You've got enough going on in your life without having my presence make you uncomfortable."

"Why don't you like me?"

His words shot through her mind and left her stunned. He thought she didn't like him. Was that true? "Did I ever say that?"

"You're not denying it."

"I'm just shocked you think that."

He released a halfhearted laugh. "Saying my girlfriend should dump me pretty much tells me you don't like me."

Should she defend herself or let it go—agree with

him and be done with it? But he wanted the truth, didn't he? Honesty was the best answer. "It's not that I didn't like you or don't like you. I didn't like the way you treated Brittany when you were dating her. She took second place to your classes and research work. You weren't there to see her disappointment when you'd forget things like her birthday or wouldn't show up for a date. Your negligence made me angry. Is that what you wanted to hear?"

Hanging his head, Max made no rebuttal.

What was going through his mind? Heather wasn't sure how to handle this situation. He had concerns about her, but he didn't want to have a new nurse. Maybe he was just overwhelmed with his diagnosis. She would manage this somehow. "Whatever happened back then can't be changed. The only thing we can do is move forward."

Max raised his head and met her gaze. "Thanks for your truthfulness. I know I have to move on."

"So we're good?"

Max nodded but didn't say a word.

Had he always been this quiet? In reality, she'd never been around him that much. They'd exchanged greetings when he came to see Brittany or finally showed up for dates. She didn't know Max that well at all. Getting to know him was part of her job so she could give him the best possible help. "Okay, then. Let's get started."

"With what?"

"I need to know your circumstances."

"Like what?"

"Your job, living arrangements, support groups. This information will guide me in giving you the assistance you need." Heather read the hesitation in Max's eyes. He wanted to shut her out. His expression told her that a battle raged in his mind. "The more I know, the better I can help you."

"Reminds me of the big bad wolf in *Little Red Riding Hood*."

Heather wrinkled her brow. "What are you talking about?"

"You know the lines from the story, 'The better to' whatever—'see you, smell you, eat you.'"

Shaking her head, Heather chuckled. "I've never had a patient compare me to the big bad wolf."

Max shrugged. "Guess the story was on my brain after doing a video call with my younger brother. He's six and wanted to read that story to me to show me how well he could read."

Max's statement further emphasized the fact that Heather didn't know much about him. His having a six-year-old brother gave her pause. She'd met his mother at Brittany's wedding, but she hadn't met any of his other relatives. With a brother over twenty years younger, what kind of family dynamic did he come from? "So how did your family take the news about your cancer diagnosis?"

Max dropped his gaze again and let out a harsh breath. "I haven't told them."

Somehow his confession didn't surprise her, but

she had to know why. "Why not?"

"I don't want to hear my mother's reaction. I hate to do it over the phone, but telling her in person might be worse."

"Would you like me to help?"

Max shook his head. "I'll deal with it."

"Okay, but tell me about your family."

"Is this stuff you have to know?"

"Yes. I not only help you, but I help your family cope with the situation."

"But they're on the other side of the country in Washington State."

"They still need to know how to work through this with you." Heather wanted to show Max that she cared—to wipe away the animosity from the past, but she resisted the urge to reach out and touch him at this point. He might not appreciate the personal contact. "So please fill me in about your family."

Despite his reluctant expression, Max nodded. "My mom, Beth, married Clay when I was in high school, and he adopted me. I never knew my real father. He died before I was born."

"I'm sorry."

Max shrugged. "Don't be."

Heather didn't know what else to say. His response said a lot. Too much resentment bubbled around the edges of that statement. "Tell me about your siblings."

Max smiled for the first time today. "I have a half sister, Abby, who's four, and my half brother, Alex. They keep my mom busy. She's also a kindergarten teacher, and my dad works as a consultant."

Heather nodded, glad to hear Max volunteer at least this much information without her having to coax it out of him. Maybe he was beginning to feel a little more comfortable. "What do you think they'll say about your situation?"

"I know my mom will be upset. That's why I've put off telling her. The kids maybe won't understand, or maybe they'll understand, and the news will scare them." Max stared over her head as if he was thinking.

"What about your dad?" Heather tried to read Max's expression. What kind of relationship did he have with his adopted father?

"My dad's a rock. He keeps the family steady. I'm glad he married my mom. They're good for each other…"

Heather sensed a "but" coming. However, he didn't say anything else. She couldn't expect him to open up completely on this first visit, especially since he didn't seem to want to talk at all. She had to be patient. "What about your job? Have you told them?"

Max shook his head. "I wanted to know more before I said anything."

"That seems reasonable. I'm here to assist you with that kind of thing, too." Again Heather sensed Max's unwillingness to accept her help. "I'm planning to set you up with a dietician and a counselor, who will give you good advice during your treatments."

"What if I don't want to use them?"

"That's up to you, but I'd think you'd want to avail

yourself of everyone who can support you." How was she going to convince this man that he needed more than chemotherapy? "Cancer's a tough disease. The treatment takes a lot out of a person. You need a support group—people around you who will give you encouragement when you need it."

"I don't like people hovering. I like my space."

"No one's going to hover, but you do need people you can reach out to, especially since your family lives so far away. Do you live by yourself or share a living space with someone?"

Max's expression descended into annoyance. "I live alone. I have a studio apartment over in Oakton, where I work."

"You live in Oakton?"

"Yeah, why?

"I live there, too. I can't believe I haven't run into you. Oakton isn't that big." Heather knit her eyebrows. "How long have you lived there?"

"A couple of months. I got a great research job."

Heather didn't know why, but she suspected once again that Max wasn't giving her the whole story. "That's a big move—Montana to Massachusetts."

Max chuckled. "Who are you to talk? You made the same move, and for the same reason. A good job in your field."

"Yeah. There are a lot of jobs in and around Boston in the medical field. I love my job here."

"You like working with sick people—people who might die?"

"I don't like it when people die, but I like helping patients beat cancer or live to the fullest in the time they have left."

"I want to be in the former group—the ones who beat cancer. The doc says lymphoma patients have a ninety percent recovery rate. Guess that gives me a lot of hope."

"True. You should think positively." Heather handed Max a pamphlet. "Here's some information, including the anticipated schedule of treatment that Dr. Duffey talked about. Most likely you'll have eight chemotherapy treatments administered every other week. Then probably four weeks of radiation treatment. But we'll have more certainty after you take the tests I have scheduled for you. Any questions?"

"Dozens, but I'm too overwhelmed right now to ask them."

"When you're ready, ask away. We're done for today, but promise me you'll talk to your family. You can call me anytime. My number's in the information I gave you."

"Thanks." Max sighed as he stood. "I know I need to call my mom, but I'll have to work up to it. The call won't be easy."

"I know that, but I'm glad you realize the necessity of letting her know." Heather followed him to the door. "We'll see you in a few days for your tests."

Heather watched Max walk down the hall toward the reception area, clothes hanging loosely on his six-foot-plus frame. Would he do what she'd asked? She wanted to believe that he would talk to his family. The Max she'd known in Montana might let it slide. Was he still the guy who had thought of himself first and left Brittany dangling all too often? Heather hoped not. She couldn't let the past color her perception or his. Was that possible?

***

After Max left the clinic, he sat inside his car without opening the window even though the sun beating through the glass made him perspire. Or maybe the heat had nothing to do with it. The fact that he had cancer was the real reason he was breaking out in a sweat.

Staring straight ahead, he gripped the steering wheel and let out a harsh breath. What did he do now? He didn't want to go home—back to his lonely one-room apartment. It was even gloomier than his current health situation. Right now he didn't want to make any decisions. He didn't want to drive around in this rattletrap of a car either, but he couldn't sit here in the parking lot forever.

Max finally started his car and headed in the direction of home. As he drove the familiar tree-lined road toward the small town where he lived and worked, he remembered his recent trip to the Wayside Inn in Sudbury. They served wonderful meals at the historic inn, which dated back to pre-revolutionary times. The nearby grist mill offered a peaceful setting. He needed some tranquility, and that spot was the perfect place to get it.

As he turned onto the road leading to the inn, he was thankful for the folks at work who had introduced him to the place only weeks ago. He needed to find something to be thankful for. He found a spot along the road to park. The area was nearly deserted late on a weekday afternoon. He welcomed the quiet as he walked along the path that led to the grist mill. The sun warmed the day as he sat on the ground and leaned against a tree. The gurgling water turned the grist mill's giant wheel. A slight breeze rustled the tree branches overhead. Birds chirped. A dog barked in the distance. Everything about life seemed the same—everything except him.

For a few moments, Max drank in the serenity of the place. Maybe this was exactly the spot where he should talk to his mom. He pulled a cell phone from his pocket and glanced at the time. He grimaced. The three-hour time difference was always a problem when trying to phone the West Coast. She wouldn't be home from the school for at least another hour.

Maybe he should call Clay. After all, he made his own work hours and was often easy to reach on his cell phone. But what would his mother say when she found out that Max had talked to Clay first. That probably wouldn't go over so well.

Max closed his eyes again and listened to the sound of the water rushing over the spillway. He needed someone to talk to.

Brittany.

Her name popped into his head, but he couldn't call her. She was married to someone else now, but she should've been his wife. His heart still ached when he thought about it. Seeing Heather today brought back all the old hurt.

He'd dated Brittany for over eight years in high school and college, but he'd let studies and work interfere with their relationship. He'd paid the price for his neglect—losing her love. Heather was right about one thing. His inattention to Brittany was inexcusable.

More than anything he missed Brittany's friendship. Technically they were still friends, but he didn't think her husband would appreciate it if she were to get a phone call from her ex-boyfriend. Besides, she would probably tell him that she would pray for him and that he should pray, too. But right now talking to God didn't offer much comfort—only more questions. Why had God allowed this to happen?

So whom could he call? Max scrolled through the contacts on his phone. Pinecrest Elementary. The name jumped out at him. He'd forgotten that his mom had given him the number so he could reach her in case of an emergency. This was an emergency, wasn't it? He convinced himself it was as he poked the screen.

When a woman answered, Max hesitated for only a second before he blurted, "This is Max Reynolds,

Beth Reynolds's son, and I need to talk to her. It's an emergency."

"Certainly. I'll call her to the office right away."

"Thanks." Max waited what seemed like hours rather than minutes.

"Max, what's wrong?" Although filled with worry, his mom's voice strummed across his troubled heart and gave him a sense of peace that he hadn't expected.

"Mom, I'm sorry to disturb you at school, but I had to talk to you before you got home."

"That's okay. Just tell me what's happening. Did you have an accident? Are you in the hospital? Are you in some kind of trouble?"

The last question almost made him laugh. He would probably never live down his early teen years and all the trouble he'd caused his mom. He had to thank Clay for pointing him in the right direction. Clay and Brittany had kept Max from getting tangled up with the wrong crowd.

"Max, you're scaring me. Please tell me what's wrong."

"Sorry. I don't want you to get upset, but I have bad news."

"Just tell me."

"You know how I've had some strange health issues during the last year or so and seen several doctors?"

"Are you sick?"

"Yeah, Mom. I'm sick. I had some tests run, and the doctor told me I have lymphoma."

"Lim…what?"

"Hodgkin lymphoma. It's a type of cancer."

A gasp came over the phone. "Cancer." The word came out in a cry. "Oh, Max. How can that be? Maybe the doctor is wrong."

"Mom, the tests aren't wrong. Dr. Vargas made an appointment for me to see a lymphoma specialist. I was there today. I'll have a PET scan and some other preliminary tests, then most likely I'll start chemo treatments in a few days after that."

Max wasn't going to talk to his mom about going to a sperm bank to make a deposit. He wanted kids someday, but they wouldn't be with Brittany. Why did he have to think about her again? Everything seemed to bring her to mind since he and Heather had crossed paths.

"A few days? Why not tomorrow?"

"Mom, they do these tests to come up with the perfect treatment plan for me. It's Monday. I should have all my results by Friday. I think that's soon enough."

"But you need treatment right away. Maybe you should come home and have a doctor here treat you. Then I can help."

"Mom, calm down. Coming home would only delay the treatment. Besides, do you know any lymphoma specialists to refer me to?"

"No." Resignation was evident even in her one-word response. "But I'm coming out there. I should never have let you go to Massachusetts on that wild goose chase to find your father's family."

Max pressed a couple of fingers to his forehead. He didn't want to argue with his mother, but she was treating him like a kid—like he couldn't make his own decisions. He didn't need her permission to go anywhere or do anything. Sure she loved him and wanted what was best for him, but sometimes she tried to protect him too much.

"Max, are you still there?"

"Yeah, I'm still here. I really don't see the need for you to come all the way here." Max sighed, remembering how Heather said she was there to help the family cope, as well as him. "You can't make things better." *And you might make things worse.* The thought raced through his mind, but he wasn't going to say it and upset her further.

"You can't change my mind."

"But Mom, you only have a few weeks left in the school year. Why not wait until school is out?"

"You are more important than anything. School year or no school year."

The tone of her voice made it clear that she was coming no matter what he said. "Okay, if that's the way you want it."

"Good. I'll send you my flight information as soon as I book my ticket." A sniffle sounded over the phone. "I love you, Max."

"I love you, too. Bye." Max ended the call before things deteriorated more. He'd caved because she was upset. How was he going to deal with her being here?

He hadn't even mentioned that Heather was his nurse. He wasn't sure why. Maybe he needed to talk to Clay after all. He would make his mom see reason. At least Max hoped that was the case.

***

The following week, Max spotted his parents as they stood with their suitcases outside the airport terminal. His talk with Clay only confirmed that his mother was coming no matter what, so Max had accepted the inevitable. He maneuvered his car next to the curb, then got out. Before he could walk to the back of the car, his petite mom enveloped him in a big hug, her light-brown hair tickling his chin.

She stepped back. "You've lost a lot of weight."

Max nodded. "It comes with the territory."

Clay hugged Max, too, then stood eye to eye with him. "It's good to see you. Wish it were under better circumstances."

"Me, too." Max reached for his mom's suitcase.

"Let me take care of these." Clay stepped in front of Max and hoisted the luggage into the trunk.

Max didn't want them to treat him like he was helpless, but he didn't want to start an argument. He was perfectly capable of putting the suitcases into the trunk, but he knew his mom would give him a lecture about not overdoing. She would probably be giving advice at every opportunity.

As he drove away from the airport toward

downtown Boston, he turned to Clay, who sat in the front passenger seat. "You guys want to eat at one of the Italian places in the North End?"

"That sounds good to me." Clay turned to the backseat. "What about you, honey? Sound good?"

"Whatever Max wants is fine with me."

"Then Italian it is." Max hoped his mom would continue to have that attitude instead of trying to tell him what to do.

Max considered himself fortunate when he snagged a parking spot on one of the narrow streets that sported the Italian eating establishment where he'd gone with coworkers. This was one more time when he was thankful for the people at work who had introduced him to another great place to eat.

As they walked toward the restaurant, his mom put her arm through his. "Are you sure you should be walking this much?"

Max wanted to roll his eyes and shake his head, but he resisted the urge. His mom had been with him less than an hour, and she was already getting on his nerves. He should be grateful that she cared about him, but couldn't she realize that he wasn't going to keel over at any minute? How was he going to deal with her?

"Beth, Max knows how much he can do." Clay stepped in and took his wife's hand. "Don't smother him. He's a grown man and can take care of himself."

Beth frowned at her husband. "But he's sick. Very sick."

"And he'll let you know when he needs your help."

"Will you guys quit talking about me as if I'm not here?"

"Didn't mean to do that." Clay clapped Max on the shoulder. "I only want you to realize how tough this has been on your mom."

"I know that. It's tough on everyone, and I do appreciate your concern." Max motioned to the building to their left and hoped they would quit talking about his cancer. "This is it. They have great food."

"Good, because I'm starved." Clay opened the door for Beth and Max.

After they were seated and had their menus, they studied them in silence. Finally, Beth put her menu aside. She reached across the table and placed one hand on Max's arm. "I'm sorry, Max. I don't want you to be angry with me."

Sighing, Max stared at his mom as her blue eyes swam with tears. "I'm not angry. I'm glad you're here. Thanks for coming."

"It's such a relief to hear you say that." She blinked hard as she pushed a strand of her hair behind one ear.

"Who's taking care of Abby and Alex?" Max hoped to lighten the mood by steering the conversation in another direction.

"Grady and Maria. The kids are excited about staying with their aunt and uncle for the week."

"What does Kelsey think about having her two

young cousins invading her space?" Max chuckled.

"You know Kelsey. Nothing bothers her." Beth patted Max's arm again. "Grady, Maria and Kelsey all send their love and prayers. In fact, the whole church back home is praying for you."

"I appreciate that." Max pretended to study his menu some more. He didn't want to look his mother in the eye. The church back home prayed for him, but Max hadn't been able to pray about this situation at all. God seemed very far away.

Would Clay guess that Max was struggling with his faith right now? His dad had a way of knowing these kinds of things, while his mom had no clue. Clay had been the one to share his faith and help a rebellious teenager know that he needed faith in Jesus, too. Now, over ten years later, Max still needed that faith—faith that God could bring him through this.

Before anyone could make another comment, the waitress took their order. She returned moments later with a basket of warm bread. Conversation ceased as the threesome helped themselves to the bread. Max welcomed the respite from any further discussion of his health issues. He wanted this to be just another evening like so many he'd shared with his parents through the years. More than likely, that wasn't going to happen.

"Speaking of prayers, we kind of dived into this bread without giving thanks." Clay reached out his hands to Max and Beth. "We've got a lot to talk to God about."

Smiling wryly, Max reluctantly joined hands with his parents as they bowed their heads. He wasn't sure about praying in the restaurant. Had he become a closet Christian? Maybe so. Clay wasn't going to hide his faith. He never had.

Clay's prayer of thanks for their safe trip and for the food they were about to eat reminded Max that he had a lot to be thankful for—a family who loved him and doctors and nurses who knew how to treat his problem. Clay prayed for God's healing hand to touch Max. God definitely had Max's attention, but what was God trying to tell him?

CHAPTER THREE

Sunshine streamed through the window near the bed in Max's apartment. He glanced at the clock.

Six-thirty. He didn't have to get up yet, but he couldn't sleep. Today he would have his first chemo treatment. He shifted on his bed and stared at the ceiling. He had to admit he was nervous. He just wanted to get through this day without complications. Was that possible?

Despite his initial reluctance to have his mother come, Max appreciated having her nearby. At least he'd convinced her he'd be okay if she and Clay spent the night in a nearby hotel. There was barely room for him in this apartment, much less company. She wasn't thrilled that the closest decent hotel wasn't in Oakton, but Clay had assured her that being fifteen minutes away wasn't too far.

Max sat up and swung his legs over the bed. He sat there for a minute. Unexpectedly a prayer formed in his mind. *Lord, let the healing begin today*. He closed his eyes and allowed the words to soak in and hoped the doubt would flee, but it still niggled at the corners of his thoughts. What did God have in store for him?

The catchy tune he'd programed into his cell phone

sounded and broke the silence. He grabbed the phone off the nightstand. His mom. He should have known. "Hello. I didn't expect to hear from you so early. It's three-thirty back in Pinecrest."

"Yeah, but I couldn't sleep."

"Me neither."

"Can we take you out to breakfast?"

"I can't chow down on pancakes, bacon, and eggs like I usually do." Max reached over to the nightstand and grabbed the pamphlet Heather had given him. He flipped through it. "It says here in the instructions for pretreatment to eat light, high-fiber foods and drink lots of fluids, but nothing with caffeine."

"We'll be sure to take you to a place where you can eat like you should." His mom's voice wavered. "How about we come by in an hour?"

"That'll be fine. See you." Max ended the call and flopped back onto his bed. What side effects would he feel from this treatment? Should he prepare himself for the worst, or should he have a positive outlook?

Before Beth and Clay arrived, he'd managed to pick up his apartment so it was in reasonable shape. He didn't want his mom to see that he usually had dirty dishes in the sink and at least one pizza box decorating his coffee table.

After he finished cleaning, Max paced the floor, unable to relax. Finally, he stood by the front window of his second-floor apartment and looked out at the street and watched for his parents to arrive in their rental car. He couldn't blame Clay for not wanting to drive the beat-up ten-year-old sedan that Max claimed as a vehicle.

Two-story clapboard houses in muted shades of gray, green, blue, and yellow lined the street where he lived just off the town square. Crab apple and plum trees festooned the yards with blossoms. Spring brought longer days and the chance to get out and enjoy the outdoors. What a rotten time to be fighting a possibly lethal disease. He'd planned to join a softball team and had been looking forward to going to a Boston Red Sox game at Fenway Park. Would he get the chance to do any of that now?

Clay's rental car pulled up in front of the house. Max didn't wait for his parents to come inside, even though he'd gone to the effort to make the place presentable. He just wanted to get out. He bounded down the stairs and met Clay and Beth at the front door of the century-old house.

"I wanted to see your place since we didn't get to see it last night." Beth pushed past Max. "Show me the way."

Max grabbed one of his mom's arms and stopped her from going further. "You'll get to see it after my treatment. Right now we need to go. We don't know how long it will take to eat, and we don't want to be late for my appointment."

Beth sighed. "Oh, all right. Your treatment and the meeting with the doctor and nurse are the most important things."

"Let's get going." Clay helped steer Beth back to

the car.

As Max settled in the backseat, he thought about the meeting with Heather before his treatment. Why was he reluctant to mention her? He'd never said anything to anyone about his quarrel with her, and he certainly wasn't going to say anything now. His mom would probably have her radar up and wonder why he hadn't revealed that Heather was his nurse. Failing to mention her would put a lot of questions in his mother's mind.

Beth looked at Max. "I found a nice little breakfast place not far from your treatment center. I called—"

"You called?"

"Yes, they open at six." Beth waved a hand at him. "I asked about their menu, and they assured me that they'd have just the right kind of food for someone who's receiving chemo treatments."

"Thanks, Mom." Great. Now even the staff at the restaurant knew he had cancer. What would she do next? Tell people they had to treat him in a special way? He closed his eyes and took a deep breath. *Be thankful for her concern.*

"Are you all right, honey?" Beth's anxious voice drew Max from his thoughts.

Max opened his eyes. He was going to have to develop a happy facade for his mother's sake, or she would worry herself sick. "I'm fine. Just thinking about the day ahead."

"Everything will work out." Beth smiled at him.

Max almost let his mouth drop open. The smile

was a surprise, like the sunshine popping out from behind a big black cloud. One minute she sounded apprehensive and the next she was telling him that all would be okay.

"The restaurant's right here, and there's even a parking spot near the front door." Clay slowed the car and maneuvered it next to the curb.

Max followed Clay and Beth into the eating establishment that reminded Max of the Pinecrest Café back home, with its faux red-leather booths. The place bustled with folks of all ages enjoying breakfast and congenial conversation. The smell of brewing coffee, cinnamon rolls, and fried eggs permeated the air.

Max's stomach rumbled, but he couldn't eat any of those things. What would be his choices? He hoped his mom wouldn't announce to the waitress that he had cancer. He didn't want people staring at him or feeling sorry for him. He just wanted to be normal. Would that ever be the case again?

When the middle-aged waitress brought the menus, Beth waylaid her. "We're looking for nutritious whole-grain, high-fiber items. Could you show us those on the menu?"

"Absolutely." The waitress pointed to the bottom of the second page. "Right here are our heart-healthy items. I love the waffles. They're made with whole grain, but they're light and come with the best fruit toppings."

Beth nodded. "Thanks so much."

The waitress took their drink orders. "I'll be back with your drinks and then take your food order."

Max breathed a sigh of relief. His mom hadn't announced to the whole place about his cancer. He looked over at Clay, who had been surprisingly quiet today. Clay was usually the talkative one, while his mom was quiet.

"So how's everything back in Pinecrest?"

"Same as always. Not much changes in a small town." Clay took a gulp of his coffee.

"Yeah, I suppose you're right." Was that how it was in Oakton? Max didn't know much about the small town where he lived now. He'd spent most of his waking hours at work, except the few times his coworkers had coerced him into joining them for dinner, and even then, they'd gone to places outside of Oakton. Max had used the rest of his free time searching on the computer for his father's family without any success.

"You said we'll be meeting with the doctor and a nurse before your treatment, right?" Beth's question made Max's stomach take a nosedive.

His mom had just handed him the opportunity to let her know about Heather. He couldn't back away now. "Yeah, Mom. By the way, do you remember Heather Watson, Brittany's friend?"

"Should I?"

"I don't know. You met her at Brittany's wedding. Heather was the maid of honor." Max hated talking about one of the most miserable days of his life—right up there with the day he'd found out he had cancer.

"Oh, sure." Beth nodded. "Why do you ask?"

"She's my nurse."

"She is? How wonderful!" Beth wrinkled her brow. "Why didn't you mention it before now?"

Max shrugged, hoping his discomfort didn't show. "I don't know. Maybe because the opportunity hadn't presented itself until now, and I've had other things on my mind."

"You certainly have. Too much for you to bear alone." Beth squeezed Max's arm, her lips pressed together.

Max hoped she wouldn't cry here in the restaurant. At that moment the waitress arrived with their orders. As she placed the plates on the table, his mom appeared to find her composure. After the waitress left, Clay reached for Beth's hand, and just as he had done the night before, he said a prayer. This time Max didn't care what the other diners thought. He needed the prayers.

For a few minutes, they ate in silence. Then the conversation turned to more events in Pinecrest and the antics of Abby and Alex and his mom's kindergarten students. For a few minutes, everything seemed normal while he ate the waffles. The waitress had been right to recommend them.

"How are things at work? What did they say when you told them you have cancer?" Beth pressed her lips together.

Was his mom going to cry again? Her eyes were

dry, but whenever she looked that way, he was pretty sure she was on the verge of tears. "Mom, I love my job, and they're very understanding about the situation. I'm going to work as much as I can during the treatments."

"Promise me you won't overdo, okay?" She knit her eyebrows in that little frown Max had seen so often on her face since she'd been here.

"I promise. I don't have any idea how the chemo is going to affect me."

"Beth, don't borrow trouble." Clay gave his wife an indulgent smile. "Max is right to try to keep his life as normal as possible. I think our meeting with the doctor and nurse today will help ease your mind."

Max wanted to thank Clay for trying to calm Beth's nerves. As always, Clay was the one to take charge and bring serenity to the situation. Max knew his mom would always do what she thought was best to defend him, to take care of him, to be on his side. Clay was the steady one who would give Max the advice he needed to negotiate his problems. That's the way it had been since Clay had come into their lives.

While Max continued to eat, he wondered what Clay thought about the purpose of Max's move to Massachusetts. Did Clay resent having Max search for his biological father's family? Clay had been a real father to Max in so many ways, and he didn't want to hurt this man he'd grown to love and respect.

Max had never discussed his move with Clay, only his mom, who had objected strenuously. But Max had ignored his mother's advice and never sought Clay's. A life-threatening disease made a person rethink his choices. Maybe this visit with his parents brought with it the opportunity to talk with Clay about those decisions and give him the thanks he deserved.

Clay pointed to his watch. "We'd better get the check and be on our way."

"The time has come." Max took a deep breath as his stomach somersaulted at the prospect of his upcoming treatment and encounter with Heather again. For his mother's sake, he didn't want to let on that he was nervous. He would think positively. Today would be a success.

***

Heather braced herself for the meeting with Max and his family as she followed Dr. Duffey into the conference room. She prayed that Max would be more amenable to her suggestions than he'd been during their last encounter. She was grateful that Max had decided to tell his family about his cancer, but would the presence of his parents help or hinder the situation?

Dr. Duffey introduced himself to Beth and Clay Reynolds, and Heather introduced herself to Clay. After the introductions, she took a seat at the table next to Dr. Duffey and tried to surreptitiously study Max's reaction while the doctor launched into an explanation of the test results, charts and procedures.

Max kept glancing between the doctor and his mother. Heather guessed that Max was gauging his mother's reaction to what the doctor was saying. He really cared about his mom.

When Max looked Heather's way and caught her watching him, a blush crept up her neck and heated her cheeks. Her pulse quickened. The reaction came as a surprise. Assessing the patient was part of her job, so why was she bothered that he noticed her interest? Maybe the bad blood between them still colored their relationship. She vowed to keep personal thoughts out of her professional evaluation.

When Dr. Duffey finished, he stood and gestured toward Heather. "Ms. Watson will take over from here."

Heather didn't miss the frown on Beth Reynolds's face as the doctor left the room. She looked at Max. "Why is the doctor leaving? Why are you left with just a nurse?"

With chagrin painting his features, Max glanced in Heather's direction, then immediately turned to Beth. "Mom, this is Heather's job. She knows what she's doing."

Heather couldn't believe Max was defending her. She definitely needed to ease his mother's mind about how things worked in the clinic. "Mrs. Reynolds, Dr. Duffey has made all the assessments and ordered the treatments, but I monitor them and help Max by making sure he's surrounded with all the people who can help him."

"Yeah, Mom. Listen to her. She's here to support us."

"That's right." Heather shot Max a quick smile. After their meeting last week, she would never have guessed he would be so agreeable today. What had changed? "I'm here to help you and Mr. Reynolds, as well as Max."

Beth frowned. "So how do you do that?"

"I can arrange for you to see counselors, who will be of assistance to you during Max's treatment."

"But we don't live here, and I can't possibly stay for as long as these treatments last. I have two small children at home who need me." Beth pressed her lips together. "Who will take care of Max when we leave?"

Clay Reynolds reached over and took his wife's hand. "Beth, we'll work it out. Ms. Watson is here to assist us."

"You're right, Mr. Reynolds. We can talk about that right now, if you'd like."

"Mom, Dad, Heather." Everyone looked at Max. "Do we have to be so formal? Is it all right to call each other by our first names?"

Heather nodded as she glanced at Max and his parents. "You're welcome to call me Heather rather than Ms. Watson."

"Okay by me. What about you, Beth?" Clay put an arm around her.

"Whatever Max wants."

"Good." Max leaned forward. "I know you're

worried about me, Mom, but I can take care of myself."

Heather cringed at Max's statement. She had no idea how he would react to the chemo. Could he accept the fact that he might not be able to take care of himself? She had to bring up that possibility. "Max, I know you want to handle this on your own. You made that quite clear during our last meeting, but there is the possibility that the chemo will make you quite sick. You have to make arrangements for someone to be with you after your treatment. You may need someone to drive you to and from the appointments."

"See what I mean." Misery painted Beth's face. "How can I leave you here alone? If only you hadn't moved here to go on that wild goose chase, you could be close to us for this care."

Wild goose chase. Heather wondered what that was all about. Was it something she should know as a part of the family dynamic in Max's treatment? Knowing or not knowing, she had to take charge of this meeting and find some solutions. "Max, is there someone at your church who would help out after your parents leave?"

Running a hand through his mop of dark hair, Max looked uncomfortable, seemingly at a loss for words. He glanced at his parents, then back at her. "I haven't found a church here. I've attended several but never felt at home in any."

"Have you tried the Oakton Community Church?"

Max shook his head. "Is that where you go?"

"I do. You should give it a try. I think you'll like it. They have a very active singles group because of the nearby colleges."

"I don't remember seeing that church. Where is it?"

"Actually, we're meeting in a storefront one block off Main Street near the edge of the business district. Our current building, which is over a century old, is undergoing extensive renovations, so we can't have services there."

"Oh, yeah. I've seen all the scaffolding on that church just off the square. Is that the building you're talking about?"

Heather nodded. "But we're not here to talk about my church's renovation project. We need to find someone to help you while you're undergoing treatment."

"What about friends or coworkers?" Beth asked.

An uneasy expression etched its way across Max's features, his coffee-colored eyes conveying his anxiety. "I haven't been here long enough to make friends—at least friends I could count on to do this."

"There must be someone you can ask." Beth's voice raised a pitch.

Heather took in the fact that his mother's question had forced Max to admit he hadn't made any close friends since moving here. Just like in Montana, his focus was on his work and research. Heather wanted to dispel Beth's distress, but Max's penchant for living in his own little world could make that difficult.

"I might have an idea." Leaning forward, Clay waved a hand in the air as he looked her way. "Heather, what about someone from your church's singles group? Could you talk to them?"

"I can." Heather nodded. "In fact, your suggestion brings to mind a couple of guys I know who are looking for someone to share their apartment."

"You want me to move?" Disbelief and antagonism punctuated Max's response.

"I—"

"You can't expect him to move when he's going through chemo treatments." Beth was like a mama bear protecting her cub.

Heather wondered whether it was safe to speak again without getting cut off. Before she could think of a way to deal with the volatile situation, Clay stood. Heather's heart jumped into her throat. Now what?

Clay placed the palms of his hands on the table as he leaned forward and looked back and forth between Beth and Max. "Okay, you two, I know this is hard on everyone, but Heather is trying to help you, so give her a chance to explain." Clay sat down and gestured toward Heather. "The floor is yours."

Heather smiled at Clay and remembered how Max had described his dad as a rock. Not only was the man a rock, but his take-charge style had a strangely calming influence. If only Max could take a few lessons from his father. "Thanks. We don't have an ideal situation here. I'm trying to search for the best answers, so I'm making some suggestions. Let's talk about them before we reject them out of hand."

"Are you saying I should move?" Max's voice was calm, but his narrowed gaze told a different story.

"We'll have to see. Let me explain." Heather glanced around the table. "Luke and Jeremy live in the first-floor apartment of an older home across the street from where I live. Peter, the third occupant of the apartment, is getting married this coming weekend. So he's moving out. I think they're still looking for someone to take Peter's place, but I'm not sure. I'll have to talk to them. So you see. It was just a thought."

"Even if these guys are looking for another roommate, are you sure they'd be willing to take in a cancer patient?" Max grimaced.

"I don't think that'll be a problem. We're all on a PMC team together."

Beth frowned. "What's PMC?"

"Pan-Massachusetts Challenge. It's a bike ride to raise money for cancer research." Max's gaze slid from his mom to Heather. "So you ride in the PMC?"

Heather nodded. "This will be my third year."

"I was going to ride this year, but guess I won't be doing that after all." Max let out a harsh breath.

"I should hope not." Beth looked wide eyed at Max.

Heather noticed the worry etched on Beth's face. Maybe it was going to be a good thing she lived far away. Max needed support, but he didn't need to be kept in a cocoon. "You're right, Beth, Max probably isn't going to ride in the PMC, but he should be as active as possible during his treatments—walking, short bike rides or even some weight training will be good for him."

"Won't that make him more tired?"

"Actually, the exercise will help improve his quality of life during his treatments. He shouldn't overdo, and he should rest when necessary, but he definitely shouldn't become a couch potato."

Max gave Heather a lopsided smile. "I'm glad to hear you say that."

"There are lots of things you need to do—eat right, get the rest you need, and relax."

"Lots of orders there."

"You'll learn I'm very good at giving orders."

"Somehow, I think I already knew that."

"Why don't you have Heather introduce you to these guys and explain the situation?" Clay's question made Heather realize that for just a few moments she'd forgotten there were other people in the room besides Max and her.

"I suppose it won't hurt anything, but there's one problem. I have four more months on my lease." Max looked at her. "What do you think, Heather?"

"I'll check with Luke and Jeremy. If things work out with them, then we'll see what we can do about your lease. You really would be better off living with someone." Heather stared at Max. Was that a twinkle in his eyes? Her imagination was playing tricks on her. She turned her attention to Beth and Clay.

Heather shook the question away as a nurse technician entered the room. "Is Max ready to check out the infusion floor?"

"He is." Heather stood. "Lindsay is one of our nurse technicians, and she'll give you a tour of the infusion area and get you settled in a room. When she has everything in order, I'll be up to check your vital signs and start your treatment."

Max and his parents followed Lindsay, but he stopped in the doorway as the others went ahead. He grinned. "See you in a few minutes, big bad wolf."

Heather stood glued to the spot, a smile she couldn't contain curving her mouth. Yeah, he was flirting with her. She hadn't imagined it earlier. Maybe he was only trying to find some humor in a scary situation. Cancer patients often went into their first treatment with a lot of trepidation.

Heather's guard went up. No way should she have an interest in Max. She was his nurse, and besides, she was wise to his ways. So often when he would forget to show up for a date with Brittany, he would come over later and use that same bantering tactic with her. Heather had witnessed his apologies time and again where he'd say he was sorry in his goofy duck voice and have Brittany laughing and forgiving him in seconds. Heather wouldn't let that scheme work on her.

Max didn't fit her criteria. So why should she worry about his attempts to flirt with her? She wouldn't. That was a promise.

CHAPTER FOUR

Max bowed his head. While the pastor prayed to close the worship service, Max hoped the upcoming meeting with Heather wouldn't be awkward. He'd certainly blown it when for some inexplicable reason he'd attempted to flirt with her on his first treatment day. What a stupid move. She was the last woman he should be flirting with.

Chemo brain? No. He hadn't had a treatment when he'd flirted with her, but chemo brain did exist. It made his thoughts fuzzy and his execution of speech feel as though the words came out of his mouth in slow motion.

Everyone was right. He couldn't have handled all this stuff alone. He hated being so dependent on other people, but he had to get used to the prospect in the weeks to come. Although he felt better today, he'd had a rough few days after his first treatment. He was certainly glad his mom was staying behind to help him after Clay returned to work. Max regretted never finding the time to talk to Clay alone.

Last week he might as well have been a human pincushion when he'd gone to the clinic for shots to boost his white blood cells. He'd also received his port for future treatments. Nothing like having a hole punched in your chest. It reminded him of how the breakup with Brittany had punched a hole in his heart, and that fact alone made his flirting with Heather even more crazy. She had everything to do with the demise of his love life.

During his visits, Heather had been all business and a little distant. Could he blame her?

The prayer ended, bringing Max's scattered thoughts to a halt.

As the congregation spilled out of the rows of folding chairs, Max spied Heather near the front as she talked with a group of teenagers. Even without her nurse's smock, she looked like she was in charge. He had the bad feeling he was going to get railroaded into moving, not only by Heather but his mother as well. After his mom had seen his less-than-stellar apartment, she'd changed her mind about the move.

Max detested having people tell him what to do. He liked living by himself. That way he didn't have to answer to anyone. But as things stood now, his life wasn't his own anymore. Everything had changed, so he'd better get used to the idea.

"Max, don't just stand there. Let's go see Heather." Beth prodded Max out of the row of chairs.

He nodded in Heather's direction. "Can't you see she's busy?"

"She's just talking, and she's expecting us."

"Sure." Max manufactured a smile even though he was frowning on the inside. He would somehow deal with these people who were trying to help, but it felt as though they were trying to run his life. He only had to remember not to do something stupid—like flirt with Heather again.

Max let his mother lead the way as they walked up the aisle. Despite his disconcerting feelings toward Heather, he couldn't help watching her interact with the teenagers. She waved her hands while she talked, her expression animated. Yeah, she'd always been that way. She never missed a chance to say what she thought or try to push someone into doing whatever she thought was best. Well, he wasn't going to let her push him around.

While he was giving himself a pep talk, Heather glanced in his direction. The look in her eyes told him that standing up to her wasn't going to be easy.

"Hey, Max and Beth." Heather waved as she walked toward them. "I'm so glad you made it."

"Thanks for inviting us." Beth extended her hand to Heather.

"Sure. I talked with Luke and Jeremy, and they're willing to have you as a roommate as long as you feel comfortable with the arrangement." Heather glanced around the room. "They should be here somewhere."

Max hung back, not saying a thing. He wasn't sure he wanted Heather to find Luke and Jeremy, but Max figured his mom was determined to secure roommates for him. She'd told him more than once how much she hated having him so far away. So if his sharing an apartment with these guys made her feel better, he would go along with it.

"Oh, there they are." Heather waved wildly as she looked at the back of the room. "Luke, Jeremy, come on over. I want to introduce you to Max."

Max turned. Two guys about his age sauntered toward the front. The tall one with bright-red hair grinned at Heather. Max wondered whether this guy had a special place in Heather's life. Annoyed with himself for even thinking about it, Max dismissed the thought. Heather's love life wasn't his concern. The other guy was nearly a foot shorter with dark hair and glasses. Max guessed that Jeremy was the redhead.

When Heather made the introductions, Max congratulated himself on his correct guess. He smiled and shook hands, hoping these guys wouldn't feel sorry for him. He didn't want pity, but he was afraid that was what he would get from people as soon as they learned he had cancer.

"You can stop by now and check out the apartment." Jeremy eyed Max.

"That sounds wonderful." Beth stepped in before Max could answer.

While his mother made arrangements for him, he wasn't sure whether he was surprised or annoyed that his usually introverted mother had taken it upon herself to answer for him and take charge of the upcoming events.

"Okay." Jeremy nodded. "We'll meet you there. Heather can show you the way."

Max stood there, still trying to sort through the way the people around him were directing his life. Maybe that's what cancer did—made your life everyone else's business.

"Let's go." Beth prodded Max toward the door.

Max obediently followed his mother and Heather outside as if he didn't have a will of his own. He stared at the back of Heather's head. This whole thing didn't make him happy, but he didn't want to make waves. He just wanted his old life back—the one with Brittany in it. Why did he keep going back to that impossible wish? Maybe just the fact that 10 percent of people with his kind of cancer didn't conquer the disease had him wishing he could go back and change the way he'd caused the demise of his relationship with her.

"Max, are you okay?"

He gazed at his mother. "Yeah, why?"

His mother stopped next to his beat-up car. "You seem distracted."

"I have a lot to think about." He didn't want his mother to worry, so he'd better get his act together and quit thinking about might-have-beens.

"I'm sure you do." Beth patted his arm, then turned to Heather. "You lead the way, and we'll follow."

"You could just ride with me, and we can swing back by here afterwards so Max can get his car, okay?"

Beth glanced at Max. "What do you think?"

Max shrugged. "Whatever."

"That sounds good to me." Beth headed toward Heather's car.

Max again followed. He slipped into the backseat as Heather got behind the wheel. For his mom, riding in Heather's late-model sedan was much better than riding in his old rattletrap.

During the short trip, Heather and his mom gabbed. He'd never seen her so talkative. Leaning his head back, he promised himself that he wouldn't let Heather or his mother run his life. But he feared he wasn't going to keep that promise. Right now he wasn't much of a match against the two females.

While he was trying to sort out the mess of his life, Heather parked her car in front of a three-story clapboard house with a porch that wrapped around one side. The second and third stories had balconies that looked out on the quiet tree-lined street.

Heather and his mom were out of the car and on the sidewalk before Max could get out of the backseat. Was the cancer making him slow, or was he reluctant to check out what would surely be his new residence? His mom was already exclaiming over the place without even stepping inside.

"The houses in this block are all what they call triple-deckers. They were built around the turn of the twentieth century, but most of them have been updated." Heather pointed across the street. "I live in the green one just down the block."

Max glanced toward her residence. Was she trying to show off her knowledge or just being informative? Would living this close to her always remind him of Brittany? Here in this new place he needed Heather's friendship, but that fact annoyed him. He was afraid her presence in his life would bring to mind his failures. It was hard enough to see her on his treatment days, and having her for a neighbor might be more than he could handle.

Was he losing his mind? Why couldn't he stop thinking about Heather?

As Heather strolled up the front walk, Jeremy and Luke walked out onto the porch. She waved. "We're ready for the grand tour."

Jeremy chuckled. "I don't know how grand it will be, but we'll give you a tour. We even threw out the old pizza boxes before you got here."

Max smiled as he stood beside his mom on the porch. Maybe this wouldn't be so bad after all. He felt right at home with pizza boxes. He suddenly realized why this whole scenario bothered him. Other than his freshman year in college, he hadn't had roommates. He'd lived by himself. Even growing up, he'd been an only child. His half brother and half sister were born after he'd gone away to college. Sharing a space with other people was something he would have to get used to doing again.

Luke opened the door and stood aside as he waved a hand toward the entrance hall. "Max and Mrs. Reynolds, after you."

Max let his mom go first. On the right was a staircase that led to the apartments on the second and third floors. On the left was the door leading into the first-floor apartment—possibly his new home. Luke led the way, and Max stepped into the hallway just inside the door. He caught his first glimpse of the living room straight ahead. Dark wood floors and woodwork filled his vision. A comfortable-looking sectional curved along two walls, and a big-screen TV sat on a stand on the opposite wall.

"Oh, this is lovely." Beth slipped her arm through Max's as she looked up at him. "Don't you think so?"

Max couldn't mistake the excitement in his mother's voice. "Yeah. It's nice."

"It's nicer than my place," Heather said. "This apartment has been completely updated."

Jeremy moved down the hall to his left, then looked back at Max. "This is the room you'd have if you decide to move in here."

"Max, this is great." Beth walked toward the window, her steps echoing in the empty room. She looked out before turning back to him. "You have a view of the front yard."

He nodded, not sure he shared his mom's enthusiasm for the place. It was appealing. So what made him hesitate? Heather?

"You have to see the rest of the place. It has a fantastic kitchen. It's too bad it's wasted on guys who order pizza too many times a week." Heather chuckled.

Pizza sounded fine to Max. He wasn't much for cooking. Did they each cook for themselves? He would have to learn the logistics of sharing this space. That's why it had always been easier not to have roommates. He'd been responsible for everything. While his thoughts roiled, Max followed the group down the hall until they came to the kitchen. Although it wasn't large, it had the updated appliances and a solid-surface counter. Someone had put a lot of money into this rental property. Maybe the rent was going to be more than he could afford even if it was split three ways.

"This is a wonderful kitchen." Gesturing around the room, Beth looked at Luke and Jeremy. "With this kitchen, none of you cook?"

"Peter was the one who cooked when he had time." Jeremy glanced at Heather with a wink. "We invite Heather over from time to time so she can show us her culinary skills in our fabulous kitchen."

Grinning, Heather nodded. "It's a treat."

"With Heather around to cook, maybe you won't starve." Beth eyed Max.

"I hardly think Heather wants to cook for me." Max tried to smile as he glanced Heather's way. She showed no reaction to his comment. His mom, on the other hand, was probably remembering the pizza boxes she'd seen stashed in the trash at his apartment.

Beth grimaced. "I didn't mean that she'd be cooking for you. I was just thinking that at least once a week you'd have something good to eat."

"Are you saying I'm a terrible cook?" Max put an arm around his mother's shoulders as he looked down on her.

"I'm not saying you're a bad cook, but I know you don't take the time to do it. That's all." His mom extracted herself from his embrace as she glanced between Heather and him. "It's nice that you've had a chance to reconnect with a friend from Montana. So you should take every opportunity to get together."

Great. His mom was pushing Heather on him. Not only did she live across the street, but they invited her over on a regular basis. Was God trying to send him some kind of message? First the cancer. Now Heather at every turn. Clay had always told Max that God's plans weren't always our plans. God's plans were best. Max had tried to keep that in mind, but the last couple of years he'd struggled with that idea.

After they'd finished looking at the rest of the apartment, and Jeremy and Luke gave Max the details about rent and utilities, he could come up with no argument against moving here except one. He had a lease to fulfill.

Max shook hands with Jeremy and Luke. "Thanks, guys, for the tour. I'll have to see what I can do about my lease. Then I'll let you know as soon as possible whether I can move in. In the meantime, if you find someone else, don't worry about me."

"I don't see any problem with waiting for your answer. We haven't had any responses to our ad for a roommate, so I'm sure we're good till you make your decision." Jeremy nodded.

"We'll deal with Max's lease even if I have to pay it off myself." Beth patted Max's arm.

Max resisted the urge to roll his eyes. He wouldn't argue with his mother in front of these other people.

Heather stepped forward. "I think the social worker

assigned to Max's case can help with that situation. I'll talk to her tomorrow."

Max suppressed an angry retort. They were planning his life again. He wanted all these people to quit meddling in his world. He wanted to feel in control again. He wanted his old life back.

"Thanks, Heather. I'm grateful for your help." Beth surveyed the group. "Let me take you all to lunch."

"Thanks, Mrs. Reynolds, but Luke and I have our regular Sunday lunch dates." Jeremy glanced at his phone. "I don't mean to rush off, but we're going to be late if we don't hurry."

"Don't let us keep you. Thanks for showing us the apartment. I appreciate everything you're doing for Max. It puts my mind at ease to know he won't be alone."

"We'll keep him in line." Luke smiled as he led the way to the door.

"Thanks." Beth smiled in return.

Even though his mother had smiled, Max didn't miss the misty-eyed expression behind her smile. And if Jeremy and Luke had regular Sunday dates, maybe he'd imagined Jeremy's interest in Heather. Max didn't know why he was concerned about it anyway.

As they walked to the car, Beth turned to Heather. "At least let us take you to lunch."

Wonderful. Just when he thought he would have some time to himself. More time with Heather isn't what he needed.

"What about you, Max? What do you think?"

Heather looked at him as if she knew that he wasn't excited about the prospect of having lunch with her or moving to a new place. Or was he reading something into her expression?

Max shrugged. "Whatever you guys plan is fine with me."

***

Heather was pretty sure Max wasn't enthused about sharing lunch with anyone, but especially with her. He'd been quiet today. He was obviously going along with whatever people said or asked just so he didn't upset anyone. She wasn't sure whether she should accept the lunch invitation, but she would be rude not to. Max would just have to deal with it.

"I'd love to go to lunch." Heather opened her car door. "Do you mind if I make a suggestion?"

"Please do." Beth settled into the front passenger seat as Max climbed into the back again.

"There's this place over in Hawthorne. It's a bed-and-breakfast, as well as a restaurant. I met the couple who owns it during the PMC last year. They were giving out coupons for free meals at the end of the ride."

"That was nice of them," Beth said.

"A bunch of us went out to dinner there, and the food was fabulous." Heather started the car and maneuvered it into the street.

"Sounds wonderful." Beth turned to Max. "Okay

with you?"

"Yeah."

Heather guessed that Max's one-word answers were going to be a common occurrence this afternoon. His demeanor spelled discontent. Was it just because of the cancer, or were other issues bothering him? Did she have any hope of drawing him out when he probably wished she weren't there to begin with? Maybe if she talked with Beth, she could elicit some conversation out of her son.

While they drove through Oakton toward Hawthorne, Heather asked Beth questions about life back home. Beth gladly answered all of Heather's inquiries, but Max said nothing. She tried to surreptitiously catch a glimpse of his expression in the rearview mirror. He was staring out the window, seemingly ignoring the female conversation. What had Brittany ever seen in Max? Heather had no clue. They'd dated for nearly eight years, so there must have been something.

As they arrived at the Hawthorne Inn, Heather pushed her troubling thoughts aside. She was going to enjoy this lunch no matter how Max acted. She hoped for Beth's sake that he wasn't sullen.

In minutes the hostess led them to a table on the side porch of the grand Victorian house. "This is beautiful. Next time we come to visit Max, we'll have to stay here." Beth turned to Max as he pulled out her chair. "I wish you'd told us about this place."

Grimacing, Max took his seat. "I didn't know

about it."

Beth nodded. "I forgot that you haven't lived in this area that long. Sometimes it seems like just yesterday that you moved here, and other times it seems as though you've been gone forever."

Max laughed halfheartedly. "Mom, I haven't lived at home for a long time."

"I know, but at least you were closer when you lived in Montana."

Heather took in the conversation as she gained more insight into Max's relationship with his mother. He obviously cared for his mom, but he wanted his own life. She couldn't blame him. She'd traveled from Montana to Massachusetts to do work in the oncology field so she could help people deal with their cancer. Now she had a patient who would test her abilities. During this lunch, she hoped to discover more about Max. Would he open up or continue to brood?

The waitress appeared and explained the daily specials while Beth and Max studied the menu. Deciding to order the special, Heather laid her menu aside.

"The special sounds good to me," Max said.

His statement surprised Heather. He'd actually spoken a complete sentence, not a one-word answer.

"That's what I'm having, too." Beth looked Heather's way. "What about you?"

Heather smiled. "Looks like it'll be three specials."

After the waitress brought their drinks and took their orders, Heather twisted the napkin in her lap.

What could she ask Max in order to get him to talk? If she talked to Beth, Max would sit there without saying a thing, just as he'd done on the ride here.

"Max is feeling pretty good today. He really only had one bad day after his treatment. Will that be the case with every treatment?" Beth's eyes brimmed with worry as she waited for Heather's answer.

As usual, Max didn't say a thing. Heather guessed that his tight-lipped expression meant that he wasn't particularly happy that his mother was discussing his condition.

"That's probably the way things will be for the first couple of treatments." Heather eyed Max. "You'll most likely find that with each successive treatment, you'll have more bad days. It's an accumulative effect."

"Yeah, I figured that."

Oh, good. A multi-word response. Heather treated this as a positive sign. "How do you feel about that?"

Max shrugged. "Comes with the territory."

Heather took a deep breath and chanced another question. "How are things at work?"

He nodded and gave another shrug. "Okay. Everyone understands about my health. Since I haven't been at my job very long, I was a little reluctant to tell them. I didn't know whether they might consider letting me go. But I figured in the long run, I'd have to explain the absences."

"I'm glad you told them. It's important that the people you work with know what's going on in your life. They're as much a support group as anyone else." Heather hated sounding like she still had on her nurse's cap, but she wanted to encourage him to reach out to as many people as possible.

"I'm hoping since my treatments are on Friday that I won't miss much work."

Beth sighed. "Max, you can't overdo."

He frowned at his mother, but he didn't say anything. Heather guessed that he figured whatever he said wouldn't make any difference. She wished she could reassure Beth that Max was in good hands, but a mother's worry was hard to overcome. While Heather stewed over the mother-son dynamic, the owner of the bed-and-breakfast approached their table.

"Hi, Molly.

"Heather, it's so good to see you." Molly glanced around the table. "You've brought some friends with you today."

Heather nodded. "I'd like to introduce you to Beth Reynolds and her son Max. I knew Max when I lived in Montana. He's living here now, and Beth is visiting from Washington State. Max, Beth, this is Molly Jansen."

"It's good to meet you." Molly shook hands with Beth and Max. "Beth, you're a long way from home. How do you like Massachusetts?"

"It's beautiful, but different from the beauty out west." Beth gestured toward the flowering trees growing next to the porch. "The spring flowers are lovely here, and your inn is charming."

Molly smiled. "Thanks. My husband and I own and run the Hawthorne Inn, so I hope you enjoy your meal. We appreciate your patronage."

As Molly hurried away, the waitress brought their meals to the table. Flavorful aromas filled the air. Conversation stopped, and Beth held out her hands. "Let's give thanks for our food."

Beth grabbed Max's hand. With a twinkle in his eyes, he held out his hand to Heather as if he knew she wasn't exactly comfortable with this scenario. She had no problem giving thanks for their meal, but she wasn't used to holding hands while she prayed. Now she had to hold hands with a man who more often than not annoyed her. She'd prayed that God would take away her feelings of discomfort with Max. She thought things were getting better, but the old feelings of animosity popped up when she least expected it.

Before she could analyze her feelings further, she put her hand in his, closed her eyes and bowed her head. Although Beth's prayer was short, the warmth of his touch lingered even after they dropped hands.

Not wanting to see his expression, Heather took a bite of her food before she looked up and focused her attention on Beth. "Beth, how much longer do you intend to stay?"

"I'm hoping to see Max get moved, then head back to Pinecrest." Beth grimaced. "I hate to leave, but Alex and Abby need me back home."

Heather nodded. "It's tough wishing you could be in two places."

"That's so true." Beth reached over and touched Heather's arm. "Promise me you'll take good care of Max."

Heather didn't know what to say. Max was probably mentally rolling his eyes, if not actually doing so. She ventured a glance in his direction. He was grinning—the last thing she'd expected to see. Maybe he was enjoying her discomfort as much as he disliked his mother's interference.

Finally, Heather looked at Beth. "I'll try my best. It is my job to help him."

Max leaned back and rested his elbows on the arms of his chair as he steepled his fingers. A lazy smile continued to curve his mouth. "Mom, I know you mean well, but I'm not ten years old. Heather is my nurse, not my babysitter."

Beth shook her head. "I know. I know. But when I go home, I'll be worrying about you."

"Just pray for me."

"I know that, too." Misery etched lines across Beth's face. "But I'll still worry."

"It'll be okay." Max patted his mother's shoulder as he looked at Heather. "Tell her everything will be good."

Heather wished she could do that. Chances were that Max's treatment would go without a hitch, but nothing was certain when it came to cancer. She had to say something encouraging to Beth. "Lymphoma is one of the most treatable cancers. You can count on that. In fact, many people are successfully treated for cancer."

Blinking hard, Beth nodded. Heather recognized the older woman's efforts to fight back tears.

"Mom, it's going to be okay." Max picked up his fork. "Let's eat rather than talk about my health and your worry. Let's just enjoy this time we have together."

A little smile brightened Beth's face as she reached for her iced tea. "You're right. I should be glad for this time I have to visit with you. Thanks for reminding me."

"It's good to have you here. I'm glad you came."

"Me, too."

Heather took in the conversation between mother and son. Max's concern for his mother touched Heather, but she didn't want to get sucked in by his charm the way Brittany had. Heather wanted to help both Beth and Max, but she had to keep it all in perspective. Doing that would require a delicate balancing act. She wanted to be there when he needed help, but for her own emotional well-being, she had to keep Max at arm's length.

CHAPTER FIVE

While Max ate, he tried not to think about his mother's worries. He'd told her not to worry, but he knew she would anyway. He wondered if his own anxieties would return after his mother left, when he would have to deal with everything on his own.

Is that what he wanted—his mother gone? He wasn't so sure.

In the past couple of weeks, he'd warred with himself over his decisions. He'd made the choice to keep Heather as his nurse, and he'd made the choice to move in across the street from her. Now he had to live with those choices. His parents had served as a buffer in his relationship with Heather, whose heart was in the right place, but her tendency to take over people's lives grated on him. He had to get over it.

While Max stewed over his feelings, Molly and a young woman with blond hair approached their table. Heather smiled at the duo.

"Tara, I'm glad Molly brought you by." Heather stood and hugged the other woman. "Are you working?"

The blonde shook her head. "No, it's my Sunday

off, but Molly came and got me because she knew I wouldn't want to miss seeing you."

Heather looked over at Molly. "Thanks for letting Tara know I was here."

"You're welcome. Now I have to get back to work. I hope you're enjoying your meal."

"We are," Beth said. "I'm so glad Heather brought us here."

"Good. I'll see you later, Heather." Molly waved as she turned away.

Heather motioned to the empty chair at their table. "Tara, do you have time to visit?"

Tara nodded as she sat. "For a few minutes. Hailey's sleeping, and one of the other women is keeping an eye on her."

Heather looked up at Tara. "How's Hailey doing?"

"She's been really tired the past few days. We missed church this morning because she wasn't feeling well." Tara glanced around the table, a curious expression painting her features. "Are you going to introduce me to your friends?"

"So sorry Hailey isn't feeling well, and I'm sorry I forgot to introduce you." Grimacing, Heather shook her head. "Beth and Max, this is Tara Madsen." Heather motioned across the table. "Tara, I'd like you to meet Beth Reynolds and her son Max. Beth lives near Spokane, Washington. She's visiting Max, who used to live in Billings. So you have a Montana connection."

"It's always nice to meet someone who lived in

Montana. You don't meet many people from there." Tara smiled at Max. "Do you happen to know Parker and Brittany Watson?"

Max's stomach sank. He still had a hard time thinking of Brittany with her married name. Why was he suddenly confronted with people who knew her? He was trying to forget her, but reminders surrounded him, even here in Massachusetts. He finally nodded, but he certainly wasn't going to tell Tara that Brittany used to be his girlfriend. "Brittany and I went to school together, and Parker and I did a couple of projects together."

"It's good to meet someone who knows people from back home. Parker was the one who recommended the doctor for Hailey here in Massachusetts."

"Parker certainly is a good resource for finding physicians. I'm glad he was able to help you." Max hated praising Brittany's husband, but there was no denying that the man had connections all over the medical field.

"I know he helped us find the right doctor to treat Hailey's cancer."

Wow! Max had been feeling sorry for himself, but he couldn't imagine what it would be like to be a kid and have cancer. "How old is Hailey?"

"She's seven. " Tara tried to smile.

Max could see the hurt and worry in her eyes, and he realized it was the same look he'd seen in his mother's eyes. He had to be more understanding when his mom worried about him—when it seemed as though she was trying to run his life.

"Max, you'll have to meet Hailey. She's our Pedal Partner for the PMC. You could be a real help to her, especially—"

"You're right. I'd love to help her any way I can." Max cut off Heather's statement because he was afraid she was going to tell Tara that he had cancer. He didn't want Tara or anyone to feel sorry for him. Could he keep them from mentioning his condition? He eyed Heather and his mom as he gave his head a slight shake, hoping they both got the message not to broadcast his situation.

"Good. We need all the partners we can get. Has Heather told you about her big project?" Tara's question turned the subject of the conversation in a different direction.

Max looked at Heather. "No. What project is this? You have something going besides the PMC?"

Heather nodded. "It's a work in progress. Besides riding in the PMC to earn money for research, the singles group and youth group at church and whoever else we can recruit have been working to fund a house where the families of cancer patients can stay while they're undergoing treatment. We're really putting on a big fundraising push because we have to have the funds in two months, or we'll lose the property."

"Why would you lose it?" Max frowned.

"Someone else put in a bid for the property, but our agreement says we have ninety days to acquire the money before it goes to the other bidder." Heather sighed. "Thirty some days are already gone."

"Do you know who the other party is? Maybe if they know what the property is being used for, they'll rescind their offer."

Heather shook her head. "It's some nameless entity. No real person to talk to."

"You can't find out who's behind this entity?" Max asked.

"I suppose if we tried hard enough, but I figured I'd rather spend my time trying to raise the money rather than spending it chasing after the other bidder." Heather shrugged.

"That does make sense. I'd like to help when I can. Just tell me what to do." Max held his breath as he prayed that his mom wouldn't say anything about his health. He wanted to feel normal—not sick.

"Come help with the church youth group. They're really into this project." Heather gave him a challenging look.

"I'll do that."

Heather nodded. "Fantastic. I'm one of the sponsors, and we're always looking for volunteers."

Oh good. He should have thought about that before he made the commitment. Now he'd be spending more time with Heather, but he couldn't back out now. "The church youth group was a big part of my high school years, so I understand how important sponsors are."

"We meet on Wednesday nights, if you feel good

enough to make it."

Feel good enough. The words echoed around in Max's mind. Would Tara question Heather's statement? He didn't want to explain, but would that be inevitable—always having to explain?

"Max." His name came out of his mother's mouth in a scolding tone. "You're not going to overcommit, are you?"

"I hardly think helping with the youth group one night a week is overcommitting." Max held his breath and hoped that was the end of his mother's protests.

"I suppose you're right. Clay will be glad you're helping. You make him proud."

"Thanks." Swallowing a lump in his throat, Max nodded. Clay and the church youth group in Pinecrest had changed Max's perspective on a lot of things. Clay came into Max's life during his rebellious years and showed a fatherless boy how to be a real man. Max would always be grateful to the man he now called his dad.

Making Clay proud stood at the top of Max's list. What would Clay think about Max trying to find his biological father's family? Maybe it was a moot point now. He had more important things to do rather than chase after a family who didn't know he existed or, for that matter, might not even want to know him. Cancer certainly made him realign his priorities. Beating this disease trumped everything.

Tara stood. "I have to leave so I can get back to Hailey. Beth and Max, I enjoyed meeting you. Beth, I hope you enjoy the rest of your visit."

"Thanks. I will." Beth smiled.

Max released a long, slow breath as Tara left.

Heather raised her eyebrows as she stared at him. "Why didn't you want Tara to know you have cancer?"

The question shot straight to Max's heart. Why couldn't Heather mind her own business? He counted to ten in order to keep from saying something he might regret. Shrugging, Max narrowed his gaze as he looked at her. "I don't like to talk about it."

"I can understand that."

No, you can't, because you don't have cancer. The words were on the tip of his tongue, but he gritted his teeth to keep from saying them. "Then let it be."

"But sometimes, it's good to talk about it, especially when you could share with someone who really understands the struggle. Tara is someone like that. Hailey's such a brave little girl."

"I'm sure Tara's little girl is very brave." *Unlike you*. Max had halfway expected the words to come out of Heather's mouth, but they didn't. She didn't have to say them. Max had said them to himself. Did refusing to talk about his cancer make him a coward?

"I think Heather's right. You should talk about it." Concern painted his mom's face. "You can't keep everything bottled up inside."

Now his mom was giving him lectures, too. He didn't want to say anything that would upset her, so he'd smile and nod and pretend everything was okay.

After his mom left, he was going to have it out with Heather. He was going to tell her just exactly what he was thinking. Then maybe she wouldn't be so eager to have him talk about this rotten disease. She couldn't keep telling him how to run his life. Or could she?

***

"Did your mom's flight leave on time?" Heather maneuvered her car away from the curb.

Max nodded as he buckled his seat belt. If he didn't, Heather would be the first to remind him to do so. "Everything's going smoothly. She had a layover in Minneapolis. I talked to her just before she boarded her plane there."

"Then she should be home in a few hours."

"Yeah. Thanks for helping me get moved before she had to leave. I know that was a big worry for her."

"I think God is looking out for you. Everything just fell into place with the guys needing a roommate and your landlord finding someone to take your apartment right away."

Max forced a smile and nodded. If God was looking out for him, why did he have cancer? The question shot through his mind, but he didn't voice it. He wasn't sure Heather would appreciate his questioning God. Max didn't want to give her any more reasons for seeing him in a bad light.

"My mom was glad to see me through my first two treatments, even if she had to be away from Abby and

Alex on Mother's Day. Seeing that I wasn't completely down and out after my treatments helped to alleviate some of her worries."

Heather nodded. "I could tell she was happy to be with you on Mother's Day. And you do see that you need help, right?"

Max smiled wryly. "Yeah. You don't have to say 'I told you so.'"

"Sure I do." Heather grinned. "How's your appetite these days? Alice Mason has organized tonight's food for the teens. Her team always has the best meals."

"Aren't you supposed to leave your nurse's cap and questions at home when you're not at work?"

Heather shot him a perturbed look. "I'm asking as a friend, not your nurse."

Did she consider him a friend? That was something new and different. Another question he didn't want to verbalize. "There's nothing wrong with my appetite. As you know, the only thing that keeps me from eating is my mouth soreness, and that only occurs right after I have a treatment. Besides, I thought last week's food was great."

"So tonight's will be even better. And we've got something for you to take for your mouth pain after your next treatment." Heather parked her car. "Is everything good with Luke and Jeremy?"

"As far as I know. Have they said anything different?"

Heather shook her head. "They said everything's fine. I just wanted to get your opinion."

"Now you've got it. We're good." Max got out of the car and headed for the storefront meeting place.

Heather scrambled to catch up to him. "Are you sure? You don't seem very eager to talk about it."

Stopping, Max gazed at Heather. "They said it's good. I said it's good. Why can't you take our statements at face value?"

"Because you guys never say anything unless I ask." Heather shrugged.

Max laughed. "Guys don't sit around and talk about stuff like women do. Everything's okay, so what's to talk about?"

"Okay, okay. I get it." Heather hurried toward the door.

Max quickened his step and opened the door for her. She looked at him before they went inside. He wasn't sure whether she was pleased or annoyed that he'd held the door for her. Why did he even care? He still wasn't sure how to act around her. Did she still harbor ill will toward him? Her actions said she didn't, but maybe she was just putting on a good face in a difficult situation. He'd decided not to confront Heather about her need to run his life. He figured it wouldn't help their tentative relationship. He would just have to live with it.

Laughter and lively conversation bounced off the walls as Max and Heather stepped through the door. They maneuvered through the tables and chairs set up in a random order around the room. Delicious aromas filled the air. Max's stomach growled. He was hungrier than he'd realized.

Heather forged ahead toward the group of teenagers gathered near the front at a table that was laden with casserole dishes, bowls covered in plastic wrap, and disposable dinnerware. A couple of red-and-white thermoses sat at the far end of the table with a tower of red plastic cups sitting between them. Max stood back and watched while the kids greeted Heather. She fit right in. Why did that surprise him?

Looking his way, she waved him over. Why did he feel reluctant to interact with the group? He'd met most of these kids last week, and they'd eagerly accepted him. But in the back of his mind he wondered what they would think in a few weeks when he lost his hair. Would they feel sorry for him? He didn't want that to happen. As he joined Heather and the kids, he decided he had to start thinking of others rather than himself.

As the kids greeted him, three older ladies with graying hair and glasses welcomed him. Heather introduced him to the ladies as one of the new sponsors.

"Alice, Mary and Cheryl, it's nice to meet you." Max shook their hands.

Alice, the tallest of the three women, smiled. "It's also good to meet you, Max. Another person from Montana. Did you and Heather know each other before?"

Max nodded, knowing this whole conversation was going to remind him of Brittany again. One of these days her memory wasn't going to hurt. "Heather and I attended the same church back in Billings."

"How nice that you're able to reconnect here." Alice's blue eyes twinkled.

Max feared that twinkle might mean she thought a romance was in the works. He hoped to steer the conversation in another direction. "Heather tells me we're in for some fabulous food tonight. I hear you're a great cook."

Alice's wrinkled face turned pink. "Has Heather been bragging on me again?"

"She has, and I'm ready to taste some of that delicious-smelling food."

"It's about ready. So grab a plate." Alice hurried off with the other two women.

After a prayer of thanksgiving for the meal, Max lined up with the youngsters and soon had a plate filled with a barbequed pork sandwich, coleslaw, and potato salad. He found a seat at the table where Dave and Julie Murphy, the youth leaders, were sitting. They greeted him with handshakes and smiles. Two guys and three girls took the other seats at the table, and Max reintroduced himself to make sure he remembered their names. He was trying his best to put names with all the teens he'd met last week.

Conversation swirled around Max as the kids talked about their school and church activities. Their talk reminded him of his high school years and how he'd almost wound up with the wrong crowd. He hoped he could be a good influence on these teens and help steer them in the right direction, as Clay had done for him. Max pushed away recollections of Brittany that threatened to overtake his thoughts. She'd been a good influence on him, too, but these constant memories of her were doing him no good.

Besides, how good of an influence could he be on these kids when he had faith issues of his own? But he was working through them, wasn't he? He could see Heather was right about God working in his life through this difficult time. Was that why God had brought her into his life? Because God knew a familiar face would help?

Max glanced across the room to where Heather was sitting with another group of teens. Although he didn't like to admit it, she'd been a real help to him. For a second he wished she were sitting at his table. He banished that thought as fast as he could. Besides the fact that she didn't think much of him, her annoying habit of telling him what to do should make him want to be as far away from her as possible. Her presence always put his world on edge, but not necessarily in a bad way. He wasn't sure what that was all about.

"Max, what is it that you do?" Dave's question brought Max's attention back to the table where he sat.

He hoped he hadn't missed anything else while he'd focused on Heather. "I work in the lab at the local hospital where they conduct clinical trials. We do testing that helps scientists develop new treatments and drugs—mostly for cancer."

"You and Heather must have a lot to talk about since she's an oncology nurse."

Max wasn't quite sure how to respond to Dave's statement. What would he and all the others think when they learned he had cancer? "I only recently reconnected with Heather. We knew each other back in Montana through a mutual acquaintance."

"Nice that you ran into each other again." Dave resumed eating.

Nodding, Max wished the conversation would go in a different direction. Why did every discussion tonight bring his thoughts back to Brittany? He would gladly wipe Montana from his memory. He was here in Massachusetts, and that's where his life and thoughts should be.

Max glanced around the table at the teenagers. Maybe he could open up a new topic of conversation. "Heather mentioned that you guys were helping her raise money to buy the house where families of cancer patients can stay during the treatment period."

"Yeah. We've had bake sales and car washes—the usual stuff. Got any better ideas?" The boy with the brown hair and freckles shrugged.

"Justin, right?"

The boy nodded.

"So you need ideas. You can go on the Internet and find dozens of suggestions. I can help you go through them if you want." Max looked over at Dave and Julie. "What do you think?"

"We're glad for any suggestions." Dave finished the last bite of his sandwich. "Do you have a time when you want to do this?"

"Most evenings work for me. In fact, tomorrow night would be great." Time. Max had lots of free time. This project would definitely give him something to do—maybe help take his mind off his health issues. How would Heather react to his involvement in the fundraising ventures? There he was, worrying about her judgment again. If it wasn't Brittany on his mind, it was Heather. Brittany was unattainable, and Heather was a necessary irritation in his life.

Dave looked at Julie. "Does that work for you, honey?"

"Sure." Julie nodded. "About seven?"

Dave motioned to the teenagers at the table. "How about you guys? Can you come over to our house tomorrow to discuss it?"

The kids nodded in agreement as they got up to throw their plates in the trash. Justin stopped beside Max's chair and looked at Dave. "Do you mind if we bring some other kids who are interested in the fundraising?"

Dave smiled. "Sure. The more people we have, the more money we can raise."

"Will do." Justin sauntered away.

"Hey, thanks for jumping right in here to help." Dave extended his hand.

Max stood and shook Dave's hand. "You're

welcome. You'll have to give me directions to your house."

"You live across the street from Heather, don't you?"

"Yeah." Max had a bad feeling that this venture was going to include her.

"Good. She can give you a ride or directions— whichever works out for you guys."

"Sure. I'll talk to her." Max threw away his plate, then moseyed over to the table where Heather still sat with some teenage girls. Maybe he should just get used to having her around at every turn.

Heather looked his way as he drew near. "Hey, did you enjoy your meal?"

Max gave her a lopsided grin. "Yeah. You were right. Great food."

Heather patted the empty chair next to her. "Come over here and let me introduce you."

Max slid onto the chair. "Hey, everyone. I think I met a couple of you last week, and I apologize for not remembering your names."

"That's okay. You're new, and there are lots of names to remember." A petite redhead batted her eyelashes at him. "I'm Megan, and these are my friends Ashley, Cadi, and Sarah."

"Hi, girls. You can test me on your names next week." Max smiled, then turned to Heather as he tried not to let the little red-haired girl remind him of Brittany. "I was talking to Dave about fundraising for your project, and he's set up a meeting for tomorrow at his house."

"And I'm supposed to be there."

Max wrinkled his brow. "How'd you know?"

"Dave sent me a text while you were talking to the girls." Heather grinned. "He says you need a ride to his place."

"Or directions."

"I can drive you. No sense in taking two cars. Dave and Julie live near the town line on the west side."

"Sure." Max didn't like having to depend on Heather for a ride, but he didn't blame her for not wanting to ride in his old heap. He didn't see himself getting a new car anytime soon either. Even with his insurance, his medical expenses would eat up any saving he'd had toward a new vehicle.

"Okay, then. We're set for tomorrow." Heather surveyed the teens at the table. "Do any of you want to attend the fundraising meeting tomorrow night at Dave and Julie's?"

"Me." Megan waved her hand as she smiled at Max. "Are you going to be in charge? I'll be glad to help any way I can."

"Not necessarily in charge." Max shrugged. "I just have some ideas I'm going to share."

Before anyone else could say something, Dave stood up and whistled for attention. "Okay, everyone, we're ready for our lesson."

Max leaned back in his chair and stretched his legs out in front of him. He liked Dave's lessons, or at least the lesson he'd given last week. He knew how to talk to teens. He opened his Bible and urged the teens to do the same. Max fished his cellphone from his pocket and brought up the Bible app.

Dave glanced around the room. "Let's read from the seventh chapter of Ecclesiastes, verses thirteen and fourteen. 'Consider what God has done: Who can straighten what he has made crooked? When times are good, be happy; but when times are bad, consider this: God has made the one as well as the other. Therefore, no one can discover anything about their future.'"

While Dave expounded on the verses, Max noted they spoke right to him. He had to grab on to the happy times and deal with the bad ones because God had made them both. Max let the meaning of the words wash over him. He had to make sure to enjoy every minute of the good times in between his treatments. He shouldn't waste a minute feeling sorry for himself when the days were good. He promised himself that he wouldn't let the bad times get him down. He was seeing more and more how God had placed certain people in his life, even Heather.

After the lesson was over, the kids straightened the room, and Dave and Julie set up several board games. The rest of the evening was filled with fierce competition and laughter. Max enjoyed the challenge of Scrabble. He hadn't played it since he used to play with Brittany and her family when he was in high school. Max sighed. Everything from the games to the redheaded teenage girl, whose obvious interest in him reminded Max of Brittany. How was he ever going to get over her?

When the events of the evening concluded, Max walked out with Heather. As they neared the car, she leaned over and whispered, "I think someone has a crush on you."

Max stopped midstep and grinned at her. "You?"

The shock on her face nearly made him laugh, but she quickly gathered her composure as she shook her head. "No offense, but you're not my type."

"Yeah, I already knew that. Whose type am I? Certainly not Brittany's." He'd been biting his tongue all evening to keep from saying things he'd regret. Wishing he could undo the whole conversation, he grimaced.

"You're right about that." Heather suddenly looked serious. "I talked with Brittany a few days ago. I wasn't going to say anything to you because—"

"Because why?"

"I thought you didn't like to talk about her."

He stared at Heather. Had he ever said that to her? He certainly wasn't going to tell her that losing Brittany was like losing an arm or a leg. Besides being the love of his life, she'd been his best friend. He should be glad for her happiness, but their former relationship haunted him. He'd dream that they were back together only to wake and find reality telling him she was no longer a part of his life. "I'm sure I've given you that impression. For eight years she was there beside me."

Heather didn't respond to his statement as she

buckled her seat belt. She was probably feeling sorry for him or thinking he was pathetic for not being able to get over Brittany. Two years should be plenty of time. So what was his problem?

They rode in silence the few blocks to their street. After stopping her car in front of Max's place, Heather turned to him. "Thanks for your interest in the family house."

"I'm glad to be part of the project. It's a good thing you're doing." Max had to admit he admired Heather's helping heart, despite her meddling personality.

"Thanks." Surprise sounded in her voice. "I'll see you tomorrow night. I'll pick you up at six thirty."

"You want to eat ahead of time? My treat."

"Uh…yeah…sure." Even in the dim light, Max read the astonishment in Heather's expression. "What time should I pick you up?"

"Pick me up when I get off work at five. That should give us enough time to eat and get to the Murphy's house." Max opened the car door.

"Okay. I'll see you then." Heather gave him a little wave as he got out, amazement still registering on her face.

Max smiled to himself as Heather drove the short distance down the block. He watched her until she disappeared inside the house. He stood there in the moonlight and tried to figure out what was happening. He'd just asked the woman who had played a hand in the demise of his love life to have dinner with him.

Either he wished to subject himself to torment, or God was changing his heart. Max suspected the latter.

CHAPTER SIX

The blue numbers on the digital clock on the dash of Heather's car read five after five. She tapped her fingers on the steering wheel and stared at the hospital entrance where Max had told her to meet him. She really shouldn't have expected him to walk out the door promptly at five, but surely he wouldn't be much longer. Would she be sitting here a half hour from now still waiting as Brittany had done so often?

Heather pushed away the vexing question. She shouldn't jump to conclusions about Max based on the past. She wasn't sure what to make of his invitation to go to dinner with him. After all, he hadn't been the least bit reluctant to bring up her part in his breakup with Brittany. Heather shook her head. The man was a mystery. Maybe the cancer was making him rethink his attitudes? But if he failed to show soon, nothing about him had changed.

Ten minutes later, Heather was about ready to drive off, when Max stepped out the door. As he looked her way and smiled, her heart lurched. Why? Too many things about him annoyed her, but shouldn't she be more understanding and forgiving?

She took a deep breath. He wasn't that late, and she

didn't need to let anything about him irritate her. That would accomplish nothing.

As he drew closer, she couldn't help thinking that even gaunt looked good on him. His good looks might attract her attention, but his perpetual tardiness exasperated her.

"Hi." Max opened the door and slid into the passenger seat. "Where would you like to eat?"

Despite her annoyance, Heather produced a smile. "The Ninety Nine?"

"Should I know that place?" He buckled his seat belt.

Heather shrugged. "I forgot you haven't been here that long. Still, I can't believe you've never eaten at a Ninety Nine."

"Is this a special place?"

Heather started the car. "A local chain with good food."

"Okay by me."

As Heather drove away from the hospital, she wondered what kind of conversation she could possibly have with Max. Starting off with a mention of his lack of promptness would begin the evening with a negative mood. The past was off limits because it included Brittany. The present involved his poor health, and he didn't want people to know about his health issues. Could she convince him to share so people could pray for him, or would he get irritated if she brought it up?

Not much else was left to fill the silence. The

thought of a dinner void of conversation stretched before her like an endless game of solitaire that she could never win.

During the drive, Heather glanced at Max as he pulled his cell phone out of his pocket. So he wasn't going to talk to her. He'd rather scroll through his emails or whatever on his phone than have a conversation. Why had he asked her to go out to eat? Why was she getting herself all worked up over nothing?

Heather promised herself that she wouldn't let him irritate her. She would survive the evening no matter how Max conducted himself—silent, talkative, or somewhere in between.

After they arrived at the restaurant, the hostess immediately showed them to a booth with a rustic dark wooden table and benches. Thankfully, Max had pocketed his cell phone as soon as they got out of the car, but he still didn't say anything. He'd barely said a whole sentence since she'd picked him up, and she feared saying the wrong thing. So there they were, sitting across from each other as they studied their menus in silence.

"Any recommendations?" Max's deep voice startled her.

She jerked her head up and met Max's gaze as he stared at her over the top of the menu. Her heart did a little stutter step. There it was again—that strange reaction when she looked at him. Recommendations? Her mind went blank, and she swallowed a lump in her throat. "Anything you order will be good."

"What do you usually get?"

"Me?" She was beginning to sound like she had no brain.

"Do you see anyone else here who can give me an answer?" He gave her a lopsided grin as he waved a hand around the booth.

Heather returned his smile, feeling the tension drain from her shoulders. She pointed to the menu. "I usually have this chicken dish. You can't go wrong with anything you choose."

He nodded as he studied the menu further, then laid it aside. "Do you come here often?"

"Actually, I don't eat out a lot at night since I usually eat out at lunch."

"I usually eat lunch at the hospital cafeteria."

Heather raised her eyebrows. "And the food is good?"

Max chuckled. "It's okay. I know hospitals aren't usually known for their cuisine."

The waitress appeared, and Heather wasn't surprised when Max ordered a burger instead of the chicken. After the waitress left, they sat in silence. Could she get him to talk about himself?

"What made you decide to come to Massachusetts, other than the job?" Heather hoped the question would open the conversation again.

A hint of a frown colored Max's expression as if he didn't want to answer. Maybe his reasons were personal, and he didn't want to share them with her.

The unanswered question hung there like a cobweb in an otherwise pristine room. Was he going to say something or just stare at her? Should she say something?

"I thought you came to Massachusetts to work in oncology research. How come you're working as a nurse instead?"

So he was going to avoid answering by asking her a question. Maybe her answer would finally result in something besides silence. "Yes, my original job was in research, but I was initially led to believe that I would be working directly with patients while we were doing the research. In the beginning I did, but I began to see fewer and fewer of them. I missed having direct contact with the patients, so I took the job with Dr. Duffey."

"You like it better than your old job?"

"Totally." Heather wondered whether she could bring up her original question in a roundabout way. "Do you like your new job here better than your old one in Montana?"

Just at that moment, the server appeared with their orders. Heather's question was lost in the shuffle of plates and flatware. She unfolded her napkin and placed it on her lap. How many times could she bring up the same subject without appearing nosy?

Max glanced up from his food. "Looks good. Would you like me to give thanks?"

"Sure." Heather bowed her head and listened to Max's quick prayer.

For a few moments they ate in silence, the laughter and conversation of the other diners floating around them. If she tried again, would he finally give an answer to her question? "Are things going okay for you at work with having to take time off for your treatments?" Heather held her breath.

Max set the burger on his plate. "So far so good. I haven't had to take time off yet. I go in early on Fridays when I have my treatment, and by Monday I feel good enough to go to work."

"That might not always be the case."

Max nodded. "I know. My boss says I can have whatever time off I need, but that also means losing part of my paycheck since I have no sick time or vacation time accrued with this job."

Heather wanted to express her concern from Max's situation, but she suspected from the very beginning that he didn't want sympathy. Despite their less-than-amiable past, maybe Max's invitation to join him for dinner had a lot to do with his wanting a friend, not a nurse. But how could she be his friend if he didn't talk to her? "I'm glad things are okay for you at work."

"Yeah, me too."

They fell silent again. Max seemed content to eat without conversation. Heather hated it. His reticent behavior jogged her memory. She'd asked herself about his quiet nature during their initial interview. He'd been quiet when they'd gone out to lunch with his mom. Heather also recalled how quiet he was around Brittany. She'd done all the talking. Besides being perpetually late, he was also perpetually quiet. Not a good combination.

What could she say to start a conversation? Why was she always trying to think of something to talk about? She had to give it another try. "I understand that you have a number of fundraising ideas."

Max looked up at her as if he'd forgotten she was even there. He gave her a halfhearted smile as he nodded. "A few, but I have one that I'd like to run by you."

Heather hoped her surprise didn't show on her face. Max was actually going to confide in her? "Sure. What do you have in mind?"

"I was part of something like this in high school. It worked because one of the most popular teachers proposed it. So I don't know if it will work for me."

"What will work?"

"If I shave my head." He grinned and ran a hand through his rather shaggy dark locks.

"To raise money?"

"Yeah, you know, like I'll shave off all my hair if the kids raise X-amount of money. But they don't know me that well. So I'm not sure it will work." Max grimaced. "Besides, I don't know how long it will be before my hair starts falling out on its own."

Could she convince him that telling the kids about his cancer would go a long way in getting them behind the project? "I can't predict when your hair will start falling out, but I would say sooner rather than later."

"So not much point in making the proposal. My hair could be gone before they have a chance to raise the money." Max's shoulders sagged as he picked up a french fry and dipped it in ketchup.

Heather shook her head. "Not necessarily. Besides, I think if you let the kids know, they'll jump right in with the project."

"But—"

"But nothing. I know you've said before you don't want to talk about it because you don't want people to feel sorry for you, but this is a perfect opportunity to get people on your side. You were worried about not knowing the kids for very long. If you tell them about the cancer, that will change everything. They'll be on your side immediately and won't care when you shave your head."

Max took a big gulp of his drink, then stared at her over his glass. "You think?"

"I do." Wondering whether she could get through to Max, Heather set down her fork. "With more people knowing about your cancer, you'll have more people praying for you. Don't dismiss the power of prayer."

The set of Max's mouth telegraphed his annoyance. "I'm not dismissing the power of prayer, but I like my privacy."

Heather shrugged and decided to let Max wallow in his solitude. She should have known he wouldn't take her advice. "Suit yourself."

Heather tried not to let her exasperation with

Max's attitude fester. He had a right to privacy concerning his health issues. But why was he so reluctant to share?

"Will you explain to the kids if I tell them about my cancer?" Max's question nearly made Heather drop her fork.

She forced herself to proceed with caution. "So you're saying that you're okay with telling the kids tonight?"

A look of uncertainty crossing his features, Max sat there without saying a thing for a few moments. Finally he nodded. "If you think it'll help the fundraising for your project."

"It will. I'm sure of it." Heather couldn't help smiling. "Thanks for being willing to help out. You don't know how much I appreciate it."

"You can thank me after we've raised some money." Max resumed eating. "I want your project to be a success."

Heather nodded as she lifted her water glass. "A toast to our success."

Grinning, Max picked up his glass and clanked it against hers. "To success."

What had suddenly changed Max's mind? She didn't want him to have any regrets, especially since she'd reassured him of the teens' acceptance. If things didn't go as she expected, events would validate his earlier assessment that she had negative feelings about him. She couldn't let that happen.

***

Max strode up the front walk toward the Murphy's white clapboard house. A crab apple tree festooned with pink flowers had a prominent spot in the yard. Even the beauty of the tree didn't take away the trepidation at the thought of telling everyone about his cancer. His dinner churned in his stomach.

He turned to Heather as they went up the three steps leading to the porch that spanned the entire front of the house. "This place reminds me of the house my mom and I lived in when we first moved to Pinecrest. It had a big front porch like this."

"Do your parents still live there?"

Ringing the doorbell, Max shook his head. "We rented the apartment on the first floor, and Clay lived in the upstairs apartment. That's how my parents met. We moved to a new place after they got married."

Before Heather could comment, Dave Murphy answered the door. "Hey, good to see you. Come on in."

Max stood aside so Heather could go inside first, then followed her into the front hall. Dave ushered them into the living room on the right. Several of the teens were already there, including Megan, who immediately greeted them. Max looked over at Heather as Megan situated herself next to Max on the couch. Heather gave him a knowing look, and he wondered what Megan would think when she discovered he had cancer. What was he supposed to do with a teenage girl who had a crush on him?

Thankfully, he didn't have to think much about it, as several more teens entered the room and Dave recruited Megan to man the chart where he planned to list all the viable fundraising activities. She smiled sweetly at Max as she stationed herself next to the white board, marker in hand.

Heather poked him in the ribs and leaned closer. "The crush is alive and well."

Max gave Heather an annoyed look. "I'd venture to say not for long."

Dave let out a sharp whistle, and the group quieted. After he said a prayer, he handed out the list of fundraising ideas. "Max has provided this list for us. Take a few minutes to read it over, and then we'll discuss it and come to a consensus on the best ones to use."

While everyone looked over the list, Max contemplated his announcement. What would be the reaction? Tonight he was feeling good. Sometimes he had to remind himself that he actually had cancer. The excellent perspective for the day reminded him to embrace the good days because the bad ones were sure to come.

He'd asked Heather to dinner to run the head-shaving idea by her, but he had considered not mentioning it. When she'd started asking him questions about why he had come to Massachusetts, he'd almost told her about the search for his biological father's family. He wasn't sure whether he could find a confidant in Heather. The old animosity still lived in the dark corners of his heart. He had to learn to let go and have peace with the bossy, yet kind, nurse.

She acted like his friend, but he suspected she had reservations about his character. He didn't know for sure where he stood with her, and he wasn't sure why he cared. At times she seemed like a lifesaver in the storm of his health issues, and other times her presence was like a huge wave that inundated him with bad memories.

He hoped Heather was right in her assessment that the kids would rally around him when he announced he had cancer.

Before Max could formulate what he intended to say, several teens started making suggestions and voicing their opinion on some of the fundraising ideas. A lively conversation filled the air. After a half an hour of discussion, Megan wrote the most popular ideas on the board. The group prioritized them.

Heather glanced his way. The expression on her face told him the time had come. Did he want her dictating his actions? Stupid question. He had to get over worrying about what she thought of his actions. This whole fundraising thing was bigger than either of them.

Standing, Max waved one hand. "Dave, I've got something else I'd like to run by everyone."

"Sure." Dave smiled. "We can always use another idea."

Max took a deep breath and released it in a heavy

sigh as he turned to face the teens sitting in the semicircle. How did he start? He didn't dare look at Heather, but he couldn't stand here and look at the floor. "I'm not sure where to start with this. You don't know me that well, but I'd like to share a prayer request with you." *God, please give me the words*. Max swallowed a lump in his throat. "This group is all about helping people with cancer...I need your prayers because I've recently been diagnosed with Hodgkin lymphoma."

A collective gasp erupted. The crescendo of voices grew louder until Heather stepped to the front and waved her hands above her head. "Okay, everyone, let's quiet down. In addition to asking for your prayers, Max is hoping to gain your support with this fundraising idea. He's going to be shaving his head in the next few weeks, so he thought we could have a contest. The person who raises the most money by the end of the month gets to shave his head."

Another wave of voices filled the room until Heather drew their attention again as she picked up a clipboard and waved it in the air. "You can sign up on the sheet I have here."

As the cacophony of voices subsided, Max wasn't sure he was happy about her intervention. But that was Heather, and she probably wasn't going to change, especially for him. He looked her way. "Thanks."

Dave went to stand beside Max. "Before we sign up, let's have a prayer for Max and our fundraising efforts."

Max bowed his head while Dave prayed. Despite the prayers of friends and family, Max couldn't shake the fear this disease created in his mind. Did God want him to recover? What was the purpose in God's plan? Clay always reminded Max of the Scripture in Romans that talked about all things working for good. Somehow he had to believe there was good in this disease somewhere.

When the prayer ended, Megan was the first to sign the sheet. Afterward she came up to Max. "I'll be praying for you every day."

"Thanks." Max tried to smile as he looked over her head to see Heather grinning at him. Should he see humor in this? Maybe that was it. He had to learn to laugh at this situation—not easy.

Even after everyone expressed plans to pray for Max and help with the fundraiser, he still had mixed feelings about having revealed his illness. Their knowledge of his condition put him in a vulnerable position. He should be grateful for their concern.

He liked his space—a chance for solitude. All of that had disappeared. He had medical people, roommates, and now a group of teenagers poking and prodding around in his business. His solitude was a thing of the past. Could he ever regain his former life?

While the disconcerting thoughts whirled in Max's mind, he smiled and nodded as he spoke to each person. The whole scenario seemed like an out-of-body experience. The teens wanted to pray for him as they showed their concern, but probably no one at Dave's understood what it was like to have a life-threatening disease.

He had to quit thinking about himself. Focusing on Heather's project and the fundraisers should help to keep his mind focused on the right things. Maybe that was what God was trying to teach him.

Selflessness.

A big lesson to learn.

"That went well. Would you agree?" Heather looked at him as if she wasn't quite sure how he would answer.

Max gave her a lopsided smile. "Yeah, I guess."

Heather leaned closer. "And you still have your biggest fan."

"And what am I going to do about that?"

Heather shrugged as she gave him a silly grin. "Can't help you with that one."

"Sure you can, but you just like to see me squirm." Max put on his best annoyed look. "You like to pump me full of poison and wait for my hair to fall out."

"Are you trying to make me laugh or cry?"

"Both."

Chuckling, Heather nodded. "You did the right thing tonight, even if it doesn't feel like it."

"Thanks for the encouragement."

"Anything to help. That's my job."

"You don't have to have your nurse's cap on all the time."

"It's not just my nurse's cap. It's a friend's cap,

too." Heather eyed him with a slight grimace. "I know things haven't always been so good between us, but I hope we can leave that behind."

"I'm working on it." Max wondered how Heather knew what was going through his mind. Probably her experience with so many cancer patients made her more aware of the things those with the disease thought about. He appreciated that she was on his side. He kept trying to make that notion a major part of his thinking, but his brain was stuck in the past. He needed a fast-forward button that would propel his mind away from the toxic thoughts that kept him stuck in old hurts.

Before Heather could reply, Dave joined them as he extended his hand to Max. "I wanted to tell you that if you ever need anything, let Julie and me know. And I'm not just saying that. We're here to help you with anything."

Max shook Dave's hand. "Thanks. I appreciate that. So far things have been okay. Your lesson from Ecclesiastes on Wednesday really hit home for me."

"God put that lesson on my heart. Now I know why." Dave smiled and glanced at Heather. "So are you taking care of this guy?"

Raising her eyebrows, Heather eyed Max. "That all depends on your perspective."

"Yeah." Max laughed halfheartedly. "I like to call her my own Nurse Ratched."

Heather shot him an irritated look. "Someone has to keep him in line."

Max grinned. "I suppose that's right."

Dave chuckled. "I can see you two know how to keep things light even when a lot of heavy stuff is involved. I'll remember you both in my prayers."

"Thanks." Heather nodded. "We'll need them. Now I have to get my patient home."

A round of good-byes accompanied Max and Heather's departure. When they reached the car, Heather looked at Max over the top as she opened the door. "Nurse Ratched? Really? That's a low blow."

Shrugging, Max grimaced. "Guess I should've kept that thought to myself."

Heather got into the car and buckled her seat belt while Max did the same. What madness had made him mention his "Nurse Ratched" thoughts about Heather? Chemo brain? He couldn't keep using that as an excuse for the stupid things he said.

"No, I'm glad to know what you think of me."

Max let out a loud sigh. "Does this mean you're going to poke me with more needles to get even?"

Heather didn't say a thing as she slowed the car to a stop at a traffic light. Had he annoyed her again? Maybe he should just keep his mouth shut, or maybe he should just tell her that he thought she was bossy and barged in sometimes when she wasn't wanted. The temptation to say that very thing grabbed hold of his thoughts and wouldn't let go. He closed his eyes and prayed that he wouldn't succumb to that temptation.

"Are you all right?"

Max opened his eyes and looked over at Heather. "Yeah, just tired." *Tired of enduring your constant meddling.*

"Then I'd better get you home."

Too tired to respond, Max laid his head back against the seat and stared straight ahead. When they arrived at his house, he hopped out of the car and said his thanks and good-byes. He jogged toward the house without a backward glance. He didn't want to think about Heather and their somewhat antagonistic relationship.

Max went straight to his room. He didn't want to talk to Luke or Jeremy. The thought of conversation made Max want to hide. He plopped down on the bed and lay there staring at the ceiling as if words of wisdom would suddenly appear there. Finally, he decided to get ready for bed before he fell asleep in his clothes.

After he brushed his teeth, he stared at himself in the mirror above the sink. Thin, but he still had his hair. What would he look like without it? He'd know sooner than he'd like. So much about tonight put him in turmoil.

Sharing his situation.

Dealing with Heather.

Trying to forget the past.

Was all this emotional upheaval a result of the cancer? He wished he could say yes, but he'd never come to grips with losing Brittany. How many times had he told himself that he had to move on only to fall back into the poor-poor-miserable-me pattern that had plagued him for the last two years? Every time he promised himself he'd get over it and move on, he failed. Somehow he would change that pattern.

CHAPTER SEVEN

Nothing much was different since Heather had convinced Max to share his health issues with some of the teens nearly three weeks ago. She'd seen him through one more treatment and cooked a couple of meals for him and his roommates. During all this time, despite their relationship as nurse and patient and their shared church activities, she didn't know him much better than she did the day she'd walked into the exam room and found him sitting there. He remained a puzzle she couldn't solve because he kept everything close to the vest unless she dragged it out of him.

Preparing to head to the Wednesday evening youth meeting, Heather waited in her car for Max to walk down the block and across the street to where she was parked. She was willing to pick him up, but he'd reminded her that she said he should be as active as possible and insisted on making the short walk as long as he felt like it. This arrangement always tested her patience because he had a tendency to arrive at the last possible minute. Tonight was no different.

The sunlight glinted off the hood of her car as the sun sat in the sky just above the tree line. She squinted toward Max's place, but there was no sign of him. After waiting several minutes, Heather glanced at her phone as she let out a heavy sigh. Max was later than usual. Should she call? Just as she picked up her phone, he walked out the front door. Someone was with him. A woman with auburn hair, the reddish-brown highlights evident in the waning sunlight. Did Max have a fascination with redheaded women? This woman's hair was brown with hints of red, not the coppery color of Brittany's or Megan's hair, but still another redhead.

The woman was tall with a well-endowed figure. They stood on the porch together as they talked. Then Max walked her to her car. Before she opened the car door, she gave Max a hug, and he clearly hugged her back. Heather's heart thumped, and a flash of jealousy flitted through her mind.

Why? She had no clue. There was so much not to like about the man.

The woman drove away as Max waved and jogged down the street. When he reached Heather's car, he opened the door and folded his lanky frame into the passenger seat.

He looked at her and smiled. "Sorry I'm late. I had company."

"I saw." Heather wondered if she should ask about the woman. "A friend?"

"Ah, no. My cousin...well, my stepcousin, Amanda."

"Kissing cousin?"

Shaking his head, Max gave Heather a horrified glance. "Spare me. I wouldn't consider that in any circumstances. Cousin or no cousin. Too high maintenance for me."

Interesting. Heather started her car and proceeded down the street. Is that what had happened with Brittany? Max considered her too high maintenance? She wanted attention he couldn't give her. "What's too high maintenance?"

"You've never heard that expression?"

"I've heard it, but I was just curious as to what you meant by it."

Max shook his head. "Where do I begin?"

"I don't know. You're the one who called her that."

"Yeah, with good reason." Max grimaced. "She's spoiled and wants her own way all the time. Surprised me when she called. She said her dad told her about my cancer, and she wanted to see me since she's going to school in Boston."

"Maybe she's grown up since you last saw her."

"Maybe, but she had a long way to go. When I was in high school, she and her dad and little sister moved to Pinecrest." Max rolled his eyes. "You should've seen her flaunting her thirteen-year-old self around my friends. When she wasn't doing that, she was complaining about living in Pinecrest."

"You have to give her credit for coming to see you."

"Yeah, I suppose, but I figure there's some ulterior

motive somewhere. I never saw any change in her in the two years before I graduated and went away to college. She was in a constant pout unless she was trying to flirt with my friends."

"Guess she's not on your list of favorite people." Heather wondered whether she was on the same list, but she wasn't going to ask. "Where's she going to school?"

"Some music college. I forget." Max shrugged again. "She has a fantastic singing voice. That's the one good thing I can say about her."

"Is this the first time she's contacted you?"

"Yeah."

"Did you know she was in Boston?"

"Yeah, but I wasn't very interested in seeing her."

"So it works both ways."

"Are you trying to say I should've looked her up?" Max frowned. "My parents didn't even contact her while they were here."

"They had other things on their minds."

"I just remember her as a pain to be around."

"Maybe you should invite her to church. That might solve the problem with your biggest fan."

Max sighed. "Don't tease about that."

"I'm not teasing. I'm serious." Heather maneuvered the car into a parking place. "You don't have to tell Megan that Amanda is your cousin, step or otherwise."

Max raised his hands and waved them. "No and no again. That's a recipe for disaster. Amanda would probably foist herself on Luke or Jeremy, and then they'd hate me."

"Or they might thank you. She's a pretty girl."

"Pretty doesn't make up for the unpleasant personality."

"Okay, suit yourself." Heather chuckled as she got out of the car. "Ready to cut your hair?"

"Not really, but I guess it's better than going bald a few patches at a time." Max waved the ball cap in his hand. "Got my Red Sox cap handy."

"Are you going to the game next Sunday with the church group?"

"God willing, as my grandma always says." Max gave her a determined look. "That's pretty much my whole life these days. Depending on God to see me through this."

"My work with cancer patients confirms my faith in God. Those who rely on Him deal better with their treatments than those who don't." Heather fell into step beside Max as they made their way down the block to the meeting place.

Max suddenly turned and stopped in front of her, blocking her progress. "What do I do with the doubts? They're with me every day. And I keep asking God, 'why me?'"

Max's intense stare made Heather swallow hard. "I didn't say my patients with faith never question God, but in the end their faith sustains them."

"Is that going to happen with me?"

Heather was a bit taken aback by Max's

confession. He'd suddenly opened up and shared his feelings about this disease. Was this a breakthrough? He wanted reassurance. Could she give him some? "You've already said you've been depending on God."

"Yeah, hanging on by the thinnest of hopes. I keep trying to tell myself God will pull me through, but I'm afraid I don't believe it most of the time. How can God answer prayers when my faith is so weak?"

Hardly believing what was coming out of Max's mouth, Heather only stood there and stared at him. Had the prospect of shaving his head made him open up about his feelings? This was not the Max Reynolds she'd known in Montana or the one she'd been dealing with the past few weeks. She had to say something positive. "It's hard to let our faith rule when bad things are happening to us."

"What would you know about it?"

Heather almost smiled even though his question was caustic. Now he was talking like the Max she'd always known. "I don't know about it personally, but I've seen enough people dealing with this disease that takes a toll even when people survive it."

Max hung his head, then glanced up. "Hey, I shouldn't have jumped on you like that. Let's get to the meeting."

"Sure." Heather quickened her pace to keep up with Max, who walked like he was trying to put some distance between him and the conversation they'd just had. She didn't know what else she could say to him.

She hated to leave him hanging, but he obviously didn't want to talk or listen anymore.

When they walked into the meeting place, the teens immediately welcomed Max. They were eager to find out who had the privilege of shaving his head. Dave would announce the winner at the end of tonight's meeting.

While Heather watched the teens greeting Max, she couldn't forget her unexpected emotional response to seeing him with another woman. She didn't want to examine her reaction, but the memory hovered in the corner of her mind. He was still all the things he was when he'd dated Brittany—perpetually late, mostly reluctant to talk, and plagued with tunnel vision and forgetfulness. But she was learning that he was compassionate. Is that why a tender spot for him was growing in her heart? Is that why a streak of jealousy had jarred her peace of mind?

***

With Megan tagging behind him, Max went through the food line, then found a seat at one of the tables. Megan was right there beside him, chattering away. The one-sided conversation reminded him of the adult voices in the Peanuts animated features—a lot of undecipherable noise. He just kept nodding his head and hoped she wasn't saying something he should be paying attention to.

Maybe Heather had been right. He should invite

Amanda to church to discourage Megan's interest. Her coppery red hair always reminded him so much of Brittany when she was eighteen, but Brittany hadn't annoyed him. Probably because he'd been seventeen and crazy in love with her. Would he ever find love like that again?

"I can hardly wait to find out who won the chance to shave your head."

Megan's statement made Max turn. He gave her a lopsided smile as he ran a hand through his dark mop of hair. "I can. Not quite ready to give this up, but a bargain is a bargain."

"I think you'll look fine without it." Megan smiled up at him.

"Not much I can do about it except wear my ball cap whenever possible." Max glanced around for Heather. Could she rescue him from Megan's clutches?

Max spotted Heather sitting at another table. Had she left him to fend for himself? He didn't want to hurt Megan's feelings. He'd been hoping the fact that he'd soon be bald would make her interest wane, but after her last comment, he feared that wasn't the case.

Max smiled while he ate and barely listened to Megan's chatter. He realized how ironic his thoughts were about Heather. He hated her interference, and yet here he was wishing she would interfere. How sad was that? He gave himself a mental shake. He had to deal with his own problems.

"I'm going to start taking classes at a community

college as soon as I graduate this spring. I want to be an oncology nurse like Heather." Megan stared at Max as if she was waiting for him to comment.

Ashamed that he hadn't been listening to the girl, Max nodded. What else had she said that he hadn't taken in? "Does Heather know about your ambition?"

Megan shook her head. "I've just decided that's what I want to do. You know it's kind of hard to figure out what you want when you graduate from high school, but learning about your cancer and knowing how much Heather does to help people with that disease helped me know what path I should take."

"That's a big decision. You should talk to Heather about it." Max didn't know whether that was good advice or not. Did Megan need guidance, or did she really know what she wanted? It wasn't for him to decide. She could take his advice or leave it.

When Max finished eating, he took his paper plate and Megan's to the trash and thanked the ladies who had prepared the meal. He breathed a sigh of relief when Megan remained at the table, talking with the other girls. He longed for some time alone before he had to shave his head.

What was he going to do? Go hide in the restroom? He'd just grin and bear it. Isn't that what he'd done through all the awful stuff in his life?

Smiling on the outside and feeling rotten on the inside. That's what he'd been doing until tonight with Heather. He still couldn't believe he'd spilled his guts to her, of all people. What would she think of him now? She didn't have the best opinion of him anyway, and now she knew he was a fraud when it came to his faith. What difference did it make? He wasn't trying to impress her anyway.

While Max stood around worrying about Heather, Dave instructed the kids to make a semicircle of the chairs in preparation for the lesson. Once again Max found himself seated next to Megan. She smiled sweetly at him, and he tried to smile back. She was like a stray kitten that had adopted him, or at least it seemed that way. He wasn't sure how to handle this situation. He wondered if he should ask Clay. Something he'd been putting off because talk about the search for his father's family had to be in that conversation somewhere. He didn't know how Clay would take the information.

Max turned his attention to Dave, who stood before the group with his Bible open. "Let's look at Psalm 59:16–17. It says, 'But I will sing of your strength, in the morning I will sing of your love; for you are my fortress, my refuge in times of trouble. You are my strength, I sing praise to you; you, God, are my fortress, my God on whom I can rely.'"

As the group discussed the verses, Max knew they were meant for him. God knew what he'd needed to hear tonight. He needed to remember these words when his doubts threatened to undermine his faith. They ended the lesson time with prayer, especially for him.

Dave looked in Max's direction as he placed a

chair in the middle of the semicircle. "Are you ready to find out who gets the privilege of cutting off your hair?"

Max stood, resignation dragging on his smile. This was it. He sat in the chair and faced the group. His gaze found Heather standing at the back of the room, her arms crossed as she watched him. Without uncrossing her arms, she gave him a thumbs-up sign and a smile. His heart thudded.

Surely not because of Heather. The prospect of losing all his hair had to be the reason his heart romped around in his chest. He took a deep breath. "Okay. Let's see who the winner is."

Dave waved his wife over. "Julie has tabulated the final results. And my wife is very good about keeping a secret, so I don't even know who the winner is."

Julie sidled up next to her husband and grinned at Max. As if she were announcing the winner at an awards show, she held up an envelope. "I wanted to make sure no one knew the results before now. They are sealed in here."

"Don't keep us in suspense any longer." Dave leaned over Julie's shoulder as she opened the envelope.

Julie looked back at her grinning husband. "Do you want to read the name of our winner?"

"If that's okay with you?" Dave took the card Julie held. "Before I tell you who gets to cut Max's hair, I want to let you know how much money this group has raised to help buy the property to be used to house the families of cancer patients."

"Don't keep us in suspense." Heather raised her voice above the chatter of excitement surrounding the announcement.

Max took a deep breath and held it. This was one time he agreed wholeheartedly with Heather. He wished they'd make the announcement and get the whole thing over with.

"Okay, here's the total. Six thousand seven hundred eighty-one dollars and sixty-four cents." Dave started the applause that continued until he held up a hand for silence. "Now for the winner of the contest. We have a team of winners. Alice Mason, Mary Keefe and Cheryl Herne."

A loud cheer erupted as Max looked over at the ladies who so generously cooked meals for the youth a couple of times a month. They were all smiles as Alice waved a dark-green cape in front of her like a bullfighter. The ladies followed Alice and stood behind Max's chair while she put the cape over him.

As Alice tied the cape at the back of Max's neck, a bunch of the guys pulled chairs from the circle and placed them on either side of Max. He watched the proceedings, a frown gathering on his brow. "What's going on?"

"I guess it's time we let you in on the secret." Dave stepped forward as he gestured around the room. "After you made your announcement, the kids got together and formulated a plan to have a huge community yard sale. Alice and her group were already selling items online, so they funneled all their sales into the project. That's how they came up as the winners. In addition, all the guys, including me, are going to shave our heads. Alice's husband, Bill, is a barber, and his crew is here tonight to go to work."

As soon as Dave finished talking, a group of men entered the room. They carried more capes and barbering tools. Max looked at the group with disbelief. Why were these guys willing to shave their heads to support someone they'd known for only a few weeks?

While the young men continued to assemble their chairs in preparation for the haircuts, Max stood and shook his head. "I can't believe you're doing this for me. I don't know what to say."

"Just say thank you and sit down so they can cut off your hair." Grinning, Heather motioned for him to sit. "Luke and Jeremy are on their way to join in with the fun."

"Was this your idea?" Hoping not to come across as ungrateful, Max tried not to glare as he looked at her.

Still grinning, she shook her head. "It was everyone's idea."

Before Max could return to his chair, Luke and Jeremy walked into the room.

Luke shook Max's hand. "We're here to join in this head-shaving party."

Nodding, Max wasn't sure he should open his mouth. He feared he couldn't speak for the huge lump that had risen in his throat. The lump finally dissolved along with his trepidation, and he managed to smile. "Thanks, but you guys don't have to do this."

"Hey, we're all in this together." Jeremy clapped Max on the back. "So let's get this show on the road."

"Okay." Max shook his head as he sat down. "I'm still not believing this."

"Well, believe it." Heather stepped forward and started giving instructions as to where everyone should sit.

Max just smiled as he watched her. What else should he expect? She liked telling people what to do. He should be used to it by now.

Then Heather held up her phone. "We have to have a before and after photo, so, guys, let's hear a loud cheese."

A thunderous collective "cheese" filled the room as Heather snapped a couple of photos. Then Alice made a big production of taking the barbering supplies from her husband. She had the kids laughing as she brandished the clippers like a sword.

Alice looked at Max, then turned to the kids. "Down the middle or down the side?"

"Down the middle," the kids chorused.

Max wondered if he should close his eyes. Soon his hair would be gone, but a bunch of guys would join him. Would that make the loss any easier?

Alice stood in front of Max. "Here we go. Are you ready?"

Max took a deep breath. "As ready as I'll ever be."

The clippers buzzed like a giant insect ready to attack as Alice skimmed them down the middle of his scalp. His hair fell onto the cape, and the kids cheered. Alice gave a victory pose before she handed the clippers to her friends, who each had a turn before Alice's husband took over. The kids stomped and cheered as Bill finished shaving Max's head while three other barbers from his shop worked on the other guys.

Bill handed Max a mirror, and he sat there for a moment, afraid to look. He ran a hand across his hairless head as he looked into the mirror. He didn't look scary, but he'd be wearing his ball cap as much as possible. Maybe he'd get used to the bald look, but it would have to grow on him. Trying to smile, he glanced around as a blizzard of hair fell to the floor nearby.

Several minutes later, ten baldheaded guys stood around Max while Heather took several more photos. Afterward, everyone gathered around as Heather flicked through the photos on her phone. Max hadn't realized that she'd been taking pictures during the entire thing.

Looking at the photos reminded him that he should get over himself. Every one of these guys had done something for him. They didn't have to lose their hair, but they chose to join him so he wouldn't feel alone. He needed to think about doing something for others rather than worrying about how he looked. He was probably going to look a lot worse before this cancer thing was finally over.

When everyone was done looking at Heather's photos, Dave got everyone's attention. "Thanks, guys, for a great evening. Let's take a moment to close with prayer."

Max waved a hand in the air. "Before Dave prays, I have to thank you all again."

Dave put a hand on Max's shoulder. "We can thank God for bringing us all together to help with a very worthy project."

Max bowed his head while Dave prayed. Max prayed to be a better person—a person worthy of the sacrifice these people had made. He needed to be nicer to Heather and figure out a way to be kinder to Megan without encouraging the younger girl's interest. Not an easy task.

As Max walked to Heather's car, his mind overflowed with the events of the evening. He wasn't sure what to say to her, so he didn't say anything. He had his cap jammed onto his head, not quite ready to display his baldness to the world. Although at this point, Heather was the only one who would see it.

Heather unlocked the car, and Max slid into the passenger seat, his cap still firmly in place. Silence filled the car as Heather drove toward home. She looked over at him. "You're awfully quiet."

"I don't have much to say, except thanks. This was all your idea, wasn't it?"

Heather shrugged as she drove down the winding tree-lined road. "It might have been my idea, but as soon as I mentioned it, the kids ran with it. The parents even got behind it."

"Yeah, good thing. You wouldn't want some parents to be upset because their son came home with a shaved head."

Heather chuckled. "The best part was keeping it all a secret. I can't believe someone didn't let it slip."

"You certainly surprised me, and the best part is the money the kids brought in."

"God can do a lot when you have a little faith."

A *little* faith. Max knew that's what he had, but he wasn't going to say it again. He'd already said more than he should have to Heather tonight. What was there about her that had him admitting stuff he never admitted to anyone else? He changed the subject. "How's your training for the PMC going?"

"Not as well as I'd hoped by now. Some nasty weather on my days off and stuff getting in the way has limited my training time. But it's all good. I've got plenty of time to get in shape, and I've been working out on the stationary bike. Of course, it's not quite the same, but it's better than nothing."

"Wish I could join you guys."

"We'll make you an honorary member of the team along with Hailey, our Pedal Partner. You have to meet her."

"I'd like that."

"Tara said Hailey's not been feeling well, so they haven't been in church the last couple of weeks. A visit might be in order. Are you free on Saturday?"

"Not much going on in my life these days except visits to the clinic where some nurse pokes and prods and pumps chemicals into me."

"She must be a real pain."

Max grinned. "You know she is."

Heather smiled, but the smile didn't take away the sadness in her eyes. "I wish it could be different."

"Yeah, me, too. Who likes having cancer?"

"Is it okay if I put the photos from tonight on my blog?"

Did he want photos of him with a bald head roaming around the Internet? But hadn't he decided to quit thinking about himself? "What's your blog for?"

"It's mostly personal, but I highlight my fundraising efforts for cancer. I've got info about my PMC ride and a running total on our funds for the property. People in the fundraising community and cancer patients frequent my blog."

"Yeah, go ahead and post them." Max wasn't altogether sure he liked the idea, but he'd be ungrateful if he didn't agree.

"Thanks." Heather pulled the car to a stop in front of his place. "You should start your own blog about your cancer experience. A number of my patients have one. Or you could get connected with an online community of folks who share your disease."

Max opened the door, and the overhead light in Heather's car illuminated her face. Her expression was one of expectation. She clearly thought this was a good idea, but he didn't. She wasn't going to like his response. "I don't think so. I like to keep my thoughts to myself. I don't understand people who want to share their innermost feelings with the world, no matter what the cause."

Heather shrugged, her smile forced. "Suit yourself. It was just an idea. Maybe you should try journaling instead. Sometimes it helps to write down your experiences."

Not on your life. Max forced himself not to say what he was thinking. "That might work for some people—"

"But not for you, right?"

"You said it. I didn't." Did he dare tell her that sometimes she tried too hard to fix people and their problems? Probably not. At least not tonight. He should end on a positive note. "I'd better let you go. Thanks for everything. Guess I'll see you Saturday. Good night."

"Good night." Heather wished him well as he hopped out of the car.

He didn't look back as she drove down the block. She made him crazy with her suggestions that seemed more like demands. He had to remember that he wouldn't have to deal with her for several days. He would have his space. Why wasn't that the least bit comforting? Probably because she would be part of his life for weeks to come. That prospect was oddly reassuring. Was she growing on him, or was chemo brain turning his mind to mush?

When Max opened the door, Luke and Jeremy

stood there grinning. Their bald heads gleamed in the overhead light. "Hey, guys. How does it feel to be bald?"

Jeremy came over and clapped Max on the back. "Actually, pretty good." Jeremy rubbed a hand over his head. "Good enough to gain a little sympathy and snag us some dates for Sunday's ballgame. You ought to get one, too. How about Heather?"

Whoa. What was he going to say to that suggestion? No way was he going to ask Heather for a date. *Think fast.* "No dates for me. Cancer and dates don't mix. I'm going to invite my cousin, who goes to school in Boston."

Jeremy shrugged. "If you want to invite your cousin, that's cool."

"Thanks again, guys. I'm off to bed. Funny thing about these cancer treatments. They make me tired. Good night." Max removed his cap and headed to his room.

As he got ready for bed, he wondered why he'd said he planned to invite Amanda to the ballgame. Now he'd at least have to make an attempt to do that. Amanda's presence at the game might kill two birds with one stone. He would have a good excuse for not asking Heather, and he'd discourage Megan's interest. Which was worse—hanging around with his pain-in-the-butt cousin or dealing with Heather and Megan? He didn't have an answer, but he had to look at this as a good plan, whether it was or not.

CHAPTER EIGHT

The raucous cheers of the crowd filled Fenway Park as the Red Sox took the field. The smell of hot dogs and popcorn filled the air. The sun warmed the seats in the outfield where Heather sat between Amanda and Hailey, who had a new hero.

Max.

Hailey's pink baseball cap with the big blue B emblazoned on the front shaded her face and hid the fuzz of blond hair that was barely visible. Max was explaining the game to her, and her little face was turned up to his as if he'd built the stadium and knew all the ballplayers personally. She hung on every word he said, her blue eyes aglow with hero worship.

While Max pointed out the home team to Hailey, Heather wondered if the guy she was observing now was the one who had enthralled Brittany for nearly eight years. Not the self-centered man Heather had known back in Montana. What was there about him that captivated a little girl and a teenager and once upon a time her best friend? Heather had never seen his appeal until his interaction with Hailey last night and today. Had she been wrong about him?

The visit with Tara and Hailey last night had

served to show Heather a whole different side of Max. He'd related to Hailey in a way Heather never would have expected from the man who had disregarded Brittany's feelings so often. When he'd suggested that Hailey attend the baseball game, Tara had hesitated. Hailey had begged to go, and Max had promised to take good care of her. He was doing exactly that.

Since Max was engrossed in instructing Hailey on the finer points of baseball, Heather turned to Amanda. "So are you a baseball fan?"

"Not really, but I came because Max invited me. I thought it's the least I could do since he has cancer, and all." Shrugging, Amanda shook her head. "I can't imagine what he's going through, but he seems to be doing okay. Is he?"

"What did he tell you?" Heather didn't want to say anything to Amanda that Max wouldn't want revealed. If she wasn't his nurse, she wouldn't have to be as careful.

"Max really didn't tell me anything. Mostly I got secondhand information through my little sister, Kelsey, who got her information from my dad and stepmom." Amanda sighed. "I know he's getting chemo treatments, and he looks so much thinner than the last time I saw him a couple of years ago."

"I can't really discuss his medical condition other than to say he's doing okay for now." Heather wondered whether Amanda had any insights into Max's life that would help Heather understand him better. "Did Max contact you?"

Amanda shook her head. "My stepmom, Maria, is cool as far as stepmoms go. She insisted that I look in on Max. So I thought I'd better do it. He would never have contacted me. Max and I have never been very close."

Remembering what Max had said about Amanda, Heather wondered whether she should ask Amanda about him. The cousins appeared to come from different worlds. The younger woman's clothing, jewelry and shoes said society party, not baseball game. Heather didn't know how Amanda walked in those wedge sandals. Everything, including her flawless makeup and designer purse, said high maintenance—Max's exact description.

Maybe asking wouldn't produce much, but taking a chance could yield valuable information. "Why do you suppose you and Max aren't close?"

"You know he's my stepcousin, don't you?"

Heather nodded. "He did mention that."

"Well…I'm pretty sure he thought I was a pain when he was in high school, and I probably was." Amanda chuckled.

"Why do you say that?"

Amanda narrowed her gaze as she looked back at Heather. "Why are you pumping me for information? You have a personal interest in Max?"

The question took Heather by surprise. Personal as in really personal—like a romantic interest? No way. "I like to know as much as I can about my patients."

"Oh, so that's it." Amanda's expression conveyed

skepticism. "I hated it when we moved to Pinecrest, and I didn't hide my distaste for the little town. And Max was part of everything I hated there."

"Did you ever learn to like it?"

Amanda shook her head. "Give me the city any day. I love it here in Boston, but my real goal is to go to Nashville and become a recording artist. I've been composing a lot of songs and singing at open mic events around the area while I'm going to school."

"Is that what you've always wanted to do?"

"Pretty much. My dad thinks it's an impossible dream. We don't see eye to eye on much, but after I got my undergrad degree in business, he finally let me go to music school. I love every minute of it, even the hours of practice and music composition."

"What's an open mic event?"

"Different places have amateur musicians perform, and sometimes talent scouts discover them at these events. I'm not expecting that to happen here. I mainly use them for practice, but I'm hoping someone will discover me in Nashville." Amanda's face lit up with excitement.

"I'd like to hear you perform."

"You would?" Amanda leaned forward and looked in Max's direction. "Do you think you and Max could come and hear me next weekend?"

Heather shrugged. "I don't know. I could, but I don't know how Max will feel after his chemo treatment. You should talk to him."

"The invitation would come across better from you

than from me." Amanda pressed her lips together. "He probably wouldn't be that excited about it."

Heather chuckled as she took in Amanda's trepidation. "When it comes to Max, I think we might have a lot in common. I'm not sure he would accept my invitation either."

"What do you mean?"

"He blames me for the breakup with Brittany. He just has to tolerate me because I'm his nurse."

With her mouth hanging open, Amanda pointed a finger at Heather. "Now I know why you seemed familiar. You were Brittany's maid of honor."

"You were at the wedding?"

"Yeah. I was home from college, and I attended. It was the wedding of the year in Pinecrest. That's the last time I saw Max." Amanda leaned back and lowered her voice. "I had no idea what happened between Max and Brittany, but I could tell he was trying to put on a happy front at the wedding."

Heather didn't think she should tell Amanda about the confrontation with Max, but the fact that she recognized Max's unhappiness said a lot since she wasn't that close to him. "That doesn't surprise me."

Amanda leaned closer to Heather. "I wonder if his ears are ringing."

"If not, they should be." Heather glanced down the row toward Max. He was pointing out something to Hailey, who still had that worshipful look on her face. Heather looked back at Amanda. "At least, today he seems happy entertaining Hailey."

"Yeah, he was always good with kids. He used to entertain my little sister with his silly duck voice."

Heather wondered whether Max ever used that voice these days. She hadn't heard it, not that he'd had any reason to use it, except maybe today with Hailey. What did it matter? Heather hadn't learned anything new about Max by talking with Amanda.

"Hey, Heather, I thought you told me you liked baseball. You haven't been watching the game, just gabbing with Amanda." Max gave her a questioning glance.

Heather stared back. So he'd been watching her. What did that mean? Nothing. Absolutely nothing. Why had the question even popped into her mind? "Yeah, I like baseball, but I was getting to know Amanda. There's no score, so I haven't missed anything."

"Sure you have." Max looked down at Hailey. "Tell her what she's missed."

Hailey's eyes got really big. "The Red Sox's pitcher has three strikeouts. So far he has a perfect game. You know what a perfect game is?"

Heather smiled, and her admiration grew for the man who had taken the time to teach a little girl about a perfect game. "I do, and that would certainly be something exciting to see. I'll have to start paying better attention. What do you think?"

Hailey nodded as she looked over at Max with satisfaction. "He knows a lot about baseball. You should listen to him."

Heather smiled at Max over the top of Hailey's head, then looked down at the little girl. "Do you think he should listen to me because I know a lot about helping people who have cancer?"

Hailey eyed Max. "I listen to my nurses. You should, too."

"Okay. Let's make a pact. We'll listen to our nurses." Max held up a fist. "Fist bump on that?"

"Yeah." Hailey bumped her fist against Max's. "We could be a really good team."

"Max is going to be an honorary member of our PMC team. So you'll be partners with him, too." Heather hoped Max realized the extent of Hailey's hero worship. Did she dare tell him that he should be a good example? He really didn't like to take orders. She needed to step lightly, or she could set him on the course of rebellion that she sensed whenever he thought she was taking too much control.

"Cool." That one word coming from Hailey said it all. "You can hang out with me and my mom during the ride."

"That sounds like a good plan to me." Max nodded as he looked at Heather. "Is that good?"

"Yeah. That works." Heather waved toward the field. "Guess you'd better follow your own advice and watch the game. The Red Sox have a runner on base."

Max turned to look, then leaned over to Hailey. "We'd better pay attention."

Bouncing in her seat, Hailey clapped. "He's on first base, right?"

"Right. Let's cheer for a home run. Maybe the batter will hit it out here." Max pounded a fist into his glove. "I can catch it and give the ball to you."

Hailey focused her attention on the field. "That would be awesome."

For the next few innings, Heather watched the game and cheered and stomped her feet right along with Hailey, who was enjoying every minute. Amanda cheered, but Heather could tell the younger woman wished she were somewhere else.

Max continued to instruct Hailey. She yelled with delight when the Red Sox scored, but let her lower lip protrude when the other team ruined the Red Sox's perfect game. Heather tried to take her attention off Max and enjoy the game, but he was never far from her thoughts. She wanted to believe her role as his nurse kept him in her focus. Despite her earlier thoughts that she couldn't see what other women had seen in him, his actions today continued to chisel away at that idea.

Max didn't look much different now that he'd shaved his head, because he wore his ball cap most of the time, even when the other guys had no problem sporting their baldness. Max took off his cap when the guys all posed for a photo, but as soon as they were done, he put the cap back on.

In the top of the ninth inning, the Red Sox had two outs and were ahead four to two. The crowd rose and cheered more loudly with each strike on their opponent's batter. The game finally ended with a pop-up to the Red Sox's center fielder. The crowd roared, and Hailey jumped up and down as she clapped her hands.

As they exited the ballpark, Heather and Max walked together, each holding one of Hailey's hands. Amanda walked on the other side of Max.

Once they were outside of the park, Amanda stopped and gave Max a hug. "Thanks for inviting me."

"Glad you could meet us." Max adjusted his ball cap. "Do you need a cab to get home?"

Amanda shook her head. "I can walk. I don't live that far from here."

"You're sure?" Max glanced down at those wedge shoes.

"Positive." Amanda glanced at Heather. "Um, I was talking to Heather during the game and wondered if you guys would like to come and listen to me perform next Saturday. It's okay if you don't want to. I just thought I'd ask."

Heather watched Max's reaction, but she couldn't tell what he was thinking. She should keep her mouth shut and let him do what he wanted.

Max rubbed the back of his neck as he stared at Amanda. "Can I let you know on Saturday morning? I have a chemo treatment on Friday, and I don't know how I'll be feeling."

"Sure. I understand." Amanda waved. "Talk to you on Saturday."

Max waved and took Hailey's hand again as they

headed toward the church bus. They were one of the first of the group to arrive. Max settled on the front seat by the door, with Hailey sitting beside him.

Heather sat across the aisle behind the bus driver and glanced at Hailey. "How did you like your first major league baseball game?"

"Cool." Hailey looked at Max. "And Max is a really good teacher."

He grinned. "Thanks, kiddo. I'll have to teach you how to play now."

During the trip back to Oakton, Heather noted that Amanda's presence seemed to have steered Megan's interest toward one of the young men in the youth group. Although Heather had made the suggestion, she hadn't been at all sure inviting Amanda would work on Megan. Despite that success, Heather guessed he didn't appreciate her interference in his life, but she couldn't help herself. She wanted to see people make the best choices.

Even though Heather hadn't learned much about Max from Amanda today, this outing had been an eye-opening experience all the way around. This reticent man had made a little girl's day and made Heather reconsider her attitude about him. Still, she didn't want him to fool her in the same way he'd fooled Brittany. Heather couldn't let go of her skepticism about him that easily.

***

Two days after the baseball game, Max stared at his phone and hoped the call to Clay wouldn't be a mistake. The ring from the outgoing call sounded in Max's ear as he let out a harsh breath and waited for Clay to answer. Max shouldn't be nervous about talking to the man he'd called "dad" for ten years, but his stomach roiled, and it had nothing to do with his chemotherapy. The antinausea medicine they'd given him at the clinic had been working well.

"Hey, to what do I owe this call?" Concern came across in Clay's words. "Is everything okay?"

"Yeah, just wanted to talk." Max paced in his room.

"Great. What's going on?" The apprehension in Clay's voice faded.

"We never had the chance to have a good conversation while you were here, and there are some things I need to discuss with you." Max hoped Clay would understand why he was searching for his biological father's family.

"What things?"

"Did Mom ever tell you the real reason for my move to Massachusetts?" The silence on the other end of the conversation made a lump rise in Max's throat. "Are you still there?"

"Yeah, I'm here, and she did tell me." Clay let out a halfhearted laugh. "I wasn't sure I was supposed to know."

"It's okay." Max looked out the window. The sun glinted off the windshield of his dilapidated car and reminded him to be thankful for another good day. His car was still running, and the sun was still shining. "I didn't know how you'd feel about it. I want you to be good with it."

"I understand why you want to do it. If I were in your place, I'd want to do the same thing."

"What do I do with Mom? She isn't keen on the idea." Max started pacing again. "She didn't want me to come here. She thinks it's a wild goose chase. Now she's really unhappy because I'm sick and so far away."

Clay chuckled again. "I believe I've heard those statements more than once around this house."

"So she's still not happy?"

"She's coming to grips with your being away, but you could make things a whole lot better if you called her more often."

Max sighed, pushing away the guilt that Clay's request engendered. "I know it's not a good excuse, but the three-hour time difference makes it difficult to call her, especially during the week."

"I know that from being on the Eastern Time Zone for business, but send her some texts or emails to keep her updated." Max glanced out the window again and noticed Heather walking her bike out to the street. She was probably practicing for the PMC. Thankfully, she couldn't hear this conversation, or she would be on his case, too. "I'll do better."

"Good. So how's your search going?"

Max let out a sad little laugh. "It's not. Moving and

getting used to a new job took most of my time when I first moved here, and then I got sick and don't have the energy to look."

"Did you ever think you're not supposed to find them?"

"No." Max gritted his teeth. Clay said he understood, but he seemed to be taking the same stance as his mother. They didn't know that Max knew the unpleasant truth about his father. He'd overheard them arguing about it when he'd been home the summer Brittany got married. Two blasts to the heart in one week. But the awful events had made him more determined than ever to find the family who didn't know him and show them that he was worth knowing—worth being alive. Now he was almost too sick to care.

"If you're determined to find them, maybe you should think about hiring a private investigator."

"They cost too much, and now I have medical bills to pay on top of my normal living expenses." Max realized he was making Clay's case for him. "But that only means the search will be on hold. It's not like I have to find them tomorrow."

"True." Silence followed Clay's response, but just as Max started to say something, Clay continued. "Your mom showed me the photo of you and all the guys without your hair. I'm glad you have a lot of people supporting you. That's important."

"How did she see the photo?"

"Heather sent her something."

"That's news to me." This information made Max happy and angry all at the same time. The support of the people here had been awesome, and it buoyed his spirits every day, but Heather's interference grated on him. What right did she have to send photos to his mother without asking him? Just when he thought he might find something to like about Heather, she did something else annoying.

"Yeah, it was from the baseball game you went to. Wish I could've been there with you. Did you enjoy the game?"

Clay's question made Max's anger toward Heather subside. "I did. I invited Amanda to go, and she came."

"Good. I'm glad you two have connected. How's she doing?"

"Fine. I guess. She spent most of the game talking with Heather." Max chuckled. "I don't think she's much into baseball. You should've seen the sandals she was wearing. I'm not sure how she walked in them."

Clay laughed, too. "That doesn't surprise me. Abby would call her a fashionista."

"Good description."

For the rest of the conversation, Max and Clay talked about baseball, Max's involvement in the fundraising projects, his interaction with Hailey and the kids in the church youth group. Their discussion reminded Max of all the enjoyable things in his life and made him appreciate them more. He couldn't let

Heather or her actions diminish what was good all around him. When Max finally ended the call, his mind was in a much better place. He couldn't believe how long they had yakked—nearly an hour. He should have known speaking with Clay would be a good thing.

As Max gazed out the window again, Heather, his two roommates, and a couple of people he didn't recognize brought their bikes to a stop in front of Heather's place. They were talking and laughing as they took off their helmets. A streak of envy flashed through Max. He should be out there with that group, but his energy said otherwise.

Max forced himself to think about the good things he and Clay had discussed. Max was determined not to let envy or anger ruin his attitude. He closed his eyes and let a prayer of forgiveness filter through his mind. *Lord, let me remember the good things You've provided always.*

Max turned away from the window and wandered into the living room. Before he reached the couch, Jeremy and Luke burst through the front door.

Wearing biking shorts and a fluorescent-green jersey and holding his helmet, Jeremy looked the part of a cyclist who had just finished a tour event. "Hey, Max. We're riding into town. Want to join us for ice cream?"

Luke motioned toward the street. "Yeah, it's not too far, and we've got a bike and helmet for you to use."

Max smiled. God was answering prayers almost as soon as they were spoken, and working on Max to show him the good things. "Wish I had the energy."

"Come on. We'll go slow." Luke motioned for Max to come. "Heather says you need the exercise."

Heather again. Was he going to let her dictate his life? But at the same time, was he going to let her presence keep him from a good time? He'd felt better after the outing to the baseball game. He didn't know why he felt so tired today. "Sure, but I'm holding you to that slow thing."

After locking the front door, Max followed his roommates across the street. "Thanks, everyone, for the invite."

"Glad you decided to come." Heather handed him a helmet. "Have you met Emma Butler? She's one of the nurses at the clinic."

Now that he was closer, Max remembered the blue-eyed blonde from the times he'd been in for treatments. Max extended his hand. "I'm glad to meet you, Emma. I do recall seeing you at the clinic."

"Nice to meet you, too." Emma shook his hand, then turned to the man standing beside her. "This is my husband, Ryan."

Shaking Ryan's hand, Max exchanged greetings with the other man as Luke wheeled a bike up to them. Max put on his helmet and buckled the strap. "Thanks."

"Is everyone ready to head to the Dairy Station?" Heather called out.

A collective chorus of yeses filled the air. Max pushed off along with the other riders as they started down the street. The group laughed and talked while they rode toward the ice cream stand at the edge of the town square. The sun sat just above the tree line and cast long shadows of the bikers.

Max took in the camaraderie of the group and realized how he'd cut himself off from people after his breakup with Brittany. He was seeing more and more how he'd neglected his relationship, not only with her but with all his acquaintances in Montana. He had to thank Heather for one thing. She'd pushed him out of his comfort zone and given him a group of friends here. He had to make sure he nurtured these friendships.

When they reached the Dairy Station with its train depot motif, they parked their bikes near the building and placed their orders. When everyone had ordered, the group gathered at an empty table sitting under the overhang that resembled a depot waiting platform. Laughter and conversation floated through the air as other patrons enjoyed their ice cream. On the far side of the parking lot kids played in the miniature train cars.

Max ate his ice cream in silence as the others talked around him. Sitting there with his newfound friends should make him happy, but instead, it reminded him of the first encounter with Brittany back in Pinecrest. After football practice his sophomore year, he'd gone to the local ice cream stand with a bunch of the football players and cheerleaders. Brittany, who was a year older, had been with the group. He'd been fascinated with the cute little redhead from the moment he'd met her, but it had taken a whole year before they actually started dating.

Why couldn't he get her off his mind? Would thoughts of her haunt him forever? Was there a chance he could find someone else? Hardly. At least not while he battled cancer. What woman would be interested in him now?

"Max, did we wear you out on the ride?" Heather looked at him over the top of her ice cream cone. "You're awfully quiet."

I like the quiet. Max let the phrase slip through his mind but kept his mouth shut. She didn't need to know what he was thinking. Why did it bother Heather that he wasn't the talkative kind? He toasted her with his ice cream cone. "Just enjoying this. Thanks for inviting me."

Jeremy gestured around the table. "We want you to be part of the team even though you can't ride with us."

"Hailey and I will be your honorary members." Max hoped that didn't entail much, because he didn't know how much energy he would have at that point.

"I heard Hailey say she wanted you to hang out with her and her mom during the ride. Are you cool with that?" Heather asked.

"If that's what I have to do." Max shrugged. "Where do you stay on the first night?"

"We camp in tents at the Mass Maritime Academy."

"The church I attended in Pinecrest used to have a campout every summer up on the Pend Oreille River." Another memory that brought Brittany to mind. Max wished somehow he could turn off the memories.

"Then you should join us." Heather eyed him. "There are a lot of cancer survivors who make the ride. You'll get a lot of encouragement from the experience."

Was Heather trying to run his life and tell him what to do—what to experience? He had to quit thinking of her that way. She was probably right. "Yeah, I'd like to do that. Just let me know what to do."

"We'll get it all worked out." Jeremy nodded. "This is going to be the best year ever for our fundraising. We have lots of sponsors, and some of us have already exceeded our goals."

"That must give you a feeling of accomplishment." Max ate the last bite of his ice cream cone.

"Finishing the ride is the crowning jewel in the accomplishment." Luke reached over and patted Heather on the back. "And our little mother here is the one who prodded us into doing this last year. So we're all here doing it again."

"And she talked me and Ryan into joining her team." Emma shook her head. "I can't believe how far I'm able to ride already."

Max listened to the conversation with a little smile

on his face. So he wasn't the only one who had
Heather hovering in the background telling them what
to do. She liked to be in command and organize
people's lives. Did her efforts annoy anyone else, or
was he the only one who found her bothersome? He
was stuck in a rut of memories and irritation. How
was he going to get out of it?

CHAPTER NINE

Musical tones filled the air. Heather fished her phone out of her purse. Jeremy. Why was he calling? "Hello."

"Hey, Heather, Luke and I have had tickets for this concert for months, and we're leaving to pick up our dates in a few minutes. We were wondering whether you wanted to look in on Max."

"What's going on with him?"

"I'm not sure, but he seems more out of sorts tonight than he has after any of his other treatments. He says he's fine, but I don't think so." Jeremy sighed. "You know how he is."

"Yeah, I do. He doesn't want to put anyone out or ask for help."

"You got it. So what do you think?"

"I'll stop in, but don't tell him I'm coming. Just go out and have fun."

"Are you sure?"

Heather wasn't sure, but she refused to say so. She had to hope Max wouldn't guess the reason for her visit. "I'll deal with it. Thanks for letting me know."

"It's the least I could do. Hope you have a good evening with your reluctant patient."

"Me, too." Heather chuckled as she ended the conversation and glanced out the window toward the first floor of the triple-decker where Max and his roommates resided. She let out a long, slow breath as she picked up the DVD she'd planned to watch tonight and stuffed it into her purse. Could she get Max to watch it with her? It wasn't exactly a guy movie, and it wasn't a recent feature.

Heather continued to watch out the window until Jeremy and Luke drove away. She didn't want to arrive at Max's too quickly, but she didn't want to wait too long. She was beginning to think like her own version of Goldilocks. There was no sense in waiting around. She grabbed her jacket and headed down the stairs and across the street.

Reds, oranges, and yellows painted the sky as the sun sat low on the horizon, barely visible above the houses lining the street. Moments later Heather stood on the front porch. She hesitated before she knocked on the door. *Please, Lord, let Max take my visit as a good thing.* She took a deep breath and rang the doorbell. She stood there waiting, but no one came to the door. Had something happened to Max after Jeremy and Luke left?

Just as she was ready to punch the doorbell again, the front door opened a crack. "We don't want any."

Heather couldn't help laughing even though she wasn't sure whether Max was joking or not. "I'm not selling anything."

Max opened the door a little wider. "Oh, it's you."

At least he hadn't closed the door in her face. "You didn't recognize me?"

"I wasn't actually looking at you."

"I don't know what to think about that." Heather cocked her head. "Are you going to ask me in, or do I get the boot like someone trying to sell you magazines?"

Max let out a strangled laugh as he rubbed a hand down his face. "I guess you can come in."

"Such an enthusiastic welcome."

"I'm not in a welcoming mood."

"I can tell." Heather stepped into the front room.

"Did those guys send you over? I don't need a babysitter."

"I know you don't need one, but I thought you might like some company." Heather manufactured a smile. "I'm probably not the company you'd pick on your own, but it's better than sitting around alone."

"Alone sounds good to me."

"Seriously?"

Pale and haggard, Max stared at her as if he was going to respond, but instead, he walked over to the couch and plopped down. His baseball cap hid his features.

Unsure whether to follow him, Heather stood rooted to the floor.

"Well, if you're going to stay, don't just stand there."

"Okay." Heather sat at the other end of the sectional and wondered what to do next. Max didn't really want her here. "How are you feeling?"

"You know you don't have to be on duty twenty-four seven."

"I'm asking as a friend, not your nurse."

"I've heard that before. Nurse. Friend. What difference does it make?"

"So you're not feeling so good, huh?"

The sound coming from Max's mouth couldn't be classified as a laugh or a moan. "Yeah, I'm feeling…I can't describe it. I slept most of the day after my treatment."

"Did you eat?"

"Yes, Nurse Mother."

Heather stood. "I'll be glad to leave."

He looked up at her with a slack-jawed expression and sleepy eyes. "Don't."

Contradictory. She'd had the same feeling when he'd first come to the clinic and had insisted on not having a different nurse. She sat down again and pulled the DVD from her purse and held it up. "I brought over a movie."

If Max's face could get any paler, it did. Shaking his head, he held up one hand. "I can't watch that movie."

"*August Rush*?" Heather put the case containing the DVD on the coffee table and wondered about the wisdom of asking him why. "I know it's kind of a chick flick, but it's not that bad, is it?"

"I've seen it." He eased back onto the couch and laced his hands behind his head. "With Brittany. I don't need any reminders of her tonight."

"I'm sorry. I didn't know."

"Not your fault that I can't get over her." He closed his eyes and took a deep breath as he laid his head back.

Heartache chiseled his features. She didn't know how to relate to his pain, because she didn't know what it was like to have a long-term relationship fall apart. In fact, she'd never had a serious relationship at all. Her list came to mind. Was she too particular?

She wanted to sympathize with Max, but he didn't want her sympathy or anything else from her except her nursing skills.

Finally, Max removed his cap and rubbed a hand over his bald head. "The movie not only reminds me of Brittany and all that went wrong there, but it was right during that time I blew out my knee and my football career came to an end. I loved playing football."

Heather opened her mouth to respond, but Max held up a hand as he slapped the cap back on his head with the other. He narrowed his gaze. "Don't say you're sorry. You don't care whether I played football, lost Brittany, or have a disease that's keeping me from finding the family of the father I never knew. The little boy in *August Rush* is looking for the parents he never knew. That movie brings back a boatload of unpleasant memories."

Wow! The words tumbling out of Max's mouth flabbergasted Heather. Maybe she should change the subject to put a lighter mood on the conversation. "Do you wear that cap to work?"

He looked at her as if he couldn't believe she'd asked that question. "No. I can't wear it in the lab."

"Do you wear it all the time when you're not at work?"

"Most of the time."

"When you sleep?"

He gave her a lopsided grin. "Yeah. My head gets cold."

"I could knit you a cap to wear like they put on newborns."

His grin grew wider. "You knit me one. I'll wear it."

"Deal."

He flicked the brim of his cap with one finger, making it sit back on his head. He steepled his fingers and hung his head. "I shouldn't have blown up at you like that."

"I'm here for you to blow up at."

Max shook his head. "No. You don't deserve the brunt of my jumbled life. This thing with Brittany is as bad as the cancer that's attacking my body. Thoughts of her assault my brain. I can't stop thinking about her, wishing I hadn't messed up our relationship and longing for the hurt to go away."

"Have you talked to the counselor we have available for you?"

He pounded a fist into his chest, then glanced over at her. "I am a mixed-up person, but I don't want to talk to some shrink."

"Have you found the advice from the dietician to be worthwhile?"

Max nodded.

"Then why not use the counselor?"

Max grimaced. "Maybe."

"Could I ask you a question?"

"Sure, but I don't guarantee an answer."

"That's fair." Heather scooted forward as she placed her hands on her knees. "Can you tell me about the search for your father's family?"

A muscle worked in Max's jaw as he stared at her, indecision radiating from his eyes. "What do you want to know?"

A question for a question. What did she want to know? Everything, but he probably wasn't going to do that. "What prompted you to look for them?"

"Why do you care?"

Another question—one she wasn't sure how to answer. Why should she bother? If he wanted to wallow in his losses and refuse to talk about his life, what was it to her? But she did care. She didn't know why or how it had happened, but she was actually beginning to like Max Reynolds. She could never tell him. And what would Brittany think? Heather could only imagine. "I care because I want you to beat this thing called cancer. Keeping everything bottled up inside isn't going to help you."

"Oh, so now you're a shrink in addition to being the nurse that fills my bloodstream with that poison cocktail every other week."

"At least you still have a sense of humor."

Max gave a halfhearted laugh. "A sense of humor. Yeah, I'm real humorous, especially when I'm pumped full of drugs. Gallows humor."

"Okay. Don't tell me anything." Heather grabbed her purse and DVD off the coffee table. "I'll just take my movie and go home. You can have that alone time you wanted."

Sitting forward, Max reached out and laid a hand on her arm. "I don't know why I'm giving you such a hard time. I don't...I don't want you to leave."

His touch sent prickles down her arm and made her heart beat a little faster. Was it the realization that her feelings for him had somehow grown beyond the nurse-patient relationship? Heather wasn't sure what was going on with her or with Max. For the second time tonight, he'd asked her to stay. Did she want to stick around and chance more of his ill humor? "I'll stay if you tell me what I want to know."

He looked down at the floor while that muscle worked in his jaw. His silence beckoned Heather to leave, but she waited and hoped he would open up again. Finally he glanced up. His Adam's apple bobbed as he looked at her. "When Brittany broke up with me, my whole world came crashing down around me."

"And you blame me for that?"

"Yeah, at the time I did. You've pointed out that my inattention to her was a big part of the breakup, and I know that." Max looked down again. "But I'm not the bad guy you made me out to be. I loved Brittany, and I'm afraid I still do. My head says to get over her, but my stubborn heart doesn't want to comply. It's irrational. Why can't I be rational?"

"I wish I could tell you why we do things that don't make sense." What Heather was feeling definitely didn't make sense. Max's declaration of love for Brittany pricked Heather's heart. Crazy. That's what this feeling was—almost as crazy as Max's inability to get over Brittany.

"I was only trying to make sense of everything in my life. The breakup prompted me to take a good, hard look at myself." Max got up and started to pace, almost as if he was talking to the walls instead of to her. "I decided I wanted to find my father's family. I wanted to know them and for them to know me."

"That was over two years ago."

Max stopped pacing and turned to look at Heather. "Yeah, I didn't know where to start, so I talked to my mom the summer Brittany got married. She didn't offer up much information. She told me from the beginning that my father died before I was ever born, but that was about the extent of what I knew about him."

"No photos?"

"None." Max released a harsh breath. "She wouldn't have had any. She was sixteen when I was born, and my father didn't want me."

Heather frowned. "Did your mother tell you this?"

"Not directly."

"Then how do you know?" Heather watched Max pace back and forth in front of the coffee table. "Why don't you sit down?"

He stopped and gave her a laser look. "It's easier to talk this way, especially about this part." With a heavy sigh, he started pacing again. "After I asked my mom for information about my dad, she and Clay must have discussed it. One night I came home after visiting with my former youth pastor, and I heard my parents arguing."

"And you listened in?"

"Yeah. I had to listen after I heard my mother say, 'I can't tell Max that.'" He jammed his hands into the pockets of his baggy jeans. "The gist of the conversation centered on whether to tell me about my father. My mother insisted that she couldn't say anything good about him. I can still hear her saying, 'How can I tell Max that his father gave me money to have an abortion?'"

Heather placed a hand over her mouth. The shock of Max's statement punched her in the gut. How would she feel if she learned something like that about one of her parents? "I would've listened, too. Obviously, they decided not to tell you."

"But I knew anyway, and I couldn't get it off my mind." Max stopped again and stared. "I decided I had to find the other half of my family. I wanted them to know I existed and that my existence was a good thing."

"And your mother doesn't approve?"

A little frown knit Max's eyebrows. "How do you know?"

"It's obvious from your story, and besides, I remember your mom calling it a 'wild goose chase.' I didn't know what she was talking about at the time, but now I do." Heather couldn't imagine the hurt Max carried, and she'd contributed to it. But wasn't his breakup with Brittany a good thing? She was happy now with Parker, and despite the bad things in his life, Max didn't have an excuse for the way he'd neglected Brittany. "What does Clay think about it?"

"I talked with him a few days ago." Max shrugged as he finally joined her on the couch again. "I got a mixed message from him."

"How so?" Heather listened to Max's recounting of his conversation with Clay. "I don't think he's discounting your efforts to find your father's family. Maybe he wants to encourage you to pray about your decision."

Max slouched, his long legs stretched out in front of him. A pinched expression created a frown. "Yeah. Pray about this. Pray about that. Do I get any answers? Who knows?"

Heather wasn't sure how to address Max's obvious doubts. Cancer could do that to a person's faith. Even knowing so much more about Max's life couldn't help her go back and undo the past. "I don't know. Sometimes it's hard to know what God wants for us. When bad stuff happens, it's twice as hard to figure it out."

"And I've had more than my share of bad stuff."
Max stared straight ahead as he shook his head. "But I
should be thankful that my mom had the fortitude to
stand up for my life and the courage to stand up to her
parents, who wanted her to give me up for adoption.
Maybe I would have had a great adoptive family, but
I'm glad my mom chose to keep me."

Heather took a deep breath as she watched Max's
expression soften. She'd seen how much he cared for
his mother. He obviously had a special bond with her.
"Would you tell me about that?"

Max gave her a sideways glance. "Not much to tell.
She kept me against her parents' wishes."

"How did she manage?"

"Her parents sent her away to live with a great-aunt
until I was born. I don't know this for a fact, but I
figured that my great-aunt Violet was an advocate for
my mom and helped her keep me. When Violet died,
my mom inherited what little estate her great-aunt
had. She had no other heirs. That's when we moved to
Pinecrest, where my mom got a job through a friend
of Violet's. I'm named after Violet."

"Violet's your middle name?"

"No. Maxwell. That was Violet's last name."
Max's wry smile morphed into a chuckle. "I didn't
appreciate the struggle my mom had as a single parent
until Clay came along. He helped save me from
myself. I was headed in the wrong direction."

"How did he do that?"

"He caught me coming home drunk after a party."

"Wow! How did this happen, and what did he do?"

"He'd moved into the apartment upstairs from the one my mom and I lived in. He saw me when I came home and confronted me. Made a deal with me—if I went to church and youth group functions, he wouldn't tell my mom."

"Did you take the deal?"

"Reluctantly, but that came back to bite him when we finally had to confess the incident to my mom. She was so angry and told Clay she didn't want to see him again. I was angry at her because I thought she was being unfair to him. But Clay never gave up on me or my mom. He helped my mom reconcile with her parents."

Heather listened as the words poured out of Max's mouth. At the beginning of this evening, she would never have guessed how much she would learn about him. "So your mom was estranged from her parents because of you?"

"Yeah, pretty much. Thanks to Clay, things are good with my grandparents now, but they weren't for many years."

"Do you suppose prayer had anything to do with that?"

Max let out a heavy sigh as he nodded. "I know it did. Thanks for reminding me."

Heather's mind whirled. He hated asking for help. He hated accepting help. He hated to admit that he needed help. How was she going to get around the barriers he'd set up? If she volunteered to search, how would he react? "You said you've been too tired to think about searching for your father's family. I could do it."

Like a kaleidoscope, mixed emotions colored Max's expression. He sat up straight. "And how could you do that?"

No answers populated Heather's thoughts. She'd spoken before she'd formulated a plan. Not smart, especially where Max was concerned. "Do whatever you were planning to do."

"And what if I had made no plans?"

Heather sat back and pressed her lips together. Typical Max. No plans. Was he just going to wing it and hope something turned up? She forced herself not to say what she was thinking. "Then we can make some."

"Why do you want to do this?"

"Because I want to help."

"Yeah, like you helped me with Brittany? No thanks."

"Are you ever going to let that go? I thought for a few minutes here tonight, you were finally looking at me as a friend instead of an enemy." Heather placed her hands on either side of her head as if doing so could hold all the angry thoughts inside. "All I want to do is help, and all you want to do is be difficult."

"You know what, Heather? You can't be Ms. Fixit for everyone who comes into your life. Sometimes, you have to let people make bad choices. They learn from them. So quit trying to fix me."

Heather stared at Max, a lump rising in her throat. Was that what she'd been trying to do? Fixing Max? Fixing Brittany? Fixing everyone except herself? In reality, only God could do the fixing. She had to let Him work in her life and everyone else's life instead of trying to take over for Him. She twisted her hands as her voice pushed past the lump. "I'm sorry you feel that way. What's wrong with trying to help people?"

"Nothing, if the people want help."

"But sometimes people don't know they need help."

"And you know when they do?"

"Sometimes."

"And sometimes you butt in where you're not wanted."

Maybe she'd overstepped in people's lives in the past, but she couldn't see why Max was so upset about her offer to search for the family he didn't know. "Why don't you want help finding your family? Why is that butting in?"

Max released a harsh breath as he hung his head. Only the hum of the refrigerator filled the awkward silence. He finally looked up. "Because I don't know what I'll find."

Understanding seeped into Heather's brain. Was Max afraid they would reject him as his father had done? Was Max afraid the family he didn't know consisted of unlikable people—people he would be sorry he'd searched for? "That's why you need someone to stand with you."

"And you're going to do that? Be my advocate—vouch for my character?"

Heather wasn't sure of Max's meaning, but the sarcasm dripping from his words gave her a pretty good clue. "I can do that."

He let out a half grunt, half laugh, displaying his disbelief. "Yeah, like you did with Brittany."

Heather finally came to the conclusion that Max didn't want her help or her presence. She was done. "Yeah, like with Brittany. I saved both of you from a disastrous relationship, whether you want to believe it or not. If you want to wallow in your self-pity, go ahead. I won't stop you. And don't ask me to stay this time, because I'm leaving. You can't change my mind. And since you don't want my help, I'll talk to Dr. Duffey on Monday about having another nurse take over your care. I think that will be better for both of us. Then I won't be tempted to fix you."

Max didn't make a move as Heather grabbed her purse, DVD, and jacket. She refused to look back as she headed for the door. As she touched the doorknob, she wondered whether Max would come after her, but she wasn't that surprised when he didn't. Her stomach tied in knots, she closed the door, resisting the urge to slam it. She raced across the street and up the stairs to her apartment. Once inside, she leaned back against the door as it closed. She covered her mouth with her hands and let the tears flow.

She didn't want to believe she was crying over

Max Reynolds, but she was. Every time he brought up Brittany, it pierced Heather's heart. She had to face the fact that he would never look at her as someone other than the person who had destroyed his love life. How had she let herself get caught up in his life?

She couldn't become involved with a patient. That was asking for trouble of all kinds. She hoped Dr. Duffey wouldn't question her request to be removed from Max's care. She should have been wise enough to realize right from the beginning that she couldn't be his nurse, but she'd let him persuade her otherwise. Now she had to put her plan into action no matter how disruptive it seemed. Max would be better off without her. Why didn't that make her feel any better? She couldn't kid herself. She knew the answer. She'd let herself care too much for the most unlikely man.

***

After Heather had rushed out, Max pushed himself up from the couch and plodded to the door. He opened it and stepped onto the porch. The street lamps illuminated the nearby houses and cast shadows in every yard. A cloud floated over the moon while he stared into the night. As he looked toward Heather's apartment, a light came on. His peevish behavior had chased her away. Why had he dismissed her help?

Heather had been nothing but supportive since the day she'd walked into the exam room and announced that she was his nurse. He, on the other hand, had done nothing but give her grief. He could apologize, but he wasn't sure she would listen. Could he drag himself to Amanda's event tomorrow night and seek Heather's forgiveness? Maybe she wouldn't even attend, because she didn't want to be around him. He wouldn't blame her if she did just that.

Max's stomach roiled, and his heart ached. His father didn't want him. Brittany didn't want him. Now he'd pushed Heather away, and she didn't want him, as a patient or anything else.

As Max leaned against the porch support, weariness grabbed hold of him and wouldn't let go. The exhaustion wasn't only physical, but mental and spiritual, as well. He was tired of fighting this disease, fighting himself, and fighting his feelings. Feelings of uncertainty, inadequacy, and whatever he was feeling about Heather. He couldn't make up his mind whether he was pushing her away because she made him angry or because he was starting to care about her too much.

Max couldn't believe how he'd divulged so much to her tonight—everything from his heartache over Brittany to his drunken episode as a teenager. His messed-up life probably confirmed to Heather that she'd done the right thing when she'd persuaded Brittany to dump him.

Brittany's happiness was something he wanted, despite his own heartache. A recent post from a friend on social media confirmed that she was. She and Parker were going to have a baby. She loved someone else and had a wonderful life. Her well-being made

Max sad and happy at the same time. Could Heather help to heal his heart as well as his body? Did he want to find out?

The unfathomable thought of falling for Heather scared him more than the cancer. How could he have romantic feelings for a woman who had come between him and Brittany? Were his mind and heart playing tricks on him? Was he one of those patients who had an attraction to a nurse?

The feelings he had for Heather didn't make sense. Ridiculous. The word tattooed itself on his brain. Caring about Heather Watson would take him on a straight path to heartache. Whatever had caused his attraction to her couldn't be good.

Max stood there, his thoughts as unclear as the cloudy sky overhead. Nothing made sense. Brittany. Heather. The two were like night and day. What prompted his interest in two such different women?

Should he talk to a counselor? He shook his head. He couldn't talk to a counselor about Heather.

Jeremy or Luke? Not hardly. They were almost strangers still.

Clay? Clay was always there to confide in, but Max feared that Clay wouldn't understand Max's inability to let go of his heartache over Brittany.

God? He should be the answer, but Max had his doubts. Even though he attended church and helped with the youth group, too often God seemed far away and impersonal. Max looked heavenward. The clouds, the stars, the moon—all God's creation. God was there. Max only had to reach out to Him.

Lord, you know my thoughts. I need Your forgiveness and Your help. Max bowed his head and confessed his sins, asked for guidance, and poured out his heart to God. Tomorrow was a new day. Tomorrow, with God's help, Max promised himself that he would make better choices.

CHAPTER TEN

The eating establishment located on the square of the neighboring town hummed with activity.

Heather made her way to the table where Amanda sat near the small stage that sported three microphones. When Amanda looked in Heather's direction, she waved.

Heather wasn't sure what to expect from Max's cousin. Was it too much to hope that the younger woman could tell Heather more about why Max couldn't get over his breakup with Brittany? Heather didn't know why she even cared after the way he'd acted last night and the way she'd walked out on him, but something inside wouldn't let her dismiss him.

Amanda stood and gave Heather a hug—a good sign. "I'm so glad we could get together, but I'm sorry Max couldn't make it."

"He wasn't doing very well last night when I saw him. He was really tired." Heather knew she'd had every reason to leave, but the guilt for doing so hadn't gone away.

Amanda grimaced. "I still can't believe he has cancer. He seemed pretty good at the baseball game."

"By the day of the game, it had been over a week

since his last chemo treatment. So he'd had some time to recover. The first few days following the treatments are usually the worst." Heather's mind buzzed with the hope of getting more information about Max. "What are your plans for tonight?"

"The organizers will announce the acts. They'll put out a white board a little later so the performers can sign up." Amanda motioned toward the stage. "Each performer gets ten minutes, so I'll have time to do a couple of songs. Then I'm also part of an ensemble group from the music school. I enjoy working with them. We're going to perform one of my original songs."

"That's terrific. You write your own material?"

"Some of it." Amanda nodded. "I'm going to perform one original solo song, too. I really appreciate your coming tonight. Thanks."

"You're welcome. I've been looking forward to this."

A waitress stopped by their table, took their drink order and handed them menus. Amanda glanced at the menu, then back at Heather. "There aren't very many selections, but the food is usually good. My favorite is the burger."

"I'll order that on your recommendation." Heather laid her menu aside. "I know we touched on this a little at the baseball game, but I'm trying to understand why Max can't get over Brittany. Can you give me any clues?"

Shaking her head, Amanda narrowed her gaze. "I

told you that we weren't very close. I was shocked when I came home and found out she was getting married, but not to Max."

"So you didn't even know that they'd broken up?"

"No, I was away at college in California." Amanda shrugged. "They dated in high school. Brittany was a year older, so when she graduated, she went to the community college in Spokane during Max's senior year so they could be together. He got a scholarship to play football at some college in Montana. When he went to Montana, Brittany went, too. I saw them for a few weeks every summer while I was still in high school, but we didn't hang out or anything. When I went away to college, I only came home for a week or so between sessions. I always went to summer school because I hated living in Pinecrest. I wish I could be of more help."

Heather smiled. "That's okay. I don't understand him. Maybe you can relate. Have you ever broken up with a longtime boyfriend?"

Amanda wrinkled her nose and vigorously shook her head. "Guess I'm not very good at relationships. The longest I've ever dated anyone is about six months, and I was glad when that one ended. Since I've been here, I've pretty much been hanging out with a group. I don't want to get involved with someone, because I want to concentrate on my music, and relationships take up time I don't want to surrender. What about you?"

Heather nodded. "Those are pretty much my

thoughts, but I have all these well-meaning friends who keep trying to fix me up. What a disaster!"

Amanda laughed. "So far I've managed to avoid the well-meaning friends and their matchmaking."

"Not me. I have this one friend I work with who is constantly arranging dates for me. So I made this list of requirements—a really crazy list. I told her if she could find someone who met all the qualifications, I'd go out with him, but otherwise, she shouldn't bother."

"Did it work?"

"So far."

"Then you aren't interested in Max?" Amanda grimaced. "I'm not trying to be nosy, but I was just curious because you keep asking questions about his old relationship with Brittany."

Amanda's question caught Heather off guard. How could she answer honestly?

Before Heather could respond, the waitress returned with their drinks and took their orders. Heather thought maybe she had a reprieve on the question, until Amanda cocked her head. "So what's the verdict on Max?"

Heather took a deep breath and let it out slowly. "I'm not sure."

"Not sure?"

"I care about Max because he's one of my patients, and I'm afraid his inability to leave his relationship with Brittany in the past will affect his treatment. That's why I was hoping you could give me some insight into their relationship."

"Are you sure that's all it is?" Amanda gave Heather a curious look. "You did tell me that he blames you for their breakup, right?"

"Yeah, he does, and he can't seem to forget that."

"So now that you've discovered you actually have an interest in Max, you don't know what to do about it. And you can't begin to explain it." Amanda's look challenged Heather to deny her statements.

Shrugging, Heather released a heavy sigh. She didn't want to confirm or deny what Amanda said. "I don't know. He seems so miserable without Brittany that it makes me feel guilty. But I honestly thought they weren't good for each other. He really didn't seem to care about her. He was always standing her up or forgetting something important like her birthday. She'd cry. Then he'd come over and apologize. She'd forgive him, but then he'd do it all over again."

"So you thought you'd step in and save her?"

"Yeah, and last night Max accused me of trying to fix things for everyone, including him." Heather hesitated, trying to ward off the unpleasant memory. She pressed her lips together and blinked back the tears. Even now his accusations hurt. Her heart twisted. She had probably pushed him one time too many.

"And he made you cry."

"How'd you know?"

"You don't have a very good poker face. I can tell that talking about last night put you on the verge of tears."

Heather gritted her teeth and shook her head. "And it shouldn't. I saw how Max treated Brittany, so I don't understand how I can be attracted to him. What's wrong with me?"

Amanda chuckled. "Nothing. Max leaves a trail of broken hearts in his wake, and he doesn't even know it. At least that's the way it was when he was in high school."

Heather frowned. "I thought you said he only dated Brittany in high school."

"True, but he was a star football player—tall, good looking, and half the girls in high school were in love with him. He didn't have a clue. He only had eyes for Brittany."

The waitress returned with their food, and for a few minutes they ate in silence. Heather worried that she would never make sense of her tangled feelings for Max. She wasn't some high school girl with a crush on the local football star. She knew all of Max's warts and foibles, and yet, here she was, falling for him anyway. Could he read her as well as Amanda? Could he tell that a look or touch from him made her insides a jumbled mess?

Amanda set down her burger. "So what do you plan to do about Max?"

"Nothing. I don't want to discuss him anymore. It won't accomplish a thing."

Amanda gave Heather a skeptical look. "Maybe you should talk about it."

"He has no interest in the woman who, as he put it,

'destroyed his love life.'"

"He said that to you?"

Heather nodded. "He cornered me at the wedding reception and told me off."

"Wow! What did you do?"

"Just let it go. I wasn't ever going to see him again, or so I thought."

"He didn't seem that angry with you at the baseball game. In fact, I would never have guessed there was any animosity between the two of you."

"I think I would describe his behavior as Dr. Jekyll and Mr. Hyde. I never know which one I'm going to confront." Heather shook her head and explained how she happened to be with Max the night before. "When I was there, he morphed between the two fictional characters more than once—telling me off, then begging me not to go."

"Maybe his feelings are as conflicted as yours." Amanda raised her eyebrows, then popped a french fry into her mouth.

Frowning, Heather shook her head again. "That's a completely wild thought. He's not conflicted about me. I know exactly what he thinks of me, and he's not a fan. You should see how pained he looks when he talks about Brittany."

"That's his problem, not yours."

"Let's talk about something else." Heather attacked her burger and hoped the enjoyable meal would obliterate thoughts of Max.

"Yeah, I think you're right." Amanda drained the

last of her soda as she glanced toward the stage. "I see some other folks are signing in, so I'd better get my name up there."

As Heather watched Amanda, a couple of guys and another girl joined Amanda while she signed in. When she returned to the table, the others came with her. "Heather, these are the other members of the ensemble I was telling you about. I'd like you to meet Sean, Morris and Claire."

Heather shook hands with Sean, whose light-brown hair hung over the collar of his shirt. He sported a neatly trimmed beard. The other guy was clean-shaven with dark-brown hair. The blond woman appeared older than the rest of the group, and she carried a couple of instrument cases. After they all exchanged greetings, they settled at the table.

Moments later, the waitress took more drink orders. Amanda explained that Heather was an oncology nurse. During the discussion, Heather learned that Sean and Morris were also riding in the PMC. When the talk turned to Heather's efforts to raise funds for cancer research and the house for families of cancer patients, Amanda suggested that the group could play a concert as part of the Fourth of July fundraising festival Heather had planned.

"That would be fantastic, but what kind of a venue do you need?" Heather asked.

"I don't know. It would have to be someplace where people have to pay to gain admission," Sean said.

"We could probably get some other groups to participate." Amanda glanced around the table at the other members of her group. "What do you guys think?"

"I'm sure we could find some others who would love to show off their talents for a good cause. I'll ask around," Sean replied.

"I'll check around to see what might be available." Heather wondered what she could come up with on short notice. Would the storefront where they met for church work? "Amanda, could you help me look for venues? You would know what kind of space you need better than I do."

"Sure." Amanda nodded. "Max said I should visit the church where you guys attend. We can get together to discuss it tomorrow?"

"Good. The sooner we get started the better." Heather tried not to worry about Amanda's visit bringing Max into the mix. Even if she wasn't his nurse, he was intertwined into her life in more ways than she wanted to count.

***

Applause swallowed the last strum of a guitar as Max followed Jeremy and Luke into the crowded café. A spotlight flooded the raised platform on the side of the room farthest from the door. Hoots and hollers joined the applause as two guys with guitars took another bow. Despite the spotlight, the rest of the place was dimly lit with candles flickering in jars on each table.

Max turned to Jeremy. "Do you see Amanda or Heather?"

Jeremy squinted as he looked around the room. "Too many people. Since you seat yourself in this place, maybe we can stand here at the back for a while until we can spot them."

"Works for me." Luke leaned up against the wall between two windows.

Max joined the two guys, his stomach roiling at the thought of seeing Heather after their acrimonious parting last night. He wished he could blame his sour attitude on the chemo, but he couldn't. Fear had made him push Heather away. He didn't understand his attraction to the I-know-what's-best-for-you woman, but he couldn't resist wanting to show her that sometimes, he knew what was best. Probably a prescription for disaster. He'd had enough prescriptions in recent weeks, so what was one more?

While they stood there, the next act, a lone female with a guitar took the stage. She sang a couple of acoustic bluegrass numbers. She was good, but not as good as Amanda. That was one of Amanda's saving graces—her singing voice. He was glad she'd finally made it to music school. Besides, she'd been rather pleasant at the baseball game even if she hadn't been dressed for one.

As the woman finished her last song, Max spotted Heather sitting at a table in the far corner near the stage. She was laughing and talking to a guy with longish hair and a beard. Jealousy flashed through his mind like the strobe light above the stage.

The crazy mixed-up feelings from the night before still afflicted him. Sometimes, he thought he should just kiss her and get it over with—see what kind of reaction he got out of that. Another crazy, crazy thought.

"Hey, there's Heather and Amanda." Luke motioned toward the other side of the room.

"Yeah, I see them." As the next performer headed toward the stage, Max followed the other two guys and hoped Heather wouldn't ignore him.

Jeremy came up behind Heather and leaned over. "Can you find three more seats?"

Heather jerked her head around, then smiled when she saw Jeremy. "Where'd you come from?"

"Max asked us if we'd like to hear his cousin sing. So we decided to see what this open mic thing is all about. Sounded like a fun evening." Jeremy nodded toward Max.

Max tried to smile when Heather looked his way. Curiosity radiated from her eyes. He welcomed the chance to look away as he searched for a chair. Finally, the three guys rounded up the chairs they needed and squeezed around the table. Max sat on the edge of the circle where he had a good view of Heather, who seemed to be ignoring him.

After he settled in his chair, Amanda came over and hugged him. "I didn't think you'd get to come.

Are you feeling better?"

Max smiled wryly. "Better than last night, so I talked Jeremy and Luke into bringing me. We didn't miss your performance, did we?"

"No, there are two more after this one before I go on, and our group is going to perform, too." Amanda introduced the three newcomers to the other musicians.

Max eased back in his chair and focused his attention on the next act, a guy who sang a foot-stomping song that got the crowd clapping. Every once in a while, Max glanced over at Heather, who was clapping and mouthing the words to the familiar number. As it ended, she looked his way and caught him staring. His first reaction was to avert his gaze, but he refused to surrender to his fears. He smiled, but she only stared back at him. Could he blame her? He had some big fences to mend.

Heather looked away as the next performer took the stage, a guy with a harmonica. He played a couple of songs and recited some humorous original poetry in between the tunes. Was she wishing he wasn't here? How was he ever going to talk with her in this crowd? He was discovering he didn't have as much energy as he thought when they'd left the apartment.

After the poet, a trio consisting of two men and a woman sang a love ballad with one guy playing a guitar and one a banjo and the woman singing lead. When the group announced the second love song, Max was sure it must be aimed at him. As the woman and the guy on guitar harmonized, the words to "Foolish Heart" shot straight to Max's emotions. Every line seemed to hit him right where he was living. Was he a fool to think he could find love again?

Once again applause filled the room as the trio finished. Then Amanda picked up her guitar and made her way to the stage amid cheers from her table. After she stood behind the microphone, Max gave her thumbs-up. He hoped this would be good since he'd coerced his roommates to come.

Jeremy leaned closer as Amanda adjusted the microphone to her height. "She doesn't look nervous at all."

"She's always had a stage presence. Her voice could capture a crowd even when she was thirteen."

"Is that when you first heard her sing?" Jeremy asked.

Max nodded as Amanda introduced her first number. "Hi, folks, glad you've come out tonight to hear a lot of good music. This first song is one I wrote a few years ago. I hope you'll enjoy it."

More applause filled the room as she strummed an introduction on her guitar. She hummed a few bars before her voice came through the sound system loud and strong. Within seconds the murmur of the crowd that had never completely gone away during the other performances died. The only sounds in the place came from Amanda's guitar and her song. The same thing had happened when Amanda was thirteen and sang at a church work camp, impressing all in attendance. She was doing the same thing tonight as her melodic tones and the words of the song filled the air.

"How do I know
When to let go?
How do I know
When to love again?"

Max listened to the words. It was as if Amanda had written the song as a message to him. That was ridiculous because she wouldn't have known about his inability to get over Brittany when she wrote it. The song's parallel to his love life was only a coincidence.

The final notes were drowned in the ovation from the crowd. Amanda smiled and thanked them as she picked up the microphone and made her way to the piano on the left side of the stage. She sat on the piano bench and adjusted the microphone. "Thanks so much. I hope you enjoy this next song—one of my favorites from Vanessa Carlton. It's called "A Thousand Miles."

The first piano chords of the song resounded through the café as the crowd listened intently. Max was vaguely familiar with the song that was popular some years ago, but he wasn't prepared for the words—words that talked about needing and missing someone, drowning in memories and not being able to let go. He had the insane urge to cover his ears so he didn't have to listen to Amanda sing a song that flooded his mind with thoughts of Brittany. Wasn't he miserable enough already without having to listen to this?

He looked away from the stage and found Heather watching him. She obviously guessed the impact the song had on him. He didn't want her to know, but he could tell by her expression that she did. He looked away, swallowing hard, but there was no hiding from Heather. The other night he'd blathered on and on about his feelings but not the ones he had for her. He didn't know how to decipher them.

When Amanda came back to the table, Max joined the others as they congratulated her on her moving performance. He enjoyed watching his cousin accept the praise with gratitude and humility. She'd come a long way from the snarly kid who had moved to Pinecrest when he'd been in high school and she in middle school. Max realized he had more in common with Amanda than he thought. Both of them had come out of some rebellious behavior and managed to become responsible adults.

"Congratulations! That was terrific." Max clapped Amanda on the back. "Has any of your family seen you perform?"

"Not lately." Amanda smiled and leaned back in her chair as the next act took the stage.

The chance to talk further was lost as the male guitarist started his first song. Max sat through two more acts, wishing he could leave. His energy seeped away as if someone had punched him full of holes and it was draining out of his body. Even though Amanda was going to sing with her group, he was ready to call a cab to take him home so the others wouldn't have to leave. Maybe he could hang on until Amanda sang again.

After another singer finished, Max leaned over to Amanda. "When will you perform again with your group?"

"We're up after this musician." Amanda gave him a questioning look.

"Good. Because after you sing again, I'm going to catch a cab home. I'm wearing out."

"You don't have to stay if you're too tired. I understand."

"No, I can make it." Max forced a smile, hoping Amanda wouldn't be concerned.

Thankfully, the next act started, so she didn't have time to question him further. He sat back in his chair and closed his eyes. He didn't want to listen to the words to this song either—another song about love gone wrong.

Did knowing that he obviously wasn't the only one suffering over love make things better or worse? A lost love should be the least of his worries. Cancer made everything else unimportant. Except his heart wasn't getting the message—a cruel set of events of his own making.

Applause made Max open his eyes. Had he fallen asleep? He looked around to see if anyone had noticed. It appeared that no one had, until he saw Heather looking at him with concern. She averted her gaze, then grabbed Amanda's arm and said something.

Amanda whispered something to Heather before going up on the stage. Were they talking about him, or was he being paranoid?

He had to get over himself. He sat up straighter in his chair and focused on Amanda as she took her place at the piano while the others in the group with their guitars and banjo in hand gathered in front of the microphones at the front of the stage. First, they sang one of Amanda's original songs.

Max's thoughts brightened when the song talked about a happy love—one that brought joy. Still, the words resurrected the question about whether he could find love again and planted it squarely in his thoughts.

When the guitar chords of their second song started, Max wished he hadn't stayed. The rendition of Tim McGraw's "Just to See You Smile" didn't put a smile on Max's face. He'd deleted the song from his playlist not long after Brittany broke up with him because every time he heard it, he thought of her.

So much of the song really didn't fit their story, but the part about doing anything to see her smile always hit home. Too often he hadn't made her smile, and that had been the problem. So when she'd married someone else, he'd told her he was happy for her. Had it been a lie like in the song? He'd convinced himself it wasn't. Her happiness meant a lot to him, but he wanted to find happiness, too.

Max glanced at Heather, who once again was mouthing the words. Just before the song ended, she glanced at him and smiled. His heart took a little jog around his chest. She was getting to him again. Where did he go from here? Could she help him forget Brittany, or was he so desperate for someone to love and someone to love him that he was looking at the wrong woman?

He was tired. Tired of second-guessing himself. Tired of wondering where he belonged. Tired of fighting his feelings. He had to get out of here.

Standing, Max congratulated Amanda and her group on a great performance. He told Jeremy and Luke he was going to catch a cab for home so they could stay. They protested at first, but he persuaded them that there was no sense in ruining their evening because of him. He waved, then made his way to the door.

Stepping outside, he took a deep breath. The coolness of the evening soaked into his bones, and he pulled his jacket closer around him. The full moon took a snapshot of the town hall in the middle of the square while wispy clouds raced through the stars. He grabbed his phone from his pocket and started searching for a cab company.

More music from inside the café filtered out to the sidewalk. Max punched the link with his finger, and the phone started ringing. As he stared off into the night, someone tapped him on the shoulder. He jerked his head to the side. Heather stood beside him.

"I'm going to give you a ride home." Heather gave him a no-nonsense look. "There's no need for you to call a cab. So you can put your phone away."

Ending his phone call, Max blinked a couple of times—not sure he'd heard her correctly. He raised his eyebrows as he stared at her. "You're giving me a ride home. Why?"

"Because I like to tell you what to do."

He couldn't miss the twinkle in her eyes and the smile that lurked at the corners of her mouth—a very kissable mouth. He was in trouble for sure, but somehow the idea of a relationship with Heather didn't seem as scary at this moment. Maybe it was all those love songs he'd heard. Max knit his eyebrows, still not making sense of her offer. "But why would you want to do that after the way I treated you last night?"

"Because I'm a nice person." She gazed at him, still trying to fight a smile.

"Nicer than me. That's for sure."

Her near smile morphed into a grin. "I'm glad you recognize that."

Chuckling, Max couldn't believe she was joking about his bad behavior as if he hadn't been a real meathead last night. He'd been waiting all evening for a chance to talk to her and make amends, but now that they were alone together, his brain was mush. He couldn't get his mouth to work. He looked down at his phone to make sure he'd actually ended his call. The screen was blank, like his mind. "Okay. Thanks."

"Would you like to walk with me to the car, or do you want me to come by and pick you up?"

"I'll walk."

"Are you sure? You looked a little on the tired side this evening."

"You were watching me?" Max tried to act surprised, but he wasn't. He'd caught her looking at him several times. Would she admit it?

"Yeah. You said you didn't have enough energy to come, and then you show up." She shrugged.

"I wanted to support Amanda."

"I'm glad. She has a wonderful talent."

"She does. I hope she can succeed, but it's hard to get discovered in the music field, even though you have talent."

"She seems to have a lot of determination." Heather pointed toward the square. "My car's parked on the other side of the town hall. So let's not just stand here. We can talk on the way."

"Sure." Max fell into step beside Heather.

They walked across the street and down the block without saying a word. Did she have something to say, or was her statement only an expression to get him to move? He should start the conversation with an apology, but he didn't know where to begin. He'd never been very good at saying he was sorry or following through on any apologies he'd made, especially with Brittany.

When they reached Heather's car, she looked over the top as she opened the driver's side door. "I hope you don't mind if I stop at the grocery on the way home. I have to pick up a couple of things."

"No problem. You're doing me a favor, so I can't

complain." Max slid into the passenger seat. She was conversing as if he'd never been rude to her. Was she feeling bad about walking out on him? No. Couldn't be. She'd had every right to walk out. He deserved her disdain, but she hadn't mentioned it.

Heather maneuvered her car into the street and drove around the square onto the main route through town. She pulled the car to a stop at the traffic light at the edge of the business district. She looked his way. "Amanda and I had dinner together tonight, and we talked about our fundraising efforts. She said she was coming to church on Sunday, and afterwards we're going to search for a venue where we can have a concert to raise funds. She said she and her band would play. She also indicated that she could get some others to join them. What do you think?"

"I think that's great." So this was what Heather wanted to talk about—not a word about last night. Max took in the news with a shake of his head. Amanda hardly seemed like the same teenager he'd known back in Pinecrest. Why should he be surprised that Amanda had grown up? He wasn't the same kid who had knuckled under to peer pressure and did a lot of things he wasn't very proud of.

After Heather pulled away from the traffic light, they rode in silence to the grocery. She brought the car to a stop in the nearly empty parking lot, then glanced at him. "I'll only be a few minutes."

"Hey, could you get me a carton of eggs? I'll pay you back."

"Sure."

"Thanks." Max pressed the button on the side of the seat, and it slowly reclined. He closed his eyes as the car door slammed shut. Somehow he had to get the courage to ask for forgiveness for his behavior.

The click of the car door startled Max as he blinked against the car's dome light. He must have fallen asleep in the short time that Heather was in the store. He quickly straightened the seat to a more upright position as he pulled some bills from his pocket. "Here's some money."

Heather glanced down at the cash he'd shoved into her hand. "That's too much."

"That's okay." Max waved a hand at her.

"If you insist."

"I do."

Heather started the car. "Did you get some sleep?"

Max chuckled. "Guess you caught me napping."

"It's a good thing that I'm taking you home. No telling what would have happened to you if you'd taken a cab." She gave him a pointed look.

"Thanks to you, I don't have to worry about it." Max closed his eyes again. He hadn't meant for his comment to come out in such sarcastic tones. "You can dump me out if you want."

"Now why would I want to do that?" Heather drove onto the road.

"Because I don't deserve your help."

"And why do you say that?"

Max opened his eyes and looked at her in the

moonlight coming in through the windshield. "I haven't been much of a friend, patient, or Christian in the way I've treated you."

"Are you trying to say you're sorry for last night?"

"Yeah. I am."

"But will it mean a change in your behavior in the future?" Heather gave him a sideways glance before she returned her attention to the road.

Did she not believe he was sincere? Did he dare ask? "I hope so. Are you still planning to resign as my nurse?"

Nodding, she pressed her lips together in a firm line. She let out a heavy sigh. "You aren't going to change my mind by saying you're sorry. You run hot and cold. You say you're sorry, but then you do the same old stuff over and over again. I saw the pattern with Brittany too many times, and I got a taste of it last night."

Heather's statement bruised his ego, but it was true. She'd nailed his behavior. Why did he have an interest in a woman who detested him? He wished there was some way to change her opinion of him. Was that possible when he constantly did the wrong thing? "I suppose it wouldn't help if I told you I came to see Amanda tonight just so I could talk to you and make amends?"

"If I thought you could follow through on your amends. Maybe." Heather stopped her car in front of his house. She didn't look at him but stared straight ahead. "Nothing you can say will change my mind about being your nurse. I should've had someone else assigned to you right away, but I thought the past wouldn't get in the way. And you insisted that you wanted me to stay on as your nurse, and I did so against my better judgment."

"So who's going to take your place?" Even with all the times he'd wished her out of his life, the thought that he wouldn't have a built-in appointment with her every other week left him feeling at a loss. Was he losing his mind? No. He was losing his heart.

"I don't know, but it'll work out."

Max put his hand on the door handle and wished his time with Heather didn't have to end even though he was tired. What would she say if he invited her in? Could he hope for a second chance? "Thanks for the ride."

"You're welcome. Get some rest."

"I intend to." Max opened the door and got out.

As he started up the walk, a car door opened and closed. "Wait, Max. You forgot your eggs."

Max turned around as Heather came toward him with a plastic bag dangling from her hand. The light from the full moon captured her beauty. He couldn't look away. When she handed him the bag, for one insane second, he had the urge to kiss her. Thankful for the brim on his ball cap that kept him from leaning in and kissing her, he stepped back so quickly that he stumbled on the edge of the sidewalk. Heather reached for him. He grabbed hold of her. They stood arm in arm in the moonlight, the eggs nearly forgotten.

Max still wanted to kiss her, and this time he wasn't going to let anything get in the way—cap or eggs. He tilted back his cap, then pulled her closer until their lips met. At first, she was rigid in his arms, but as he deepened the kiss, she slowly melted into him. He was kissing Heather Watson, his nemesis, and liking it—liking it a whole lot. Was he crazy?

When he stepped away, Heather stood there wide eyed, looking thoroughly kissed. "Did you do that on purpose?"

"Not the stumbling, but the kiss was definitely on purpose." Max held the bag containing the eggs as she continued to stare at him as if he'd suddenly morphed into some kind of alien creature. "I suppose I shouldn't have done that, but I'm not going to say I'm sorry because I'm not."

"What are you trying to do?" Heather shook her head. "I don't understand you."

"I don't understand me either." Shrugging, Max gave her a silly grin. "Would you like to give understanding me a try?"

Heather shook her head again. "Do you think that's possible?"

Max laughed. "You know how to put a guy in his place."

"I wasn't trying to do that." Heather looked at him with a pained expression. "I'm very confused."

"That makes two of us."

"So you don't know why you kissed me?"

"Do you know why you kissed me back?"

"A momentary loss of sanity?"

"I was thinking the same thing." Max laughed. "But I want to untangle all that's going on between us. What do you think?"

Heather took a deep breath and let it out slowly as she continued to stare at him. "How do you plan to do that?"

"Do you want to come in to discuss it?" Max motioned toward the house. "I promise there won't be a repeat of last night."

Max could read the hesitation in Heather's expression.

CHAPTER ELEVEN

Could Max keep a promise? The question rifled through Heather's mind. But that doubt paled in comparison to the nameless reason for the way she'd kissed him. Sure she'd let herself care too much about him, but that kiss had taken things to a whole new level—a level she wasn't sure she was ready to deal with.

That was one amazing kiss. She'd asked herself over and over again why Brittany had stuck with Max for so many years. Heather was finding more and more reasons for Brittany's attachment to him. The pieces were all beginning to fit together. Despite his faults, there was a great deal to like about Max Reynolds, and it had nothing to do with the way he kissed. That was just an added bonus.

Heather took a shaky breath. "I'm not sure that would be a good idea. You're tired, and I don't know what I'm doing."

"I do. You're coming with me, and we're going to talk this through. I suddenly feel not quite so tired."

Max reached out his hand and took hers. She didn't resist as he led her up the steps and into the house. After he put the eggs in the fridge, he sat on the couch and brought her with him. For a few seconds, they sat side-by-side without talking. Heather wasn't sure what to say. She wasn't making any sense of what he'd done tonight.

Scooting forward on the couch, Heather turned to Max. "Last night you said you were still in love with Brittany. If that's so, why did you kiss me?"

Max blinked, then laid his head back against the couch. A muscle worked in his jaw as he stared into space. He said nothing.

"Rebound?" Heather watched for his reaction.

"I'd hardly call two years after the breakup a rebound."

"Have you dated anyone since your breakup with Brittany?"

Max turned his head without lifting it from the back of the couch, his gaze narrow. "No."

"So maybe I'm right. It's a rebound, and you don't want to admit it."

He finally sat up straight as he shook his head. "I…" He released a harsh breath and closed his eyes. "Maybe I overstated my feelings for Brittany. I only know it still hurts, but I want to move on in the worst way."

"So you're using me to get over your hurt? Kissing me to make you forget?"

Max opened his eyes, his expression guarded. "No, I don't go around kissing women for the fun of it or to help me forget anything." Max waved a hand back and forth between them, then rested a finger on his chest. "As hard as it is to explain, I've had this crazy need to stay connected with you even though you reminded me of the hurt, didn't like me, kept telling me what to do."

Max's words were far from comforting. Doubts and questions crowded her mind like the cancer cells that invaded Max's body. Was this all about his cancer? Was he reaching out to her because he was one of those patients who fell for his nurse? But if he had all these negative thoughts about her, why did he even like her?

Heather frowned as she stared at him. "So what are you trying to tell me?"

"We should see where this whole thing takes us."

"I'm not sure I want to go anywhere with you."

"Then why'd you kiss me back?" He raised his eyebrows. "You can't deny it."

She couldn't. He was pulling her in with some unnamed force that she couldn't resist. She put a fist in front of her mouth as she tried to gather her thoughts—formulate an answer.

Heather's stomach took a nosedive as she relived the kiss. She couldn't deny the chemistry between them, but they needed more than chemistry to make a relationship work. They had to actually like each other.

"Is it that difficult to give me an answer? Either you want to see where this goes, or you don't. It's that simple."

"It's not simple at all." Heather shook her head as

she let her hand drop to her lap.

"Does my cancer complicate things?"

"My reluctance has nothing to do with your health." Heather stared at him. "Why do you want to do this when you hold me responsible for the demise of your relationship with Brittany?"

Without saying anything, he got up and started pacing much the same as he'd done the night before. But last night seemed ages ago—as if they were in a time warp of some kind. He stopped and gazed at the floor, apparently reluctant to look her in the eyes. "The breakup was my fault. I didn't give her the attention she deserved. I wanted someone to blame, so I blamed you. You were only pointing out the truth."

Wow! He was acknowledging the reason why Brittany ended their relationship. "Thank you for admitting that."

"It's time I faced the truth and owned up to my inconsiderate behavior." He lifted his head. The pain in his eyes said so much.

Heather's heart sank to her stomach. No matter what he'd told her, he wasn't over the heartbreak. Did she want to help him move on? Did this confession mean he'd changed? "So what are you saying?"

"The same question. We obviously have an attraction to each other. Are you willing to see where it could lead?"

Last night he was bemoaning the loss of Brittany. Tonight he was asking her to consider seeing where a relationship with him might go. Did she want to take a chance on a man who could break her heart in the same way he'd broken Brittany's? Did she want to play second fiddle to an old love? "If I say yes, what does that mean?"

"I see you're still reluctant to give me a straight answer. Guess I can't blame you." A smile slanted one side of his mouth. "I don't exactly have a great track record."

Heather returned his smile, feeling a little bit better. "Let's just admit there's something going on between us and keep doing what we've been doing— working together on various projects, seeing each other in a group setting and letting a friendship grow."

Max shoved his hands into the pockets of his pants as his stare pinned her to the couch. "So you're trying to let me down easy, is that it?"

"I didn't say that." Heather didn't want to jump into this thing with both feet. She wanted to wade into the relationship. "Amanda told me that you and Brittany were just friends for a year before you started dating. Why can't that work for us?"

"I was sixteen." Max shook his head. "I'm not waiting that long to see where this goes."

"And I'm not saying we should, but let's ease into it—get to know each other better."

"We can't do that on a date?"

Heather let out a heavy sigh. "Are you asking me out?"

"Yeah. I am." Max pulled his cell phone out of his pocket and studied it as he punched at the screen.

"This coming Saturday night. Are you free?"

Her heart pounding, Heather plucked her phone from her purse and checked her calendar. Saturday was blank, as blank as her mind. "Yes."

"Then it's a date. Dinner. I'll pick you up at 5:30."

"Do you mind if I drive?"

"Okay. I can understand that you don't want to ride in my car." Max grinned. "How about the Hawthorne Inn?"

Heather nodded. "I'd like that."

"Good. Then we're set."

"All except one thing."

"What's that?" Concern colored Max's features.

"I want you to be okay with the fact that I'm going to have Dr. Duffey assign you another nurse."

Max knit his eyebrows. "Still?"

"Yeah. It's even more important now that you have another nurse. I think it's better if I'm not dating one of my patients."

Max gave her that crooked smile again. "And here I was just getting used to having you pump me full of poison every other Friday."

"I'm still going to be looking out for you as a friend, and I'm probably still going to be telling you what to do." Heather stood. "I'd better get going."

"Don't go." Max stepped closer to her and took her hand.

"I thought you were tired."

"I am, but I want to sit here with you for a while." He picked up the TV remote and turned on the TV.

"We can watch something."

"Okay." Heather wasn't sure why he didn't want her to go—just like last night. Had the guy who liked to take care of himself, liked his privacy, liked his solitary life, suddenly morphed into a person who needed people? Or maybe he just needed her.

More questions. Her interaction with Max always raised more questions than it answered.

Max plopped back down on the couch and patted the seat next to him. "Sit by me."

As Heather sat down, Max tuned into a rerun of the situation comedy *Home Improvement*. She didn't say anything as he put an arm around her shoulders and pulled her closer. About fifteen minutes into the show, Max's head lolled off to one side. He'd fallen asleep. Heather's heart thumped. He looked so peaceful while he slept. She hated to wake him, but she wasn't sure what to do with him.

Ducking her head, Heather carefully lifted his arm from around her shoulders. She stood and looked down at him. Surely he would have a crick in his neck if he slept that way all night, but she couldn't move him by herself. She could send Jeremy a text and let him know about Max, but first she should get a blanket to cover him.

Heather went down the short hallway to his bedroom. She stopped in the doorway and looked around. His room was much neater than she would have expected. In fact, the place was spotless, small and Spartan, but she saw what she needed—a throw folded at the end of his bed. She grabbed it and went back to the living room.

With the throw folded over one arm, Heather stood there for a few moments and watched Max sleep. A warm sensation filled her chest. She couldn't untangle the gamut of feelings that inundated her as she stepped closer and placed the throw over him. She'd better get out of here before she did something stupid like lean over and kiss him.

When Heather picked up her purse from the floor, a hand reached out and touched her. She let out a little yelp before she realized it was Max. She looked at him with a frown. "Were you playing possum?"

"No. I didn't mean to fall asleep." He picked up the throw and shook it. "What's this?"

"I thought you needed a cover while you slept."

Max got up from the couch and stood inches away from her. "Were you planning to sneak out of here without saying good night?"

Heather swallowed hard. "I didn't want to disturb you."

"You can disturb me anytime." Max smiled and put his arms around her, pulling her close. "We should say a proper good-night."

As Max leaned in, her resistance fled, and she welcomed his kiss. She'd seen Max at his worst, and yet, she was on the verge of letting her heart rule her head. Was this a prescription for disaster? Was there anything in their future besides a date?

***

Like a protective army, oaks, elms, and maples, along with tall pines, surrounded the ornate pale-blue Victorian house with the white trim. An equally ornate sign near the front walk displayed the name, Hawthorne Inn, with dark-blue lettering trimmed in gold across a light-blue background. A huge wraparound porch invited visitors to sit on any of the white rocking chairs and enjoy the pleasant summer evening.

Going up the front walk, Max looked over at Heather as he put a hand to her back. She smiled, but it didn't take away the uncertainty in her eyes. He didn't know why he was second-guessing himself now. He'd talked her into this, so now he had to make it good. Maybe part of his qualms about the situation lay in their history—one of acrimony. He was still trying to figure out why he had an attraction to the woman he'd blamed for the failure of his former relationship.

Max opened the door for Heather. "Ready for a special meal?"

"What else could I expect from Molly and her crew?" Heather stepped into the foyer.

Molly Jansen greeted them. "It's so good to see you again. I've got a special table for you two out on the side porch."

"Thanks." Nervous energy buzzed through Max's mind as he followed Molly and Heather through the dining room and out to the porch.

After Molly left them at the table for two at the far end of the porch, where one of the turrets created a little alcove, a young woman immediately filled their water glasses. Flatware and napkins graced the table along with a jar candle flickering in the shadows of the nearby trees. Max had rarely been attuned to romantic settings, but he recognized this one. Maybe that had been his problem with Brittany. He'd never really romanced her. Their relationship had become so comfortable that he'd forgotten to include a little romance. Could he do better with Heather?

Max picked up his menu. "You've eaten here more than I have. What's good?"

Heather gazed at him over the top of her menu. "Molly's dishes change from season to season. She has her summer menu now. I haven't seen this one before, but I'm sure the lobster dish or the sea scallops are fabulous."

"So you're saying I can't go wrong no matter what I choose?"

Heather nodded. "I think you can count on that."

As Max set his menu aside, Tara Madsen appeared from around the curve in the turret. "Hey, Heather and Max. Good to see you. I'm your server for this evening."

Max grinned. "How's Hailey?"

Tara nodded. "She's doing really well this week. She still talks about going to the baseball game. You're her hero."

"She's the real hero." Max didn't consider himself much of hero compared to the little girl who was so brave in spite of her cancer.

"She has a big crush on you and talks about you all the time."

"Quit telling him stuff like that, or he'll get a big head." Heather chuckled.

Tara laughed in return. "I thought he ought to know before the PMC ride that one little Pedal Partner can't wait to team up with Max."

"Well, I'll try to do my best to be a good example to her." Max produced a smile that he didn't feel as he rubbed a hand over his bald head. "I'm just getting used to this cancer thing myself."

"Hailey prays for you every night."

"Tell her thanks. I'll be praying for her, too." The little girl's prayers humbled Max. He'd prayed for her, but not every day. He had to make a better effort to look outward instead of inward. He'd been thinking of himself rather than others. How many times had he said this to himself but had made little effort to change his behavior? A small child was showing him the way.

"I'll let her know." Tara smiled. "Now I'll tell you about our specials for tonight."

Tara's explanation of the specials barely penetrated the fog of Max's mind. Images of a cute little seven-year-old girl with fuzzy blond hair filled his thoughts. He vowed to take time each day to pray for her.

After Tara took their orders, Heather looked at him as she wrinkled her brow. "Are you okay?"

"Sure. Why?"

"You look like you're far away, or at least your mind is."

Max wasn't sure he wanted to explain where his mind had been—at least not the part about his self-centered thoughts. "I was thinking about Hailey and how tough it is for a kid her age to have cancer."

"And it's hard on the moms whether their children are young or old."

Max nodded. "I know it's been hard on my mom, but she's getting better with it, or at least better about hiding her worry."

Heather took a sip of her water, then looked at Max over the top of her glass. "You have a way of collecting crushes."

Max gave her a wry smile. "There's only one crush I'm interested in collecting. Yours."

Shaking her head, she set the glass down, her finger creating a line in the condensation. "I'm still not sure I understand the big switch from disliking me to…to this."

Max leaned back in his chair and took in Heather's troubled expression. "Did I ever say I disliked you?"

"Not in so many words." Shrugging, Heather chuckled halfheartedly. "Seems to me I remember you asking me the same thing. We both had a bad impression of each other."

"Let's not try to figure it out. I know I don't understand it either. Just go with it and see what happens."

"I'm not sure that works for me."

"Pretend we didn't know each other before."

"Are you good at pretending? I'm not."

Max rubbed the back of his neck. "Are you saying the past is going to get in the way?"

"I don't want it to, but I can't promise it won't."

"We can't undo the past, but we can certainly move forward and leave the past behind."

Heather wrinkled her brow. "What will Brittany say when she finds out we're dating?"

So that was Heather's worry—not so much their past but hers. Was she worried that Brittany would think Heather broke them up so she could step in? Max dismissed the question immediately. Brittany would never have that thought because Heather had left for Massachusetts just weeks after the breakup. "Maybe she would think you have good taste?"

Heather shook her head as she let out a little chuckle. "Really?"

"Or not. After all, she was the one who ended the relationship."

Heather sighed. "You're right. I need to look forward and not back. In fact, let's talk about the Fourth of July weekend. Do you think the venue we have picked out for the charity concert is a good one?"

Max shrugged, wondering about Heather's quick change of subject. "I figured Amanda knows what would work the best, and she thought the elementary school gym was a good place. After all, there's a stage and lots of chairs."

Heather nodded. "I guess you're right. I'm just nervous that no one will come. After all, this was a last-minute idea."

"The whole youth group passed out flyers this week, and we still have nearly two weeks to work on promotion before the concert. Have some faith."

"You're right." Heather sighed again. "At least this time."

"Just this time? I figure I've been right…probably two or three more times in my life."

"I know something you aren't right about."

Max gave her a wry smile. "I'm sure you do."

"Yeah, you should let me help you find your father's family." A determined look painted her features.

"What can you do?"

"We could work together on a computer search."

Max shook his head as he gritted his teeth. Even though he'd come to Massachusetts to find his father's family, it didn't seem as important as it was before. Or maybe he didn't want the family he'd never met to see him in this condition. "I've already done a computer search."

"Are you sure they still live in the Boston area?"

Before Max could answer, Tara returned, carrying a food tray with their orders. With a few quick comments, she set the plates on the table, then rushed away to wait on another table. Max looked over at Heather. "You want me to give thanks?"

Heather nodded and bowed her head. Max bowed

his head, praying silently for wisdom as he voiced thanks for their food. When he glanced up, she was watching him. "I suppose you want an answer to your question."

"I do." Her expression told him she wasn't going to let the matter drop.

"I don't know."

"What has your mom said about them?"

Max let out a harsh breath as he picked up his fork. "Let's eat. Then I'll tell you everything I know about my biological father's family."

Heather nodded. "That works for me."

They ate in silence for a few minutes. Sometimes he wasn't sure he wanted to connect with these people. What if they were all like his father? What if he was like his father—a guy who used people and then tossed them aside? He didn't want to be like that, refused to be like that.

Heather laid her fork on the edge of her plate, her expression determined. "Okay, I think you've vanquished your hunger enough to tell me what you know."

Nodding, Max pressed his mouth into a grim line as he figured out where to start. "Maybe I don't know enough to find them. My mom probably doesn't know much anyway, and even if she did, she hasn't exactly been forthcoming with information."

"So what did she tell you?" Heather stabbed the asparagus spear with her fork.

"Right before her parents shipped her off to live

with Aunt Violet, my mom said she heard that my father died in a motorcycle accident weeks after his family moved from Ohio to Massachusetts."

"How do you think your mom felt about that?"

While Heather continued to enjoy her meal, Max stared at her, the question swirling through his mind and reminding him of how wrapped up in himself he'd been. He'd never thought about how his mom had felt. Had she been sad, scared or angry? He lowered his gaze. He didn't have an answer. Finally, he looked up. "I don't know, but I imagine not good from the little that she's told me."

"What was your biological father's name?"

His biological father. The phrase served to remind Max that Clay Reynolds was the man who had been his father, a real father, when he'd needed one most. A man Max could rely on. "His name was Scott Harkin."

"Do you know your grandfather's name?"

Max shook his head. "I doubt my mom ever met the guy's parents."

"Do you suppose your maternal grandparents could give you that information?"

Max had never considered talking to his mom's folks about the guy who had compromised their daughter. Max didn't want to open up old wounds. "Bringing that up wouldn't be wise."

"I thought you said things were good with your grandparents." A little frown creased Heather's brow.

"Yeah, but talking about that whole thing could unearth a lot of bad feelings. I don't want to be responsible for that." Max couldn't fathom talking to his grandparents about the mess. He didn't want to stir up trouble. He'd had enough bad news in his life and didn't want more.

"I suppose you're right."

"I know I am."

Max worried about what Heather was thinking. This date had served to teach him one thing. He still had a lot to learn about this woman who fascinated him and at the same time kept him on edge.

CHAPTER TWELVE

The last note of the song rang through the school gymnasium. Thundering applause, whistles and shouts followed. With a happy heart, Heather surveyed the overflow crowd. The fundraiser had brought in more money than she ever imagined. They were so close to the amount they needed to purchase the property.

As Heather joined Amanda's group on the stage, her gaze settled on Max. He sat in the audience with his grandparents, who had made a surprise appearance for the holiday weekend. He'd told her that everything was good with his grandparents, but she sensed tension between them.

But maybe it was Max's propensity to keep people at a distance because he wanted to fend for himself. She thought at times she'd broken through that barrier, but it reappeared without warning when she least expected it. Like his reluctance to tell her about his grandparents' visit. She wondered whether it had anything to do with their discussion about the search for his biological father's family. Or maybe he had no energy after his recent treatment. But he was trying to put on a brave face for his grandparents. What had he told them about their relationship?

A cacophony of voices and laughter filled the auditorium as the crowd dispersed. While Heather thanked Amanda and her fellow musicians, Max and his grandparents made their way toward the stage. Heather didn't miss the tired look in Max's eyes. She fretted that he was more tired than he let on because he didn't want his grandparents to worry.

Even though Sara and Allen Carlson knew Max had a chemo treatment yesterday morning, they probably had no idea how tired those treatments made him. They'd stayed at the Hawthorne Inn last night and had joined Max and Heather for dinner before the concert. Heather didn't miss that Max had barely eaten a thing. Would he appreciate any attempt to rescue him?

Max congratulated Amanda and her group on their performance and introduced his grandparents. Heather hoped to get Max alone for a moment. She waited impatiently while the group talked. She feared that Max pushed himself when he should give in to the fatigue—just like the night they'd agreed to find out where their attraction might lead.

Through all this, she was learning that she cared for Max more than she thought possible. The idea of loving him scared her. She couldn't forget how he'd broken Brittany's heart. Was she headed for the same outcome? She shook the question away. She shouldn't borrow trouble from the future. Her job had taught her to take one day at a time. She had to apply that to her love life.

Her chest filled with warmth as Max turned her way with a crooked smile. "You're awfully quiet."

She stepped closer. "I'm concerned that you're overdoing."

Shaking his head, Max grinned. "You're beginning to sound like my mother."

"No, I don't sound like your mother."

"Could've fooled me."

"Come on, Max. You can't keep pretending that the chemo isn't making you tired."

Max leaned toward her. "Okay, but I don't want to cause my grandparents concern."

"You think they aren't worried already?"

Max shrugged. "I suppose."

"They know you have a serious disease. You might as well own up to everything that's going on with you. You probably aren't fooling them."

Max sighed. "Yeah. So what are you trying to tell me?"

"Let me take your grandparents out to the Hawthorne Inn, and you can go home and get some rest."

Max narrowed his gaze. "Will you make sure they don't worry?"

Heather shook her head. "I can't do that. Their worry is their worry. But I'll reassure them that what's happening with you is normal."

"Okay. You win."

"This isn't about winning or losing. It's about

taking care of yourself."

Max nodded. "Let's talk to them."

Heather followed as Max approached Sara and Allen Carlson. "Gram, Gramps, I need to head home. Heather's going to drive you to the inn, because I'm beat."

Sara turned from where she was talking with Amanda and put a hand on his arm. "Okay. I'm so sorry we've kept you from going home."

"You're not at fault. You didn't know."

Allen joined them. "What's happening here?"

"Max is going home, and Heather will take us to the B and B," Sara said.

"Are we leaving now?" Allen asked.

Heather looked at Allen. "I have a few things I have to wrap up here. So I hope you don't mind waiting a bit."

"Not at all. We want Max to be where he needs to be."

Max hugged his grandparents, then looked at Heather. "Walk with me to my car."

"Sure." Heather fell into step beside him as they left the gym. "Did you want something?"

Max put his arm around her shoulders and pulled her close as he whispered in her ear. "A kiss."

"I think I can manage one of those."

Max grinned. "Good. Maybe I should've said two."

Heather let out a halfhearted chuckle. "I'll see what I can do."

Max stopped next to his car and put his arms around her waist as he looked into her eyes. "Congratulations on a great evening."

"And I have to thank you for introducing me to Amanda."

"I must say that my cousin has come a long way from her obnoxious teen years." Max chuckled. "I'm sure there are lots of people who think the same about me."

Heather couldn't help thinking about how her opinion of Max had changed in such a short time. "You need to get going."

"That's the second time you've said that. Trying to get rid of me?"

"No, but you need your rest."

"I have to collect that kiss first."

"I'm all yours." Heather leaned closer.

Max tightened his hold as their lips met. Everything around them faded into the background as Heather let Max's kiss steal her away to their own private place. This unlikely man had changed her world. She prayed that God would heal him so their budding relationship could grow. So much had transpired since she'd first met him back in Montana.

When the kiss ended, he held her at arm's length, a silly grin on his face. "You make me smile."

"That's because I'm not pumping you full of poison these days, as you used to say."

"Is that the reason?"

"Maybe, but you need to quit talking and go

home."

He saluted. "You may not be filling me with drugs, but you're still telling me what to do."

Heather chuckled. "I wouldn't want you to get too comfortable."

Max leaned in for another quick kiss, then opened the car door. "Take good care of my grandparents."

"I will. I…you can count on it." Heather gave him a little wave as he closed the door. She'd almost told him she loved him. She wasn't ready to admit that to him or herself. She wasn't sure why that thought had slipped into her mind.

She cared about Max a lot, but love was another thing altogether. She swallowed a lump in her throat as he drove off. She had some serious thinking to do before she could figure out whether she was in love with Max Reynolds.

Heather turned and hurried back into the gym, where she found Allen and Sara still talking with Amanda and some of the concertgoers. Heather scurried away to take care of her business and wondered whether she could talk to Max's grandparents about his plan to find his biological father's family.

After she talked with the maintenance crew and Dave Murphy, she headed toward the Carlsons, who were saying good-bye to Amanda's band. "I'm ready to go. How about you?"

Sara looked Heather's way. "We're ready."

"Great. Follow me to the car." Heather motioned

toward the door, then led the way out to the parking lot.

"How far is it to the inn?" Sara asked as she joined Heather in the front seat while Allen got into the back.

"It takes about a half hour. I'm glad we still have some daylight. It's a pretty drive." Heather maneuvered her car onto the main street.

While Heather drove, Sara exclaimed over the wonderful concert and the young people who were willing to give of their time and talent to raise money for the property. "I'm so glad Max has found such a wonderful group of friends here. Allen and I were worried when we found out about the cancer. When things like that happen, sometimes it's hard to see God in those bad circumstances."

Heather nodded. "Max is doing as well as can be expected."

Allen's heavy sigh sounded from the backseat. "I know chemo makes people tired, but it's hard to see our once robust grandson without any energy. I'm trying not to let him see my worry."

"That's good. He doesn't like to have people feel sorry for him."

Sara chuckled. "That sounds like Max."

"Did he tell you that ninety percent of lymphoma patients have successful treatments?"

"He did, but it still doesn't take away the worry. I know we're supposed to rely on the Lord and not worry, but the negative thoughts still creep into my mind," Sara said.

With all this talk about worry, Heather wondered whether she could even begin to mention Max's biological father. She didn't want to upset the Carlsons further. But this might be the only chance she would have to talk to them alone.

No. As much as Heather wanted to ask, she had to honor Max's request. If she didn't, he would accuse her of trying to fix him again. She didn't want to sabotage their newfound relationship before it even got started. She forced herself to steer the conversation in another direction. "Have you been to Massachusetts before?"

"No, this is our first visit." Sara waved a hand toward the outside where a myriad of hardwood and evergreen trees lined the two-lane road. "You're right. The scenery is lovely. How long have you lived here?"

"A little over two years."

"I was so surprised when Max moved here. I thought if he left Montana, he would move back to Spokane." Sara sighed. "He's so far away from his family. I...I've always wondered whether he moved here to—"

"Sara." Allen reached across the seat and laid a hand on his wife's shoulder. "This isn't our business to share."

Did this mean that the Carlsons knew about Max's quest? They didn't seem willing to share any information, and it wasn't her place to force the issue, even if she wanted to help Max find that family in the worst way. Heather pressed her lips together in order to keep from asking a question that would surely make Max angry. Gripping the steering wheel tighter, she concentrated on the road ahead.

"But, Allen, I think we should." Sara turned toward the backseat, her voice coming out in a strangled cry.

The hum of the car's motor filled the otherwise silent car as Heather waited for Allen's response. Would either of the Carlsons say anything about Max's search? She couldn't press, but she could pray.

"It's not a good idea," Allen said.

"Heather, I'm sorry we've put you in the middle of our disagreement, but I need to know." Sara let out a loud sigh. "Do you know about Max's...biological father?"

"I do. He told me about his situation." Heather darted a glance at Sara, knowing this was a chance to talk about this, because the Carlsons had brought it up. "He did mention his search for them here. Can you blame him for wanting to know about the people who are a clue to the other half of who he is?"

As Heather pulled her car to a stop at a traffic light, Sara put a hand over her mouth and shook her head. She turned with a pain radiating from her gaze. "That could be a terrible mistake."

"What could be wrong with Max getting to know his other set of grandparents?" Heather pressed on the gas pedal as the traffic light turned green. "What if you were the grandparents who didn't know you had a grandson?"

While Sara remained silent, Allen cleared his throat. "I see your point, but what if they don't want anything to do with him like the selfish young man who fathered him and didn't want to take responsibility for his actions? I don't want to see Max hurt."

"I don't either." Sara nodded. "Can't you talk him out of this misadventure?"

"Rather than trying to talk him out of it, I'd like to help him, and I wish you'd help him, too," Heather said.

Sara let out a deep sigh as she put a hand over her heart. "The circumstances surrounding Max's birth still bring a pain to my heart. Has Max told you anything about his upbringing?"

"He's told me how you and Beth were alienated from each other, if that's what you mean." Heather gripped the steering wheel tighter and prayed this conversation wouldn't lead to acrimony.

Sara sighed again. "All this reminds me of the mistakes we made with Beth. I don't want to repeat them with Max."

Heather slowed her car as they approached another town center. "Help Max find the family he doesn't know."

"How do you expect us to do that?" Allen asked.

"Tell him what you know about the Harkins."

"I'm not sure he needs to know about them, especially his father." Allen's voice sounded impassioned.

All the things Max had told her about his father sifted through Heather's brain. Second thoughts about mentioning this to the Carlsons rolled through her mind, but she couldn't back down now. "You don't have to say anything about his father. Just tell Max the things you know about his other set of grandparents."

"I'm not sure the information we have would be relevant over twenty-five years later." Sara frowned.

Heather turned into the lane that led to the Hawthorne Inn. "I understand that, but he doesn't know his grandparents' first names. That alone could help him in his search."

Sara wrung her hands as she stared at Heather. "Max said we're going to see the fireworks in Boston tomorrow. May we give you an answer then? I'd like to pray about it first."

Heather knew she'd appear unreasonable if she didn't agree to Sara's request. "Sure. I'll see you tomorrow."

"Thank you." Sara put her hand on the door handle. "And thanks for the ride."

"I was happy to do it."

"Thanks for taking care of Max." Allen opened the car door and stepped out, his mouth slightly open as if he wanted to say something else. But he snapped it shut.

"I try my best, but Max doesn't always want help." Heather smiled as she got out of the car and shook hands with Sara and Allen.

Allen nodded. "That's our Max. He's always had a

mind of his own, much like his mother."

But what about his father? The question sat in Heather's mind, but she wouldn't ask it. Instead, she wished Allen and Sara a good-night and watched them make their way up the walk to the front steps. They turned to wave before they disappeared inside.

As Heather slid behind the steering wheel and turned on the car, she was grateful she'd allowed God to direct the conversation rather than trying to orchestrate it herself. She prayed that the Carlsons would find it in their hearts to help Max with his search. For some reason, Heather couldn't let go of the idea that Max needed his father's family.

***

Sunlight slithered through the blinds and awakened Max. He glanced at the bedside clock. Five fifteen. Daylight came way too early here in the summer. Too tired to get up, he lay there and stared at the ceiling. Even though he was still exhausted, he didn't think he could go back to sleep. His discussion with Heather about the need to ask his grandparents about his father's family raced through his mind. Would they freak if he mentioned the guy who had been responsible for so much heartache?

Max wanted to know about the other side of his family tree. Did he have aunts and uncles and cousins? What kind of people were his paternal grandparents? Had he inherited his own rebellious teenage behavior from his father? The questions marched through his mind like a never-ending parade.

Today he would talk with his grandparents, and he would accept the consequences.

Max closed his eyes, and the next thing he knew, a knocking noise awakened him.

"Max, are you okay?" Heather's voice sounded through the door.

"Yeah. Give me a minute." Max rolled over and looked at the clock. Twenty minutes past eight. He'd fallen back to sleep. He rubbed a hand over his bald head and down his face as he sat up and swung his legs over the side of the bed. He was still getting used to not having hair on his head and not having to shave—one bright spot in the hair-loss department.

Sitting there, he contemplated how he would greet Heather. He imagined what she would say about finally deciding to talk to his grandparents. Would she give him that I-told-you-so look? Yeah, she probably would. He threw off his workout shorts and T-shirt that he slept in and grabbed a red polo shirt and a pair of khaki shorts from his closet. At least his shirt would fit into the Fourth of July theme.

After he finished dressing, he opened the door. Heather stood there as if she hadn't moved an inch since she'd knocked.

"Hi, sleepyhead."

When he saw her, he couldn't help smiling. What a contrast to that first day in the doctor's office. He was still trying to absorb the difference in his feelings. "Hi.

Guess I overslept."

"That's okay. We've still got plenty of time to meet your grandparents." Heather held up a bag. "I've packed some stuff to use while we wait to see the fireworks. Jeremy and Luke have already gone down to save a place for us."

Max frowned. "You think we'll be able to find them in that crowd?"

"They'll call and let us know where they are. We'll find them."

"Okay, if you think so." Max shrugged.

"You want to get breakfast before we pick up your grandparents?" Heather slung the bag over her shoulder and headed for the front door. "Your mom told me about that great breakfast place you guys ate at when they were here. I thought we could get carry-out and eat in the nearby square. Okay?"

"Sure." Max locked the door behind them and followed Heather to her car. When had his mom and Heather discussed restaurants? What else had they discussed? Was his mom checking up on him through Heather? He wasn't sure he wanted to know.

On the drive to the restaurant, Heather was unusually quiet, but Max made no attempt to make conversation. He didn't have the energy. Her silence suited him fine. He leaned his head back against the seat and closed his eyes.

"Max, we're here."

His eyes flying open, he sat forward as he looked her way. "Sorry about that. Didn't mean to fall asleep."

"No problem." She unbuckled her seat belt. "If you know what you want, I can get the order. Then you can stay here and rest."

Max hated having to rely on Heather, but he had to conserve his energy for the rest of the day. "Thanks. I'll have the waffles."

"Sounds good. I'll be back in a few."

Max watched Heather disappear inside, wondering why she'd been so quiet. That wasn't like her at all, but he didn't have the energy to try to figure her out. He closed his eyes. Heather's return awakened him, and he glanced at the clock on the dashboard. He'd had fifteen minutes more sleep. As he straightened in his seat, he gave her a lopsided smile. "I hope I keep awake to eat."

"Let's hope so." Heather maneuvered her car toward the square and found a parking spot.

Max followed her toward the gazebo, festooned with patriotic banners and streamers, in the middle of the square. The smell of freshly mowed grass filled the air.

After they reached the gazebo, Heather sat down on one of the benches lining the interior and handed a food container to Max. "Are you sure you're up for a whole day out? We can go later or not at all."

Max sat next to Heather and opened the container. "I'm good. My grandparents would be disappointed if they don't get to see the fireworks."

Heather gave him a no-nonsense look. "I know

they'll be disappointed, but you can't push yourself too hard."

"Honestly. I'll be fine."

"Okay."

He glanced at her. "Let's give thanks for the food."

She reached over and took his hand. "Yes."

Holding her hand, Max bowed his head and gave thanks for the food and said a silent prayer for wisdom in the search for the family he didn't know. When he finished, she squeezed his hand and smiled at him. His heart beat a little faster.

Despite their decision to see what their attraction to each other might bring, Max still had mixed feelings about Heather. Even his prayers didn't keep the old annoyance over her interference from slipping into his mind like the cancer that had silently invaded his body.

As he started eating, he stared at Heather and tried to figure out what was bothering her. Despite her question about his energy level, she seemed way too agreeable. Was he too suspicious in reading something into it?

Heather took a sip of her drink, then set the cup on the bench. "I have some news.

"What?" Max raised his eyebrows. So that was why she seemed so edgy.

"Promise you won't be angry."

Max let out a halfhearted laugh. "You know I can't do that."

Smiling, Heather shrugged. "I can ask, can't I?"

"Sure. You can ask, but I wouldn't begin to think of making such a promise." Max narrowed his gaze. "You're stalling. What have you done that's going to make me unhappy?"

Heather took a deep breath. The worry in her eyes absorbed her smile. "I talked to your grandparents."

Max knit his eyebrows. "Why should that make me angry?"

"Because they asked me what I knew about your biological father's family, and I told them."

Max leaned back against the side of the gazebo and crossed his arms over his midsection. He should have guessed. Should he make her squirm, or admit that he'd already planned to talk to them about that very subject? "What did they tell you?"

"Nothing. They wanted to sleep on it. Pray about it."

"That sounds like my grandparents. And thanks for not instigating the conversation." Max grinned.

"You don't know how hard that was."

"I can guess." Max chuckled.

Heather's brow puckered. "So you're not upset?"

"Not too much." Max sighed. "I know I need to talk to them, but it won't be easy."

Her smile returned. "I was worried about what you'd say when you found out."

Max smirked. "This way the ice on the subject is broken."

"I'm not sure it will lead anywhere." Heather shrugged. "Your grandmother didn't seem to think anything she had to say would help you because it's been so many years. But maybe talking to them about it will open a long-overdue conversation."

They ate without talking while the troubling thoughts whirled in Max's mind—not only about Heather, but about a much-needed conversation with his grandparents.

Heather looked over at him, her gaze narrowed. "Are you sure you're not angry with me?"

He stared back at her. Why was she so worried about her conversation with his grandparents? Was she keeping something from him?

"You are, aren't you? I can tell because you couldn't give me an answer immediately."

Max tried to decipher his feelings. "What difference does it make how I feel?

"Because I care about you, and I don't want you to be angry with me. Or pretend not to be when you are."

Max let out a dispassionate laugh. "Do you want me to say I'm angry?"

"No."

"Then don't keep asking." Max stabbed at his waffle.

Heather gave him a sad little smile. "Okay."

They finished the meal in an uneasy silence. With a heavy heart, Max wished he could start the morning over and not let Heather being Heather bother him. She meant well. She cared about him. She did what she thought was helpful. He should count those things on the plus side instead of putting them on the minus side.

Their conversation was minimal as they made their way back to Heather's car. As she drove toward the Hawthorne Inn, Max closed his eyes and prayed. *Lord, you know my mixed up feelings. I'm not sure what path you want me to take. Please help me to see the choices I should make.*

"Are you okay?"

Heather's question made him turn her way. "Yeah."

"Looked like you had fallen asleep again."

"Just resting, not sleeping." He wasn't going to tell her he'd been praying about their relationship. He didn't need any questions from her. Things would settle out when they picked up his grandparents.

Minutes later Heather turned onto the lane leading to the inn. As they drew closer, Max spied his grandparents relaxing on the rockers on the front porch. Would they be willing to talk to him about his father? Even if they talked, would their information yield any help? The questions twisted through his mind like the flowering vines that clustered on the trellis on one side of the inn.

CHAPTER THIRTEEN

Max said another silent prayer as Heather brought her car to a stop in the parking area near the inn.

His grandparents came down the front steps and waved as they drew closer. Max tried to shove away his anxiety as they got into the car.

During the drive, the conversation revolved around what they could expect from the day's events. Max wondered whether this was the time to ask his grandparents about his biological father. Heather had opened the door. Should he walk through it?

Sara leaned forward and tapped Max on the shoulder. "This isn't going to wear you out, is it?"

I'm going to be fine. No need to fuss over me."

Max hoped his grandmother wouldn't fret about him the whole day. He wished Heather would reassure them that he could survive the activities, but she was strangely silent. When he needed her to interfere, she wouldn't cooperate. But he had to admit that her interference wasn't all bad. It gave him an opening to talk to his grandparents about something he'd wanted to know for a long time.

"Gram, Gramps, I've got something I'd like to discuss with you. Heather told me that you talked about my biological father's family. Would you answer my questions about them?" Max held his breath. The hum of the tires on the pavement sounded loudly in the otherwise silent car.

Finally, Allen cleared his throat. "Yes, we've been praying about this conversation."

"What can you tell me?" Max glanced at Heather, but she kept her eyes focused straight ahead. Again there was silence. This conversation was probably as hard for them as it was for him.

"Max, I'm not sure where to start or what to say." Sara sighed. "I don't want to say anything to hurt you."

"Gram, I want to know the truth. Not knowing will hurt me more."

Sara let out a half cry, half laugh. "I hope you won't be sorry to hear what we have to say."

"I don't know if I'll be sorry or not, but I want to know. Please tell me about Scott Harkin."

"You're sure you want to know the good and the bad?" Sara asked.

"Absolutely." Max turned enough in his seat so he could look at his grandmother. "Maybe I should tell you what I already know about Scott Harkin."

"What's that?" Worry colored Sara's expression.

"I know he wanted Mom to get an abortion."

Sara took in a deep breath as she put a hand to her mouth. "Oh, Max, I'm so sorry you had to learn that. How'd you find out?"

"I overheard Mom and Clay talking one day. It's

not something I liked hearing, but I know Mom wanted me, and that's enough." Max held up a hand. "Mom doesn't know, and I'd like to keep it that way for now."

"Are you sure you want to talk about this while we're making this trip?" Sara grimaced as she nodded toward Heather, who couldn't see the gesture.

"This is as good a time as any." Max wanted to assure his grandparents that he didn't mind talking about this in front of Heather.

Sara sighed again and looked at Allen, then back at Max. "At first, I didn't want to discuss this with you at all, but your grandfather and I decided we should because Heather asked us to put ourselves in the shoes of your paternal grandparents."

When Max looked over at Heather, she nodded. Although she was quiet, he was glad she would hear this conversation. She'd been instrumental in bringing it about, and he was only now beginning to appreciate her tendency to meddle in other people's lives. How had he gone from hating that about her to appreciating that part of her personality? Love? That was a crazy thought. Too soon to even consider that emotion.

"Okay, what can you tell me?"

Sara shrugged. "I wish this was going to be a happy talk, but I'm afraid it won't be."

"Gram, I told you I want to know the truth. Good or bad. Delay isn't going to help."

"Okay." Sara gave him a tentative smile. "When your mother was fourteen, we moved to a small bedroom community near Cincinnati. Your grandfather had just started as the pastor of a church there. Your mother was a shy girl and had a hard time making friends and fitting in at a new school."

"I know the feeling." Max nodded. "We moved to Pinecrest when I was fourteen."

A sad little smile curved Sara's mouth. "I wish we'd worked harder to connect with your mother after you were born. Then we wouldn't have missed so many years of your life. We made a lot of mistakes."

"We can't undo the past. We have to forgive and move on." Max knew that for sure. He'd told Heather the same thing, and it was true here, too.

"Thanks, Max. A good reminder, but it's sometimes hard to do when you have so many regrets."

"I know. We all have those." He couldn't help thinking about Brittany and all the regrets that went along with the demise of their relationship, but the most unlikely woman was helping him put those behind him. He still couldn't believe he'd had a change of heart about the woman he'd blamed for his breakup with Brittany. His life had taken a lot of strange turns.

Sara leaned forward. "We love you."

"And I love you."

Allen cleared his throat again and patted his wife's arm. "I think your grandmother's trying to delay talk of Scott Harkin."

Sara frowned. "I am not. This is a difficult topic,

and I wanted to let Max know how much we love him."

"Okay, dear." Allen nodded. "If you don't mind, I'll take over."

Sara waved a hand at Allen. "Be my guest."

Allen smiled. "As your grandmother said, moving to a new town was a struggle for your mom. During her sophomore year, she started to make some friends. We were happy at first until a member of the congregation warned us about Scott. They said he was a well-known troublemaker and that his wealthy father, Robert Harkin, always bailed him out of whatever kind of fix he got himself into. The man never let his son suffer the consequences for his actions."

"So Robert Harkin is my grandfather's name?" Max asked.

"Yes, he worked in Cincinnati at some brokerage firm, and from what people said, he spent more time at his job than he did with his family."

Max didn't say anything for a moment. Did that mean his grandfather wasn't the kind of man who would be interested in a long-lost grandson? Had he pushed himself into something that would bring him sorrow? He hoped not. Despite his momentary doubt about the wisdom of his search, he had to know about the other half of who he was.

"Do you suppose that's why my father was a troublemaker?" Max remembered his own troubled teen years and how Clay had stepped in to make a difference, not only in his life but his mother's, too. Max prayed that his pursuit wouldn't hurt Clay in any way.

Allen shrugged. "You don't always know why a young person rebels. We were very involved in your mother's life, but she wanted friends—friends we didn't approve of. Maybe if we'd tried to reach out to Scott rather than forbidding your mother to see him, things would've been different."

This whole conversation reminded Max of Clay's bargain—the one that had kept Max from hanging out with the wrong crowd. Could his grandparents have changed his mother's mind about Scott Harkin if they'd applied a different approach with her? It didn't matter now. "What else can you tell me about the Harkins?"

"Not a lot." Allen shook his head. "They moved to the Boston area before the end of your mother's sophomore year, and your grandmother and I breathed a sigh of relief because we thought we didn't have to worry about her hanging around with Scott."

"So then what happened?" Max couldn't believe he was having this discussion with his grandparents. He still had a hard time thinking of his mother as a rebellious teen, but now he understood her worry about him and the people he associated with.

"When she couldn't hide her condition anymore, she finally came to me and told me." Closing her eyes, Sara grimaced, then looked back at Max with a heavy sigh. "I was so angry, so upset and so sad that she hadn't listened to us."

"Is that why you were estranged for so many years?" Max asked.

"Maybe one day you'll understand when you have kids of your own." Allen laid a hand on Max's shoulder. "We didn't handle it well. I yelled. Your grandmother cried. And in the end we shipped your mother off to live with her great-aunt, but you know about that part."

Max sat there silently for a moment, trying to absorb the information. He didn't want to think of his mother in terms of teenage hormones, but there wasn't any getting around it. Thankfully, he and Brittany had managed to keep themselves in check through eight years of dating. That hadn't been easy. The temptation to go too far had lurked like a monster waiting to strike, but with God's help, they'd managed not to succumb to their sexual desires.

If his grandparents had been successful in keeping his mom and Scott Harkin apart, he wouldn't be here. If his mom had done what his father had wanted, Max Reynolds would never have been born. If his mom had decided to give him up for adoption, he wouldn't know his mother's side of the family either. The unpleasant realities hit him as hard as his cancer diagnosis.

But none of that had happened, and here he was. Alive and trying to figure out who he was. Would finding his father's family help him understand himself better?

Allen squeezed Max's arm. "You okay?"

Max nodded. "How'd you find out about my father's death if his family had moved to Massachusetts?"

"His maternal grandparents still lived in town. A couple of weeks before your mom told us she was pregnant, I read about his death in the local paper."

"Did Mom ever say anything about it?"

"No. She never mentioned him and never told us that Scott was your father, but we knew." Her head low, Sara rubbed her forehead, then looked back at Max, her eyes swimming with tears. "Your mother was defiant, but seeing how everything turned out, I'm glad she didn't do as we requested. We're glad you're in our lives."

Max reached into the backseat and squeezed his grandmother's hand. "Me, too."

"I'm sorry we can't give you more information, but that's all we know." Allen shrugged as he patted Max's arm.

"Robert. A first name. That's at least something. And the fact that he probably works in some kind of financial service."

"If he's not retired," Allen said.

"And moved to Florida." Max's hope sank. That could be a real possibility. His father would have been forty-three if he'd lived. And his paternal grandparents most likely were in their mid to upper sixties—definitely old enough to be retired. "Do the Harkins have other children?"

"As I recall, Scott had an older brother and two younger sisters."

Max wondered if they lived in the Boston area. "Do you know the older son's name?"

Allen shook his head.

Maybe he'd moved here for nothing. Then he looked over at Heather. Was she the reason for his being here? He had so many unanswered questions about his feelings and hers. Would whatever they had survive his battle with cancer?

"You have aunts and an uncle that you deserve to know." Sara slowly nodded her head. "After your grandfather and I thought about it, we realized you have every right to know the other part of your family. Don't give up your search, even if it seems impossible."

Max nodded. "Thanks. It's good to hear that."

"And I think they're right, too. You shouldn't give up." Heather glanced his way, a little smile curving her mouth.

Max smiled back as his feelings for Heather hit him right in the chest. He shouldn't be afraid of them, but after he'd messed up with Brittany, he feared making the same mistakes again. And his cancer complicated everything. "Thanks for your vote of confidence. Now I just have to do some more searching."

"And I'll be here to help." Heather motioned toward the exit off the Mass Pike. "We're almost there. I hope we don't have too much trouble finding a place to park."

Heather's wish became a reality as they found a parking spot not too far from the Hatch Shell where the Boston Pops would play. They had a leisurely walk to the Boston Esplanade and joined Luke and Jeremy, who had saved them a spot. Max took in the celebratory sights and sounds of the day and thanked God that he wasn't too tired to enjoy this time with his grandparents and his friends.

The Boston Pops entertained the crowd in the waning light until darkness descended. The *1812 Overture* and the sound of the cannons filled the night air along with the pyrotechnics high over the Charles River. Folks stood in awe as the fireworks lit up the night sky, but they had nothing on the ones going off in Max's chest as he held Heather's hand.

Were his feelings for Heather developing too fast? For now he was going to enjoy everything about tonight. He would save the figuring out for tomorrow.

***

Very early the following morning, Max picked up his grandparents at the Hawthorne Inn to take them to the airport. They chatted with him about the wonderful time they'd had during their visit. They exclaimed over the beautiful scenery and the history of the area. Happy that they didn't dwell on his cancer, he listened with a grateful heart.

He'd enjoyed their visit more than he'd expected.

The information they'd given him about his biological father's family might help with his search, but he wasn't going to get his hopes up. He wavered between believing he could find them and fearing they no longer lived near Boston, or at worst wouldn't want anything to do with him, even if he did find them.

He'd jumped into this venture without truly thinking about it. He now realized the singular motivation behind his big move was getting away from memories of Brittany, but they had followed him here. The change did little to make him forget his heartache. Meeting Heather again had brought all those feelings about Brittany to a head, and he knew he couldn't continue on the same path.

The twist in the whole scenario came when his feelings for Heather took a completely different and unexpected turn.

The myriad thoughts crawled through his mind like the heavy traffic on the Mass Pike. The spectacular weather with its cloudless blue sky made the slow drive tolerable. "It's a good thing we gave ourselves plenty of time to get to the airport."

"Yes, this traffic's bad. I don't know if I could get used to living in or near a busy city like this." Allen chuckled. "I'm too used to small towns."

"The only time I have to deal with this is when I come into Boston. Out where I live, it's very similar to where you live in Ohio."

Allen nodded. "True. I guess it only seems worse because we made several trips into Boston while we were here."

"I'm glad you came to visit me."

"We are, too." Sara nodded. "Do you think your mom and Clay will make it for a visit before the summer's over?"

Max shrugged. "Mom keeps talking about it, but with the price of airfares these days, I kind of doubt it."

"It's too bad they aren't close enough to drive," Allen said.

"Yeah, I'd love to see Alex and Abby." Max let out a long sigh. "Even though we do video phone calls, I can't tell how much they've grown."

"I know. I hate not getting to see them, too." Sara caught Max's gaze in the rearview mirror. "Your grandfather's planning to retire next year, and we're thinking about moving to Spokane so we can be closer to your mom."

"That's nice." Max wondered if his mom agreed, but he wasn't going to ask. Even though his mom and her parents had reconciled years ago, he wondered how the relationship would work if they lived close to each other.

The question sent his mind down a trail of uncertainty about the search for his paternal grandparents. He was certain they would be shocked, but would they welcome him? Families were often messy places with people learning how to get along with each other when life didn't go as they planned. He'd learned that lesson early.

So why was he so eager to jump into an unknown complication? A simple answer—he wanted a link to every part of his existence. Is that why he'd made a connection with Heather?

"Are you serious about Heather?" His grandmother's inquiry brought his deliberations to a halt.

He knew his grandmother couldn't read his mind, but the question went right to what he'd been thinking. "Too early to tell."

"Well, I think you should hang on to her. Don't let this one get away."

Max shrugged, wondering if his grandparents were thinking of his breakup with Brittany—how he'd squandered that relationship. They didn't know what went wrong with Brittany, but he knew. That was enough. And he didn't want to go into his bad history with Heather. "We've just started dating, so this is all pretty new."

"She's a lovely young woman. Be good to her."

"I'll do my best." He certainly hadn't done his best with Brittany. Was this relationship with Heather a second chance to get it right?

"You'd better. She cares a lot about you, so treat her right." Allen clapped Max on the back.

Max nodded as he turned onto the road that led to the terminal. He wasn't sure what had prompted their concern about his relationship with Heather, but he didn't want to talk about it.

After he stopped, he hopped out and retrieved his

grandparents' luggage from the trunk. He hoped they wouldn't give him more advice about his love life. He wanted to deal with Heather in his own way and in his own time—just like the search for the rest of his family.

"You should've let me get that luggage." Allen pulled up the handle on the suitcase. "I don't want you to wear yourself out."

"I'm good. I'm learning my limitations." Max hugged his grandmother, then his grandfather. "Thanks again for coming to visit."

Sara gave Max an extra-long hug. "We love you. Take care of yourself. If you need us, we can always come back. We don't want you to be alone here."

"Thanks. I'll be okay. I've managed to make friends, and Amanda is here. They look out for me." Max realized that Heather had been instrumental in making sure he made friends, even with his stepcousin. His life was better for having Heather in it, but what did that mean for the long term? He couldn't say right now. Too many unknowns surrounded his life.

As his grandparents made their way toward the door, they turned around one last time to wave before they disappeared inside. Max drove away with his mind filled with thoughts about what his future would hold. Could he beat the cancer? Would he find his biological father's family? If he did, would they embrace or shun him? And how would his relationship with Heather play out? So many questions and no answers.

Max continued to mull over these uncertainties as he made his way back to Oakton and a day at work. Despite all the issues in his life, he had to be thankful for an understanding boss and coworkers. They allowed him to complete his projects in his own time, and he wanted to make sure they could count on him to do the work.

When he finally left the lab, he headed straight home. Even after a treatment and a hectic weekend, his energy level was up—something else to be thankful for. He wanted to get home and see what information he could find about Robert Harkin. An excited tension filled his chest as he walked into the house.

He stopped short when he spied Heather sitting on the couch with a laptop computer. She looked up. "Hey. I thought maybe you got lost."

"No. Just getting home from work." Max searched his memory. Had Heather mentioned coming over tonight? Had he forgotten? Had he fallen into the pattern that had ruined his relationship with Brittany?

Heather set the computer on the coffee table and motioned for him to join her. "Let me show you what I've found."

Max approached slowly, his radar up for Heather's criticism, but she didn't appear to be upset. "What did you find?"

"A dozen men with the name Robert Harkin, who live in the Boston area."

With a hint of annoyance bubbling on the edges of his mind, Max sat beside Heather. She was taking over—trying to fix things for him again. He tamped down the urge to tell her to butt out. She was only being helpful. "Okay, so what should I do with them?"

She stared at him. "What do you think?"

So she wasn't going to tell him what to do. Thankful that he hadn't expressed his feelings, he peered at the computer screen. How simple, if he knew which one, if any, was his grandfather. If he didn't give Heather a plan, would she barge ahead and make plans for him? "I don't know."

"Yeah." Heather paused as she bit her lower lip. "I don't know either."

Heather's response took Max by surprise. He'd expected her to jump right in with her ideas. He hadn't wanted her to take over, but now he had to make his own plans. "Can we eliminate some by their ages?"

Heather's fingers flew over the keyboard. "This other site gives ages. I think."

When the new site appeared on the screen, Heather handed the computer to Max. He read through the list. Not one who was old enough to be his grandfather. Had they hit a dead end already? Sighing, Max rubbed the back of his neck. "Guess I got my hopes up even though I told myself not to."

"Me, too." Heather leaned over and kissed his cheek. "I'm sorry the information your grandparents gave you didn't help."

"Guess it wasn't meant to be." Letting out a harsh

breath, Max laced his hands behind his head and fell back against the couch. "I thought since my grandparents had prayed and come to the conclusion that they should talk to me about Scott Harkin's family that I would find them. Maybe all God wanted me to find was a closer connection with the grandparents I already know."

Heather squeezed Max's hand. "Don't give up hope. Just pray for God's will and that you can accept whatever it is."

Yeah. Accept whatever it is. Easy to say. Not so easy to carry out. He wasn't going to say that out loud to Heather. He wanted to change the subject and focus on something besides himself. Heather's project popped into his mind. Perfect. "The deadline for your project's coming up. Do you think you'll get the funds you need?"

Heather didn't say anything and lowered her gaze. She wouldn't look him in the eyes as she shrugged. "I'm afraid both you and I are in for disappointment. We're close, but I don't see how we're going to meet our goal in less than three weeks."

Max didn't know what to say. He wanted to encourage her, but he didn't see a way to help. "How much do you still need?"

"Twenty-five thousand. Guess I was crazy to think I could raise enough money to buy that house." Heather let out a halfhearted laugh. "We nearly made it, but I can't keep begging people for money."

"Maybe it's time you tried to find out who put in

the other offer."

Sighing, Heather shrugged. "Maybe."

"It won't hurt to ask." Max put an arm around Heather's shoulders and pulled her close.

"I guess." She laid her head on his shoulder. "Thanks for your encouragement."

"Glad to help in any way." Contentment washed over Max as they sat there in silence.

Were these feeling for Heather something that would grow? Despite the people who loved him, Max couldn't forget the father who hadn't wanted him and the woman who had dumped him because he couldn't live up to her expectations. Could Heather change that? Would finding his father's family make a difference?

CHAPTER FOURTEEN

The following Saturday, Heather's phone buzzed as it lay on the nearby end table. She glanced at the screen, then grabbed it. "Hey, Parker. It's certainly a surprise to hear from you. How are you and Brittany?"

"Good." The happiness in Parker's voice came through loud and clear. "How's everything with you? Did you get into Boston to see the fireworks on the Fourth of July?"

"I did. They were wonderful, as usual." Heather decided to keep Max's presence at the fireworks to herself. Talking about him was off limits. "What's going on that you called?"

"I wanted to let you know that Brittany and I are coming to Boston."

"Wonderful! When?" The thought of seeing her good friend and her favorite uncle excited Heather until she thought about how Brittany might view Heather's new relationship with Max or how Max would react to Brittany's presence. Would seeing Brittany reignite Max's feelings for her? Heather tried to convince herself that she shouldn't worry about it. If what she had with Max was meant to grow into a lasting relationship, Brittany's appearance wouldn't affect it.

"I have an appointment with a couple of docs in Boston, and I'm going to ride in the PMC."

"Wow! That's fantastic news."

"So what's going on with you besides training for the PMC?"

Heather hesitated. She saw no point in telling Parker about Max and her now. Parker, along with Brittany, would find out when they got here. "I've been working on a lot of fundraising for the clinic house for the families of our cancer patients."

"I hadn't heard about that. Tell me more."

Heather explained, including the deadline that loomed. "That's been keeping me pretty busy."

"Too busy for romance?" Parker chuckled.

"Now why would my uncle be worried about my love life?"

"Did I say I was worried?"

"No, but you asked, and that's unusual."

Parker laughed again. "Brittany put me up to it. She's the one who wants to know."

Heather's stomach sank. Had word about her and Max made its way to Montana, or was Brittany's curiosity only that—curiosity? "Tell Brittany I've still got my list and haven't found anyone who fits the bill."

"She'll be disappointed. She thought for sure you'd snag some handsome doctor in Boston."

"All the handsome doctors I know are already

married." Heather chuckled, hoping to send the conversation in another direction. "Have you made a hotel reservation?"

"No. This was kind of last minute, so I hope we won't have trouble finding a place."

"Do you need to stay in Boston proper?"

"No, I plan to rent a car. Do you know of a place?" Parker asked.

"I do, but you'll have to check to see if they have rooms. It's called the Hawthorne Inn. It's a beautiful bed-and-breakfast."

"Sounds like something Brittany would enjoy."

Heather gave Parker information about the inn, glad they'd gotten off the subject of her love life. She'd have enough explaining to do when they got here.

After her talk with Parker, she called Max to check on him. As she listened to the ringtone, she wondered whether she should tell Max that Brittany and Parker were coming. Maybe she would come up with the right words to say during the bike ride with her PMC team.

When Max answered, Heather's heart skipped a beat. She still wasn't used to her reaction to this man. How could she explain anything to Brittany when she wasn't quite sure what was going on in her own heart and mind?

"Hey, how you doing? Are you still up for a ride to the Dairy Depot when we get back?"

"Yeah, I've been resting all morning and

preserving my strength." Max laughed. "Actually, I'm feeling pretty good today. I'm looking forward to seeing you."

"Me, too."

"Did you get that appointment with the other bidders?"

"I did. It's a company that buys older homes, fixes them up and resells them." Heather had little hope she could convince the other bidder to bow out. The sellers were eager to get a sale and wouldn't be happy with more delay. She ought to have more faith, but her doubts were winning. She couldn't admit that to Max. She'd kept telling him to have faith and pray, but she didn't follow her own advice. "I'm going to talk with them this coming Monday on my day off. We'll see what happens."

"I know you can persuade them to give way to your good cause."

"Thanks for your vote of confidence. See you in a while."

After the phone call ended, Heather picked up her helmet and water bottle and headed down the stairs. She grabbed her bike from the foyer on the first floor and wheeled it out the door. She hurried to meet the gang for their Saturday afternoon bike ride. Would twenty-five miles of pedaling give her enough time to figure out a way to give Max the information about Brittany?

When the ride ended and Max was sitting beside Heather at the Dairy Depot, she still had no idea what to say to him. The thoughts gathered in her mind like the dark, gray clouds on the horizon.

"Looks like we'd better start back pretty soon if we want to beat the rain." Emma pointed to the western sky.

"You're right." Heather jumped up and gathered her things. "No sense in taking a chance with those big black clouds."

The rest of the group followed Heather's lead and hurried to where they'd left their bikes. Heather hung back as she rode beside Max, who was moving at a slow pace.

"You don't have to ride back here with me." Max gave her a crooked smile. "I don't want you to get rained on."

"I won't melt if I get wet, as my mother used to tell me." Heather pedaled slower. "Are you trying to get rid of me?"

"If you'd asked me that a couple years ago, I would've said yes." His smile broadened into a grin. "Now I kind of like having you around."

"Only kind of?"

"Well, I don't want to go overboard."

"No, I wouldn't want you to do that." Was this the time to bring up Brittany when he seemed to be in a jovial mood and thinking about the circumstances surrounding his former girlfriend? The others were far enough ahead that they wouldn't hear the discussion. "I talked to Parker today."

Max gave her a curious glance. "About what?"

"He's coming to Boston for business, and he's going to ride in the PMC."

"On your team?"

"No, he's riding on his own. Brittany's coming with him." Heather held her breath as she waited for Max to respond.

Max didn't say anything, but he increased his speed as if he was trying to get away from her comment. She pedaled harder to catch up. They rode for a couple of blocks before he looked at her. "I suppose you're waiting for me to say something about Brittany."

"Yeah."

"I don't have anything to say." Max kept on pedaling.

Heather wasn't sure whether to press the issue. A little hurt pierced her heart. She shouldn't read anything into his hesitancy, but she couldn't help wondering what it meant.

They rode the rest of the way without talking until they brought their bikes to a stop near Heather's house. The group bid good-bye to Emma and Ryan, who hurriedly loaded their bicycles on the bike rack at the back of their car. The clouds overhead grew blacker as Heather pushed her bike toward her front stoop and forced a smile as she looked over at Max. "See you later."

"Sure." He gave a little wave and trotted across the street.

Heather parked her bike in the front hall, then took

the stairs two at a time to her apartment. She fought the tears threatening to spill onto her cheeks as she closed the door behind her and dropped onto her couch. Would the specter of Brittany always stand between Max and her?

Heather pulled her list for the perfect man from the drawer in the nearby end table. She didn't know why she still had the silly thing. She'd almost torn it up when she'd started dating Max. Why had she ever thought Max would fulfill this list? He wouldn't, but she'd started to think she didn't need it anymore.

While Heather sat there feeling sorry for herself, her phone rang. She grabbed it from the coffee table. Max.

"Hey, Heather." Max's voice made her heart flutter, despite her misgivings about him.

Heather tried to temper her voice. "What?"

"Looks like the rain missed us. Got time to come over? I'd like to talk with you."

"Give me a few minutes. I've got a few things to do first."

"Sure. I'll wait for you on the front porch over at my place."

Heather wasn't going to rush right over and give Max the idea that she was eager to see him. She decided to take a shower. After all, she'd ridden twenty-five miles. She needed to cool down—in more ways than one. She wondered whether Max was going to talk about Brittany after all. Heather hoped she wouldn't be sorry that she'd brought up Parker and

Brittany's visit.

After Heather showered and dressed, she took her time as she moseyed across the street. Max sat on one of the chairs on the front porch, his long legs stretched out in front of him. He appeared not to have a care in the world, but his appearance hardly told the real story.

"I've got something for you." Max held out an envelope.

"What's this?"

"Open it and find out."

Heather sat on the chair next to Max and lifted the flap on the envelope, then pulled out a folded piece of paper. As she opened it, a check fell out. She picked it up as she placed a hand over her heart. "Two thousand dollars?"

"Yeah, from the folks at my grandfather's church. They wanted to help with the purchase of the property."

Heather didn't want to think about how close she was to having what she needed but still too far away from the goal. She felt like a rider in the PMC who could see the finish line, but a flat tire had all but ended the ride. Did she dare hope that in the next two weeks more unexpected money would drop in her lap? "Why didn't you tell me about this earlier?"

"I didn't open my mail until we got back from the Dairy Depot, and this was a complete surprise. My grandparents never said anything about it. I wish it were more so you could have exactly what you need."

"I have to learn to be thankful for every donation, no matter how big or how small." Heather tucked the check into the pocket of her capris. "Please give me your grandparents' address so I can send them a thank-you."

"Sure. Come with me." Once inside the house, Max disappeared into his room. He returned a minute later and handed her a piece of paper. "Here it is. I know they'll be glad to hear from you. You impressed them."

Heather tucked the paper away in the same pocket where she'd put the check. "I did? How do you know?"

Max nodded. "They told me not to let you get away."

Should she make light of this or ignore it? She might as well find out where she stood in light of Brittany's upcoming appearance. "Do you intend to take their advice?"

Max gave her a lopsided grin. "I'm not sure. I'm not very good at taking advice."

"And what am I supposed to take away from that answer?"

Max took her hand. "Come over here and sit down with me."

Heather's breath caught in her throat as she sat on the couch next to Max, her hand still in his. Would he talk about Brittany? Why had she let herself care too much about this guy who went around breaking hearts? She stared at him while her pulse pounded.

"What are you going to tell me?"

Taking both her hands in his, he breathed deeply, then expelled a harsh breath. "I'm not very good at this kind of thing."

"What kind of thing?"

"Talking about how I feel. Saying I'm sorry."

Heather swallowed hard. Was he going to say he was sorry they'd started dating because he couldn't forget Brittany? Heather closed her eyes and shook her head. She was afraid if she opened her mouth, she'd cry. She would not let him make her cry.

Max squeezed her hands. "Please look at me."

Heather forced herself to look up into his troubled brown eyes.

"Don't look so worried. I was wrong to tell you I have nothing to say about Brittany."

"So you're still not over her?"

"I didn't say that."

"You don't have to."

"It's not what you think." Max shook his head. "Brittany married someone else and has a baby on the way. I don't know how I'll feel when I see her again. It's been over two years since we've seen each other."

"What are you trying to tell me?"

"I wish I knew." Max grimaced, then looked away. "I don't want to hurt you in any way."

"Like I said before, sounds to me like you're still not over her." Heather's stomach curdled at the thought. She wanted to be wrong, but she was afraid she wasn't.

Still holding Heather's hands, Max finally focused his gaze on her again. "I'd like to refute your suspicions completely, but I have to be honest. When you told me she was coming, I couldn't process my emotions. That's why I told you I didn't have anything to say."

Heather sighed. "So basically you're saying you don't know where we stand with each other."

"I didn't say that. I'm making a mess of things, like I usually do." A muscle worked in Max's jaw as he stared at her. "I'll quit before I dig a deeper hole for myself."

"Is that my signal to leave?"

Max rubbed a hand down his face. "I don't know what it is. Please don't give up on me."

"We need to put this relationship on hold until you figure out how you feel about Brittany." Heather stood and extracted her hands from his. "I don't want to play second fiddle to your old love."

Max frowned. "You aren't second fiddle to anyone."

"Seems that way to me." Heather took a step toward the door. "I'll let myself out."

Max opened his mouth as if he was going to say something, but he closed it again. He stood but didn't try to stop her from leaving. She forced herself not to sprint out of the room. She walked with deliberate slowness out the door and across the street to her apartment, her heart breaking as she went. She should be thankful he was being honest about his feelings, or at least admitting that he didn't know how Brittany's visit would affect him.

Why was her involvement with Max filled with so many ups and downs? Knowing their acrimonious history, maybe she'd been crazy to consider dating him, but a soft spot for him had developed in her heart. He'd insinuated himself into her life and made her care about what happened to him. Was an inevitable heartbreak in her future?

***

Armed with every piece of literature and information about her House for Families campaign, Heather stood on the sidewalk outside of Renovations for You, the company that had put the other bid on the house. Would these people be sympathetic to her cause, or were they all about the money they could make with the property they and House for Families both wanted?

Heather said a little prayer, took a deep breath, and opened the door. She had to convince these people to withdraw their bid. The small reception area sported rolled-arm chairs covered in a bluish-green herringbone fabric and colorful paintings on the pale-green walls. The place had a decorator's touch. She approached the desk situated near the large window with multiple panes of glass.

The woman behind the desk glanced up from her computer and smiled. "May I help you?"

"Yes, I'm Heather Watson, and I have an appointment with Dana Mahoney."

The receptionist glanced at her computer screen, then back at Heather. "Yes, Dana will be with you in a moment. Please have a seat."

Heather sat on one of the chairs and picked up a magazine from the nearby table. She flipped through the pages that featured remodeled houses and their furnishings. She prayed that this woman would listen with an open heart and mind.

"Ms. Watson?"

The pleasant female voice made Heather look up. "Yes."

The dark-haired woman, who looked to be in her late thirties, smiled and extended her hand. "I'm Dana Mahoney."

Heather stood and shook the woman's hand. "Thanks for seeing me. You can call me Heather."

"Certainly. Let's go into my office." Dana led the way down a short hallway, then stopped and let Heather proceed into the room. "Have a seat."

Heather clutched her papers as she sat on the chair next to the dark-cherry desk. "Thanks."

Dana sat behind her desk and leaned forward. "I understand you want to talk to me about the Diluzio property."

"Yes." Heather scooted to the edge of her chair. "I represent the organization that put in the first bid on the house."

Dana narrowed her gaze. "And you want me to

drop our bid?"

"Yes. I'm the chairperson for the House for Families campaign. We're trying to buy the house to provide a place for families of cancer patients at the clinic where I work. That's why I'm asking you to drop your bid."

"Why have you waited so long to make this request? It's less than two weeks until the deadline." Dana leaned back and laced her fingers as she rested her elbows on the arms of her chair.

"Because I thought we could secure the funds before then, but it looks like we're going to be short. We need more time."

"I see. So if I withdraw my bid, you won't have a deadline to raise the money."

"Unless someone else comes along and makes another bid before then." Heather nodded. "I hope you'll consider my request."

"I'll have to talk to my business partners first, but I'll see what I can do."

Heather pushed the papers across the desk. "Please show them these. It's all the information about the campaign and our plans for the house."

Dana took the packet and quickly shuffled through it. "I certainly will."

"Thanks for meeting with me and for your consideration of my request." Heather stood and extended her hand. "When can I expect to hear from you?"

Dana shook her hand. "After I have that

conversation with my partners, which I intend to have tomorrow."

"I'll be waiting to hear from you." Heather couldn't begin to guess whether Dana was willing to withdraw her bid for the property. Nothing in her expression gave Heather a clue. She would have to wait and pray.

As Heather stepped into the hallway with Dana, a tall dark-haired man with graying hair at his temples strode toward them. Heather stared at the man. Who was he? Was it her imagination, or did he have a strong resemblance to Max? Blood pounded in her head.

Dana rushed around Heather to greet the man. "Rob, what are you doing here?"

Rob. The name rattled around in Heather's mind. Could it be? Could this man be part of Max's long-lost family?

"I'm here to take you to lunch. Did you forget?" The man smiled and put an arm around Dana's shoulders. "I know you've been busy, but how could you forget lunch?"

"I don't know." Dana shook her head as she gave him a sheepish grin, then looked over at Heather. "Rob, I want you to meet Heather Watson."

Rob extended his hand. "Hello, Heather. I'm Rob Harkin, Dana's brother."

Heather managed to stifle a yelp as she shook Rob's hand. Her heart raced, and she couldn't think of a coherent thing to say. Had she shaken hands with

Max's uncle? That would be too good to be true. Finally, Heather's mind quit whirling. "Nice meeting you, Dana and Rob. I should let you get to your lunch."

"Join us," Dana said.

"I wouldn't want to intrude."

"That's okay. Rob's one of the partners I was talking about. You can present your case to him."

Smiling, Rob nodded. "I'm supposed to be a silent partner—you know, the guy behind the scenes—but Dana keeps telling people."

"I was never good at keeping secrets." Dana chuckled as she gazed at Heather. "So what do you say? Will you join us?"

"Okay. Thanks for inviting me." Heather couldn't help but hope that the invitation to lunch was a good sign.

Heather joined the twosome as they bid good-bye to the receptionist and stepped outside. Bright sunshine warmed the air and her heart, despite her questions about this brother and sister and their possible relationship to Max.

"We're going to the café down the street." Dana motioned to her right. "I hope you don't mind walking."

"Not at all. It's a beautiful day."

While they walked by stores and businesses with redbrick facades and brightly colored awnings over the windows, Dana and Rob talked about the work they'd done that morning. Heather listened, hoping to pick up any clue about their family. Would they mention a mother or father in the conversation?

When they reached the restaurant, Heather had learned nothing new about their family. The conversation centered on business only. The hostess, who knew Dana and Rob by name, showed them to a table next to the window that looked out on the main street of the idyllic New England town. But the peaceful atmosphere of the small town didn't reach Heather's mind.

A white tablecloth and a pink rose in a single white vase adorned the table. She sat in the ladder-back chair on the opposite side from Dana and Rob. Turmoil plagued her thoughts. She wanted so badly to ask them whether they had had a brother named Scott who was killed in a motorcycle accident. But shouldn't Max be the one to ask? What would Dana and Rob think if their answer was yes? They would surely wonder how she knew about their brother.

After the waitress took their orders, Rob looked over at Heather. "So what is this case you're supposed to present to me?"

Heather wished she still had the information that she'd given to Dana, but she could tell Rob about her campaign without it. After taking a deep breath, Heather once again made her plea for their company to withdraw their bid on the property.

Much like Dana had earlier, Rob leaned back and eyed her. "I see that your campaign is a very worthy cause, and we'll be sure to consider that when we make our decision."

"I would appreciate it."

Rob held up a hand. "I have no idea what the other partners will say."

Heather nodded. "I understand. Dana said she'd be talking with them tomorrow."

Rob picked up his cell phone from the table and tapped the screen. "Yes, looks like we have a meeting tomorrow afternoon."

"Now who's forgetting stuff?" Dana poked him in the ribs.

"Did I forget?" Rob gave her an annoyed look. "No, I confirmed it on my calendar."

"Okay. You didn't forget."

The back-and-forth between the brother and sister reminded Heather of the times she'd sparred with her own brother. If these folks were Max's family, they seemed like the kind of people who wouldn't reject a newly found member. Every ounce of her being wanted to ask them about Scott, but this was one time when she wouldn't meddle. Max deserved to make this connection himself without her interference.

The waitress brought their orders, and Heather wondered whether Dana and Rob would object if she asked to give a blessing. Would their reaction give Heather a clue as to their charitable thinking? "Do you mind if I give thanks for the food?"

Rob stopped his fork midair and stared at her, then laid it on the table. "No problem. Go ahead."

Breathing a sigh of relief, Heather quickly bowed

her head and said a short prayer of thanks for the food and a silent prayer that good things would come from today's meeting. During the meal, Dana asked more questions about Heather's plans for the house, and the questions buoyed her spirits. Surely their inquiries boded well for a positive outcome for the campaign.

After they finished eating, Heather thanked them as they shook hands. "I'll be waiting to hear from you on your decision."

On the drive home, thoughts of Max filled Heather's mind. He was at work, and she would have to wait several hours to talk to him. Would he be excited or be reluctant to approach them? She could hardly wait to talk to him. What could she do to fill the time until he was finished with work?

Heather decided to take a bike ride to get in some extra training. She donned her bike shorts, shirt, and helmet before she headed out the door. She tucked her water bottle in the holder on her bike and slipped her phone into the waterproof carrier mounted on her handlebars. She rode to the outskirts of town, staying on the less traveled roads.

When she was still several miles from home, the road curved and narrowed. As she rounded the curve, a gray sedan approached from the opposite direction. Then a blue muscle car coming from behind appeared in the tiny rearview mirror attached to her helmet. She moved as far to the edge of the road as she could.

The muscle car sped around Heather. For a moment, she feared that the two cars would crash into each other. At the last second, the sedan swerved to avoid hitting the muscle car that had zoomed by her. As both cars went on their way, Heather returned her gaze to the road ahead, but not in time to see the pothole that grabbed hold of her tire and stopped the bike dead.

Everything seemed to happen in slow motion. Flying over the handlebar. Hitting the pavement. Skidding along the blacktop road. Her whole body ached as the bike landed on her left leg. Pieces of blacktop and dirt were imbedded in the bloody patches on her right arm and hands. An excruciating pain shot through her lower leg. She didn't dare try to stand. Would someone drive by and find her? She couldn't wait for that to happen. She had to take action.

She managed to push the bike aside and reach the phone still attached to her handlebar. She called 911 and prayed someone would get here before the pain became too much to bear. The dispatcher stayed on the line and gave Heather encouragement while she waited. Trying not to dwell on the pain, she lay still on the side of the road, thankful she had her phone.

Even as she prayed, her heart was breaking because this accident meant she wouldn't be able to ride in the PMC. Was everything falling apart? Her chance to ride in the PMC. Lack of funding for the house. Her tenuous relationship with Max.

Did she have hope that the partners of Renovations for You would agree to her request, or that Max would finally get over Brittany?

CHAPTER FIFTEEN

The image under the microscope blurred, and Max let out a heavy sigh. This work required a clear mind, and his mind bordered on fuzzy. The time to quit had come. He glanced at the clock. Four thirty. His boss, Dr. McKenna, had told Max that he could quit whenever he felt tired. He hated to do that, but making a mistake could prove costly.

Finishing tomorrow would serve everyone better. Maybe he could spend a little time with Heather because today was her day off, and he could find out what happened in her meeting. He hoped she was successful with her request.

Max put away his work and stopped by his boss's office. "I'm a little tired today, so I'm quitting early."

Dr. McKenna came out to greet Max. "Good. You shouldn't overdo. If you don't feel like coming in tomorrow, let me know."

"I should be good. I tend to get tired toward the end of the day. Mornings are good."

Dr. McKenna clapped Max on the back. "Take care and have a good night's rest."

"I will." Max nodded, then moseyed down the hall toward the parking lot.

As he stepped through the automated doors, an ambulance pulled up to the emergency entrance. He paused and watched as they opened the rear doors and brought a gurney down the ramp. He looked at the patient, then looked again. Heather? Was that Heather? He wasn't sure from a distance.

Although his energy level was low, he jogged toward the emergency entrance. He reached the doors as the paramedics wheeled her out of view. That was definitely Heather. Why was she here?

Max approached the desk where a lone nurse sat as she typed on a computer keyboard. The clicking of the keys matched the beat of his heart. "I'm Max Reynolds, and I believe my friend Heather Watson was brought in here by ambulance a few minutes ago. Is it possible for me to see her?"

"I'll have to check when I have a moment." The nurse motioned to the waiting area. "In the meantime, please have a seat."

Reluctantly, Max sat on one of the uncomfortable-looking tan faux leather chairs with the wooden arms. The room was nearly empty. A young couple sat in the corner, while a television blared a news program from its perch in a corner near the ceiling. He watched for a few minutes, but he couldn't concentrate.

All he could think of was Heather. Was something terribly wrong with her? The thought hurt his heart. The feeling he had now reminded him of the day he'd found out about his cancer. The hopeless sensation left him anxious.

He pulled his phone out of his pocket. Would Heather have her phone with her? Maybe he should try sending her a text. He tapped out his message and sent it. He waited for a response as he stared at the phone. None came.

Still holding the phone, he got up and paced back and forth. What did his feelings mean? Was he falling in love? He'd toyed with the idea ever since the night she'd driven him home from Amanda's open mic night, but memories of Brittany sat in a small corner of his heart and polluted this new relationship with Heather. He didn't know how to process his feelings for either one of these women. Brittany was out of reach. She belonged to someone else, and he had no business thinking about her. Maybe her upcoming visit would help him figure things out.

While he tried to unravel his feelings, a nurse approached him. "Mr. Reynolds?"

His pulse pounded with worry. "Yes."

"You may go back to see Heather Watson now. Follow me." The nurse turned and led him back through a pair of swinging doors.

A lump formed in his throat at the smell of disinfectant and illness. He smelled them every day when he came to work, but when they were associated with someone he cared for, they had a different effect on him. The nurse ushered him through an area filled with medical personnel and devices until she came to a door on the far wall.

The nurse stood aside and motioned toward the

doorway. "She's right in there."

Unsure of what he would find, Max stepped into the room. Heather lay there, her eyes closed. They already had her hooked up to an IV. "Heather?"

Her eyes flickered open, and a slow smile curved her lips. "Max. How'd you know I was here?"

Max didn't miss the woozy look in her eyes. "I saw the ambulance as I was leaving work. What happened?"

"I had a spill on my bike." She closed her eyes again and pressed her lips together. "I think I might have broken my leg. They're giving me something for the pain."

Max grinned. "I can tell."

"You can?"

Max nodded. "You look a little loopy."

"I've never broken anything before. It hurt, so I'm thankful for pain medication."

"Yeah, I know it helps. I broke an arm when I was a kid and blew out my knee playing football. Pain medication came in handy both times." Max laid a hand on her arm. "Have they taken an X-ray?"

"Not yet. They'll probably be in to get me soon." Heather gave him a sad little smile. "You don't have to hang around."

"If I don't, who's going to take you home?"

"Oh, yeah. Guess I can't drive or ride a bike." Her voice hovered on the edge of slurring. "Can you talk to Jeremy or Luke about getting my bike?"

"Where is it?"

"Near that big curve on Mill Road."

"I'll send them a text."

"Thanks."

Before Max could say anything else, an orderly pushed a gurney into the room. He smiled at Heather. "I'm here to transport you to the radiation department, where they're going to take a pretty picture of your leg."

Heather nodded as a nurse bustled into the room. "We're going to give you a ride on this gurney."

With swift efficiency, the orderly and nurse transferred Heather from the bed to the gurney and whisked her away. Max sat in the nearby chair and realized he'd forgotten to pray about the situation. He'd let worry take over his thoughts. As he sat there, he bowed his head. *Lord, be with Heather and the doctors. Take away her pain, and help her to heal.*

While Heather was away, Max paced and prayed. He wanted everything to work out for her. Were his feelings for Heather growing beyond anything he'd ever felt for Brittany? He was so confused. Only weeks ago, he was bemoaning the loss of Brittany's love, and now he wasn't sure what those feelings had been. Had he only told himself he'd been in love with Brittany all those years?

As he continued to wait, he sent a text to both Jeremy and Luke about Heather's bike. Within minutes, he got an answer from Jeremy, who said they would find the bike and bring it back to their place.

After Heather returned, with the X-ray confirming

her broken tibia, the emergency room personnel prepared to put a splint on her leg.

"Jeremy said he and Luke will look for your bike." Max raised his eyebrows. "Do you want me to leave while they put on the splint?"

Heather shrugged. "Thanks for contacting the guys."

"Glad to help." Even though she didn't say it, Max got the feeling that Heather wanted him to stay.

"Will you eventually get a cast?

"Yeah. I have to see an orthopedic doc in a few days. They want any swelling to go down before they cast it."

"Got a color picked out?"

"Red for the Red Sox."

Max laughed. "I should've known. At least you still have your sense of humor."

Heather half smiled. "I don't know about that. I just want to go home."

Within minutes Heather had her splint and a pair of crutches. Max headed to the door, then turned back. "I'll bring the car around. Sorry. You'll have to ride home in my rattletrap."

"I won't complain."

"I'll hold you to that." Max grinned. "I'll wait outside the entrance."

Heather nodded while the nurse gave her instructions. Max made his way to the car and wondered whether Heather would follow the nurse's directions, or would she be a terrible patient? This would be interesting with her being the patient instead of him.

After he helped Heather into the car, he hurried around to the driver's side. He slid behind the wheel and looked over at her. "How you doing?"

Unhappiness clouded Heather's expression. "As good as can be expected, considering that I can't ride in the PMC now."

"People will still donate even if you can't ride." Max drove out of the parking lot.

"I suppose, but I was looking forward to the ride and everything that goes with it."

"You can keep me and Hailey company." Max turned onto the street that led toward home.

The statement brought a halfhearted smile to Heather's lips. "That can't be all bad."

"I was thinking it was all good."

"I'll try to adopt that attitude. I can't let our Pedal Partner see me down."

"For sure."

In a few minutes Max parked his car in front of his house, letting it idle. "We're here."

Heather glanced his way. "Do you expect me to hobble across the street to my place?"

Max shook his head. "I doubt you'll be able to get up to your apartment on those crutches."

"Then what do you suggest I do?"

"Stay at my place. I'll sleep on the couch, and you can have my bed." Max kept his eyes on the road as he waited for Heather's response. What would she say to his suggestion?

"And you think that's a good idea?"

"It's the only solution to your problem."

"Unless there's another answer that won't put you out and have me intruding on the all-male territory."

Max glanced at Heather. "So you're not comfortable staying with us guys?"

Heather let out a halfhearted laugh. "That's an understatement."

"We'll take good care of you."

Heather looked at him with an expression that was half smile and half frown. "Should that reassurance make me feel better?"

"Absolutely."

"Somehow, I have the feeling you might be looking for some payback."

Max pulled the car to a stop in front of the walk that led up to the house, then looked over at Heather as he placed a hand over his heart. "You wound me. Here I have your best interest at heart, and you think I'm seeking revenge."

"Only kidding." Heather shook her head. "Have you discussed this with Jeremy and Luke?"

"We discussed your dilemma when I asked them to find your bike, and we all agreed that you should stay here."

"Did they find it?"

Max motioned toward the porch. "Looks like someone did."

Heather glanced toward the house. "Good. I hope it

didn't suffer too much damage."

"I'm sure it can be repaired, just like you."

"At least my break was minor and didn't require surgery or any metal parts."

"Let's get you into the house. Do you need help?"

"Probably getting out of the car."

"At your service." Max jumped out from behind the wheel and hurried to the passenger side as Heather opened the door. He grabbed her crutches from the backseat.

"How should we do this?" Heather managed to swing her legs out of the car.

Max looked down at the splint, then back at Heather as he held out his hand. He had to admit he liked that she needed him. "If you think you can stand on one leg, take my hand, and I'll pull you up."

Heather nodded and reached out. Max closed his hand around hers, gently pulling her up until she was standing on the curb. Her trust created a warm spot around his heart. He quickly grabbed the crutches and helped her with them. She looked at him with a smile, and his heart thudded. He tried to tamp down his emotions. This wasn't the time to figure out his feelings for Heather.

"Thanks. That wasn't too bad." She adjusted the crutches.

"I'm right here beside you if you need me." Max shadowed Heather as she swung her way up the walk. "Can you negotiate the steps?"

Heather stopped in front of the three steps leading

up to the porch. Leaning on the crutches, she looked at him. "No doubt I'm going to need your help."

"That's what I'm here for." He stepped closer and assisted her up the steps.

Again the fact that she needed him left a tender spot in his heart. This whole episode only added to his mixed-up emotions. Maybe he was trying too hard to figure things out. He had to let this relationship develop without trying to force his emotions into a box. All his analyzing couldn't rush it or slow it down.

***

Heather leaned on Max as he assisted her into the house. The whole thing seemed like a dream. Maybe it was the pain medicine that made her thoughts so unclear. She hated feeling this way, but it was probably better than dealing with the pain from the break.

"Do you want to sit on the couch?" Max asked.

"Okay. I'm not going anywhere." Heather liked the way Max's strong arms held her as he helped her onto the couch, but she couldn't let the pain meds make her forget that despite Max's attentiveness, he still couldn't forget Brittany.

"I'll be right back." Max rushed into the nearby hallway and returned a few moments later carrying a large pillow. "Something to keep your leg elevated."

Heather smiled up at him. "You'd make a good

nurse."

"Don't think so." Shaking his head, Max helped Heather place her splinted leg on the pillow. "I'm not that good at giving orders."

Heather tried to give him an annoyed look, but a chuckle escaped instead. "Maybe you should be a comedian."

Max sat on the arm of the couch. "I'll stick with lab work. Anything else I can get you?"

"Clothes." Heather tapped the splint, then looked up at Max. "How will I get something to wear over this thing? I can't wear biking shorts everywhere I go. It'll be even worse when I get my cast."

"I'm sure there's something in your vast wardrobe that you can wear."

Heather frowned. "Why do I get the feeling that you're being a bit sarcastic?"

Max waved a hand at her. "I'm serious. Of course, I've never seen your complete wardrobe, but I know you have numerous nursing uniforms that should work."

"I suppose the legs of the pants are wide enough to go over the splint." Heather sighed. "Can you go over to my apartment and get some things for me?"

Max looked at her wide eyed and slowly shook his head. "I'm not going through your stuff."

"Then who's going to do it?"

Shrugging, Max gave her a lopsided grin. "Your landlady?"

"Mrs. Riley?"

"If that's her name. Yeah. Better her than me."

Heather tried not to laugh at Max's stricken look. "Okay. Will you please go talk to her?"

"I'm on my way." Max raced out the door as if something evil was chasing him.

After Max left, Heather lay back and closed her eyes. Suddenly she remembered her meeting with Dana and Rob. She didn't want to get his hopes up, but he needed to know what had happened. While she lay there, a half-dozen scenarios raced through her mind.

A door opened and closed. Heather blinked. Had she fallen asleep? She looked up to find Max empty handed as he stood next to the couch. "You didn't bring me anything. Was Mrs. Riley not home?"

"She was home, but she gave me strict instructions that you are not to stay here."

"And why is that?"

"Inappropriate." Max grinned as he cocked his head.

Still staring up at Max, Heather knit her eyebrows as she let out a little laugh. "Okay…but what does she expect me to do? I can't get up to my apartment on these crutches."

"Yes, she realizes that and insists that you should stay in her extra room until you're able to get up the stairs." Max raised his eyebrows as his eyes twinkled with mischief. "She's looking out for your virtue, and I don't want to cross her."

"Don't make fun." Heather shot him an

exasperated look.

"Who's making fun?" Max shrugged, his grin still in place. "Believe me. She gave me an earful. Besides, you'll probably be more comfortable staying with her than staying here with three guys."

Heather shrugged. "I'm pretty sure you guys are thinking that also, even though you were kind enough to offer."

"So you want to hang out here with me for a while or head over there?"

Heather patted the slim space beside her on the couch. "Sit down for a minute. I have something I want to tell you."

Max's eyes narrowed as he sat beside her. "Is there something wrong?"

"Not wrong necessarily, but interesting."

"What?"

"You know I had that meeting with the people who put the other bid on the property this morning."

"Oh, yeah. I forgot all about that. Did they say they'd drop their offer?"

"They made no final decision. They have to talk to their other partners."

"Did you get any hints as to what they might do?"

"Not really, but that's not what I wanted to talk about."

"Then what?" Max wrinkled his brow.

Heather took a deep breath. "The lady I met with today was Dana Mahoney, and as I was leaving, her brother arrived. His name is Rob Harkin, and his resemblance to you is considerable."

Max stared at her wide eyed as he took off his cap and rubbed a hand over his bald head. "You think these people are the Harkins I've been searching for?"

Heather shrugged. "Not your grandparents, but an uncle and aunt."

Max continued to stare at her. "I'm not sure what to do with this information."

"You could talk to them."

"And what would I say?" Max shook his head. "Hey, I think you're related to me."

"What had you planned to say to anyone you might have discovered in your search?"

A muscle worked in his jaw. "I hadn't planned that far ahead."

Max's response didn't surprise Heather. Typical Max. No plans. She pressed her lips together as she fought a caustic reply. He didn't need her criticism. "You should consider making some plans."

"Yeah, I suppose." He gazed down at her. "Were they friendly?"

"Yeah, they invited me to lunch." Heather reached over and placed a hand on Max's arm. "Would you like to meet them?"

***

Heather's question resurrected all the doubts and fears that had accompanied Max's search from the very beginning, even when it was only the seed of a thought. After the searching he'd done, she would surely think he was crazy if he didn't meet these people. Did he want to open himself up for rejection? He'd had enough of that in his life. Could he face more?

"You look doubtful."

Max gave her a lopsided smile. "I'm that transparent?"

Heather smiled back. "Not most of the time, but right now you are. So what are you going to do?"

That was a relief. Max certainly didn't want Heather knowing about his mixed-up feelings for her. One minute kissing her and the next wondering what he was thinking. It was bad enough that she recognized his fears about meeting these strangers who might be his family. Did he dare ask for her advice? She would probably be happy to give it. "How can I spring myself on these people? What would you do if a stranger claimed to be your nephew?"

Heather frowned. "You're not thinking of ignoring them, are you?"

Max got up and paced in front of the couch. "What do I say to them?"

"Lay it out there, and let them act on it."

"Easy for you to say. You're not the one they might reject."

"True, but they might reject my request to withdraw their bid."

Max stopped pacing. Here he'd been thinking only

of himself, not Heather's plans or the house that would help so many families deal with their loved ones combating a terrible disease. "I don't want my search to jeopardize your project."

Heather stared up at him. "You won't jeopardize anything. Did you ever think that God's hand is in this whole thing?"

"You mean like God brought these people into your life so I could find them?"

Heather nodded. "That's what I was thinking."

"I don't know." Max shrugged. "I don't have your confidence that this is somehow God's doing."

"Dana said she'd call in the next few days to let me know what they've decided." Heather pushed herself up to a sitting position as she swung her splinted leg over the side of the couch. "Suit yourself. You can do what you want with this information. I should go."

Not about to argue with Heather, Max reached for her crutches. He was pretty sure her curt response meant she wasn't happy with his indecisiveness. He couldn't make a decision to please her. He had to do what he thought was right. He ought to pray, but he wasn't sure how God would let him know what to do. "You want me to help you up?"

"Yeah." She grabbed hold of his outstretched hand.

As Max helped her to her feet, he had the urge to pull her into his arms and kiss her. But her apparent displeasure with him didn't invite affection. Better to forget it and help her home. They made their way across the street and into the front hall of the triple-decker. Max knocked on Mrs. Riley's door.

In seconds, the thin, gray-haired woman opened the door wide. "Heather, dear, I'm so sorry about your broken leg. Come in."

"Thank you for offering your spare room." Heather maneuvered herself through the door.

"It's nothing. Glad to help." Mrs. Riley waved a hand at Heather, then glanced at Max. "Your young man here is very thoughtful."

Max nodded and smiled, not sure how to respond to the older woman's comment. Did Heather consider him her young man? He looked at her. She was in good hands. "Have a good night, and let me know if you need anything tomorrow."

"Okay." She stared at him with those big brown eyes. "I'll let you know if I talk to the other bidders."

"Sure. We can talk about it tomorrow." Did he see a hint of regret in her expression? He'd never been good at reading women. That's how he'd messed up with Brittany. And why did he have to think about her at this moment? He pushed away the troubling thoughts. "Good night."

As Max stepped out the door, Heather managed to follow him, her crutches thumping on the hardwood floor. "Thanks again for your help today."

"Any time." Max wanted more than ever to pull Heather into his arms and kiss her, but with Mrs. Riley standing in the doorway, that wasn't going to happen. Her presence probably saved him from doing something entirely unwise.

Max loped down the front steps and across the street. When he reached his porch, he turned and waved to Heather, who was silhouetted in the light from the hallway as she still stood at the front door. She waved back, then turned to go inside. What was he supposed to do with her? And what was he supposed to do about these people who might be the family he'd been looking for?

Taking in the cool night air, Max stood on the front porch for a few moments. The stars twinkled overhead in the blackness and reminded him that no matter what troubles came, God was in charge. Max needed to remember that fact when things seemed out of control.

CHAPTER SIXTEEN

Over a week had gone by since the day Heather had broken her leg, and she'd become quite proficient maneuvering around on her crutches. The orthopedist had put a bright-red long leg cast on her left leg. She was doing so well that she was able to go back to work. Despite her injury and not being able to ride in the PMC, she'd procured more donations than ever. She supposed people had sympathy for her and decided to donate more.

These good things should make her happy, but Dana Mahoney had not called back. That made for worry and despair. The looming deadline for purchasing the house erased all the cheery events and left Heather with a hollow feeling in her heart. Where could they find funds to purchase the house in one day? She tried to tell herself that there would be another house they could use, even though it wouldn't be so conveniently located. Could God have a better place in mind?

As Heather finished recording patient information, she leaned back with a sigh. Max would be here any moment to drive her home. His promptness each day had surprised her, but he'd never said another word about the Harkins. Maybe it was for the best. If these people weren't willing to help out a charity by withdrawing their bid, maybe they weren't the kind of individuals Max wanted to know. She wasn't going to push him.

Then there was the matter of Brittany's visit. How would that affect him? Even though she was married to someone else, would he still have feelings for her that he couldn't shake? That question bothered Heather more than she wanted to admit. She didn't want to further her relationship with Max if he was still hung up on Brittany. Would he talk about his feelings as he'd done before or keep them bottled up inside and leave her guessing?

Heather shoved the question away. She had better things to do than worry about Max's feelings for Brittany. Heather looked back at her computer screen and tried to concentrate on the good things in her life—like being back at work.

"You look lost in thought."

Max's voice made Heather look up from the computer. He smiled, and her heart did a little flip-flop. How could she resist that smile? Taking a deep breath, she grabbed her crutches and pushed herself up from the desk. "Just working, but I'm ready to get out of here."

"And I'm ready to take you away." He winked.

"Let me grab my purse, and I'll be ready to leave."

"Sure. I'll be right here waiting for you."

Minutes later, Heather was swinging down the hallway on her crutches with Max beside her. She didn't want to think about how much she'd come to depend on him. She fretted about the way he'd backed away from his earlier talk of seeing where their attraction to each other would lead. Ever since their discussion about his contacting Dana and Rob, Max hadn't even tried to hold her hand. Maybe it was the crutches, but maybe it was the Harkins or Brittany's impending visit.

Heather tried to shutter her mind to the worrisome thoughts.

When they reached her car, Max opened the door and helped her in. "You all settled?"

"Yeah. Thanks."

Max slipped behind the wheel and glanced her way. "This has been nice driving your car to work every day, but I'm going to be spoiled when I have to start using my old hunk of junk again."

"You can always go back to walking or biking when you don't have to haul me to work anymore."

"True, but I'm going to miss this." He patted the steering wheel.

"I suppose so." Heather didn't dare ask whether he was going to miss their daily time together. Her insecurities were playing havoc with her thoughts today. She had to steer them in a more positive direction.

After Max parked the car in front of the triple-decker where Heather lived, he hurried around to help her out of the car. As he took her hand and pulled her up, her cell phone rang. Leaning against the car, she fished the phone from the pocket of her smock. Her stomach sank when she saw the caller ID. Corbin

Duncan from the bank was in charge of the House for Families account. Was he going to confirm the bad news that they had lost the house?

Heather punched the screen on her phone. "Hello, Duncan. Do you have news for me?"

"Yes." Heather could hear the smile in his voice. "We've had a last-minute anonymous donation that put you over the top. We have enough money to buy that house."

Emotions of every kind welled up inside Heather until she couldn't contain the happy tears that rolled down her cheeks. "Even with my doubts, God provided. What's the next step?"

Heather wiped at her eyes as Duncan explained the procedures. After she ended the call, she looked over at Max.

He gave her a lopsided grin. "Despite the tears, I'm guessing that was good news?"

"We're getting the house." Heather threw her arms around Max.

"That is good news," he whispered in her ear as he held her.

Nodding, Heather dropped her arms and eased out of his embrace as she sensed Max's discomfort. She smiled up at him and hoped her impulsive move didn't have him wishing he wasn't there. "Sorry for nearly tackling you."

He held his hands out to his side. "What guy is going to complain about a pretty woman in his arms?"

He'd called her pretty, but it still seemed so

impersonal. Why was she analyzing everything? She had to keep it light. "Certainly not you."

Max waggled his eyebrows as he picked up her crutches. "Better behave myself, or Mrs. Riley will be out here to give me a lecture."

"Do you think she's watching?"

"Wouldn't surprise me." Max handed Heather the crutches. "She's going to make sure I treat you right."

Heather tried to smile as she started up the walk. Did that remark contain shades of regret over the way he'd treated Brittany? Heather wished she could somehow purge thoughts of Brittany from her mind. The ridiculous disquiet didn't help anyone. "And what does that mean?"

Max shrugged. "I'm not sure, but I don't want to get on her wrong side. You want to hide out from Mrs. Riley over at my place and celebrate your good news?"

Yeah. But would it be wise? Maybe she was too far gone already to save herself from Max's lopsided grin and puppy dog eyes that pulled her in against her will. What had happened to the woman who had warned her friend against him?

She didn't exist anymore.

She didn't seem to have a will of her own when it came to Max, but how did he really feel about her? That was the scary question.

"Well?"

"Sure."

"Great. I'll order pizza, and we'll find a movie to

stream."

While Max accompanied her across the street and helped her up the steps, Heather tried not to put too much stake in his invitation. She couldn't shake the way he'd seemingly pulled back from his former flirty self. He hadn't tried to kiss her or even tease about it. He was treating her as if he was afraid that Mrs. Riley would come after him with a shotgun if he so much as touched her. Heather pushed the silly thought from her mind.

She had to quit analyzing and just enjoy the evening ahead. She could do that. And she promised herself that she wouldn't give Max any advice. Maybe that was where she'd gone wrong. She was always trying to tell him what to do. When it came to Max, could she ever learn to keep her opinions to herself?

***

The sun sat above the tree line as Max drove Heather's car toward the Hawthorne Inn. Heather sat stoic in the passenger seat. During the past week, they hadn't spent much time together except their trips back and forth to work. Heather had been in a flurry of meetings about the purchase of the house. They'd only discussed tonight's dinner with Parker and Brittany once.

Despite the time he'd spent with Heather last Friday to celebrate reaching her goal to buy the property, their relationship was on tenuous ground.

His stomach churned at the thought of seeing Brittany again. Each time he couldn't pinpoint his feelings put more distance between Heather and him. That couldn't be good. He was crazy for letting this meeting twist his feelings into a knot of apprehension. All of his uncertainty wasn't helping things with Heather.

As Max parked the car, he tried to prepare himself for this meeting. Brittany would be with her husband. Max had no business having romantic feelings about another man's wife, but he had a hard time putting their eight-year relationship behind him. Why had he agreed to this dinner?

Because he had to sort out his feelings once and for all.

Max glanced over at Heather, who was unbuckling her seat belt. "You need some help?"

She gave him a tentative smile as a little frown creased her brow. "Don't I always?"

"Yeah." As he walked around to the passenger side, he didn't know why he'd asked whether she needed help. Of course, she did, but he didn't want to take anything for granted. He opened the door and held out his hand. Lately, every time he did this, he wanted to pull her into his arms and kiss her. How could he be thinking this when he wasn't sure how he'd feel when he saw Brittany again?

As he and Heather made their way toward the wide front porch festooned with white rockers, he felt like he could implode any minute. Emotions of every stripe bombarded his heart and mind. He should've told Heather how good she looked in the black-and-red dress that matched her cast, but he hadn't because his mind had been consumed with worry about this reunion.

He should tell her now. Before Max could open his mouth, Parker stepped through the front door of the inn, his short dark hair combed in the same style Max had remembered from their previous encounters. Where was Brittany? Max didn't have to wait long for the answer. Parker paused for a moment while he let a petite redhead go ahead of him. Her shoulder-length hair flew as she raced down the steps toward them. Max couldn't miss her baby bump, the term he'd heard women use when discussing pregnancy.

Heather hobbled forward on her crutches to meet Brittany. The two women embraced amid laughter and a few tears of joy. Max stood off to the side, surprised and stunned that all those emotions about Brittany that had built up inside him slowly ebbed away like a wave on a calm day at the beach. His reaction. Nothing.

Her presence left him unaffected.

"Looks like the women have forgotten all about us." Parker stopped next to Max.

Max turned to shake hands with Parker. "Seems so. It's good to see you. How are things in Montana?"

"Good. Real good. How's your treatment progressing?"

"As good as can be expected." Max ran a hand

over his bald head. "You can see I've lost my hair, but I'm used to it now."

"Yeah, I saw Heather's photos when the kids in your youth group shaved their heads."

Max nodded. "Everyone's been very supportive."

Parker clapped Max on the back. "We need to break up the gabfest between these two women. Our table's waiting."

With a smile, Heather glanced their way as Parker moved in her direction. "My favorite uncle."

Managing to avoid the crutches, Parker embraced Heather in a big bear hug, then held her at arm's length. "Despite that cast, you're looking good."

"Thanks. I'm getting really proficient with these things." Heather waved a crutch. "Wish I could throw them away and still ride in the PMC."

Parker put an arm around Heather's shoulders. "Well, this way you can keep Britt company while I ride."

Max looked Brittany's way, and she smiled. "It's good to see you, Max."

Smiling back, he felt none of the things he'd expected. No regret. No heartache. No unrequited love. Instead, fondness for the woman who had shared his high school and college years welled up inside him. "It's good to see you, too."

All that angst for nothing. He'd been propping up an old dream that had actually withered and died. When? He didn't know, but a sense of peace filled him. He looked at Heather as they made their way into the inn. Here was the woman who made his heart dance, not Brittany.

This get-together with Brittany showed Max that his feelings for Heather weren't crazy after all. She'd been by his side through all this trouble. She'd seen him through his chemo treatments, first as a nurse and then as a friend. She'd listened to his laments about Brittany. Heather had put up with his inconsiderate behavior.

He'd tried to tell himself that he wasn't falling in love with Heather. Maybe it was time to face the truth.

***

Heather tried to read Max's features, but she couldn't interpret his reaction to seeing Brittany again. Two old friends? Was that what she saw, or was she only wishing that was the case?

Would Brittany guess that there was something going on between her good friend and Max? Heather wasn't sure how she would respond if Brittany asked about him. First, she had to be honest with herself before she could be honest with anyone else. Was she really falling in love with Max Reynolds, or was she just, as he claimed, trying to *fix him*?

Right now all she had to do was get through this dinner. She could face Brittany's scrutiny later.

As they entered the dining area of the inn, Tara Madsen greeted them with a smile. "Parker and Brittany, it's so good to see you again."

"Heather told us you were living here." Parker gave her a hug. "How's Hailey?"

"Hanging in there. She's a brave little girl." Tara turned to Max and patted him on the shoulder. "She really looks up to this guy because they share this cancer thing. She has a big crush on him."

Shrugging, Max gave them all a sheepish grin. "What can I say? The ladies love me."

Everyone chuckled as Tara led them to their table. Max pulled out a chair for Heather, and she wondered about his motivation. He'd admitted his mixed-up feelings when it came to Brittany. Would tonight's meeting clear things up for him? What would it mean if he decided he was still in love with her? Heather tried to shove that scenario from her mind, but she couldn't completely bury the thought.

The foursome studied their menus in silence while the muted conversation and laughter of the other diners swirled in the background. By the time Tara returned with their drinks, everyone was ready to order.

After Tara left, Max glanced around the table. "Where are Rose and Jasmine?"

"Delia our housekeeper is taking good care of them." Brittany chuckled as she smiled at Max. "The girls were really disappointed that they couldn't come with us, but Parker and I decided we should have a little vacation time for ourselves before the baby is born. Rose especially wanted to see you and hear you do your duck voice."

Max chuckled in return. "I still remember the day I gave the girls a tour of the lab in Billings. I bet they've grown a lot since then."

Nodding, Brittany whipped her phone from her purse. "I've got photos."

Max scooted closer as Brittany scrolled through the photos. Parker interjected commentary about the little girls—the girls Parker had adopted—as they all laughed about their antics. Heather took in Max's attention to Brittany while jealousy trickled through her mind. She tried to wipe it away, but it would reappear in seconds like the condensation running down the water glasses on the table.

After they finished looking at the pictures, Max leaned back in his chair. "So what do the girls think about getting a new brother or sister?"

"They're pretty excited." Brittany turned toward Heather. "And we found out earlier this week that we're having a boy."

"How wonderful!" Heather was genuinely happy for her friend. "Do you have any names picked out?"

"We're still working on that." Parker grabbed Brittany's hand. "She's got me going through a book with baby names."

"I'm sure you'll come up with the perfect name for that baby boy." Heather nodded. "I'm so happy for you two. I'm a good matchmaker."

"You're good at butting into other people's lives." Parker grinned. "But I'll have to admit that in our case, that's a good thing."

"At least I get some appreciation from you guys." Heather hoped all this talk wasn't going to stir up sad memories for Max.

Parker turned to Max. "Is she butting into your life?"

"From the moment she found me sitting in the doctor's exam room." Not even a hint of a smile crossed Max's face.

"I was your nurse. What could you expect?"

Max laughed out loud. "Is someone a little too sensitive about her tendency to orchestrate other people's lives?"

"I'm so glad you guys can all laugh at my expense. Where would you be without me?"

"Sad and lonely." Parker patted her arm, then chuckled. "We still love you even if you do like to interfere."

Heather didn't dare look at Max. What could he be thinking? After all, here she was sitting with Brittany, her husband and her ex-boyfriend. Heather wondered whether she was the only one who felt the situation and the conversation were awkward. She must be the only one. The others were all having a good laugh.

Before anyone made another comment, Tara arrived with their food. After Parker gave thanks for their meal, everyone started eating. The conversation drifted to the PMC ride and eventually came around to the House for Families project and the people who'd volunteered to lend their time and talent in making the renovations.

"You've got a lot of work ahead of you," Brittany said.

"I like to stay busy, but this thing is slowing me down." Heather tapped her cast.

"How much longer do you have to have it on?" Parker asked.

Heather shrugged. "At least another month. I'll sure be glad when I get it off."

"I'm sure you will." Parker looked over at Max. "And how long before you're done with your chemo?"

"I've got two more treatments." Max sighed. "Then we'll see whether they've been effective."

"I hope you get good news." Brittany nodded, then took a bite of her food.

"We've been praying for you, even Rose and Jasmine," Parker said.

"Thanks. I appreciate the prayers."

Heather set down her fork. "Max has come through the chemo pretty well."

"That's because I had such a good nurse." Max grinned at her. "She badgered me to eat right, rest, and exercise."

"Only doing my job." Heather wondered whether Max would mention that she was no longer his nurse. Probably not, or he would have to explain why.

Brittany looked back and forth between Heather and Max. "I'm glad you two were able to connect with each other."

Heather stared at Brittany. Was she suggesting that

Heather and Max were a couple, or was she only making an observation?

Before Heather opened her mouth, Max jumped into the conversation. "Yeah. It was quite a shock to be sitting in there and have her walk in."

"True. The last time we all saw each other was at our wedding." Brittany took another bite of her food.

Heather watched Max for a reaction. He only nodded. Was he being an excellent actor, or did none of this faze him? What would he say to her on the way home? Or would he remain silent? The questions wouldn't go away.

Heather breathed a sigh of relief when the conversation turned to more talk about the PMC and the weekend ahead. When the evening was over, Brittany and Parker suggested getting together again after the weekend's bike ride. Heather couldn't read Max's reaction to their future plans.

Brittany gave Heather a good-bye hug and whispered, "Before I leave, I want to know what's going on between you and Max."

Heather wondered what she could say and tried to avoid Brittany's gaze as they stepped away from each other. "I'm not sure there's anything to tell you."

Brittany gave Heather a knowing smile. "We'll see."

Heather waved as Max helped her into the car and hoped that he didn't have a clue what Brittany had said. Parker and Brittany stood arm in arm and waved as Max maneuvered the car up the lane to the main road. The headlights illuminated the darkness ahead, but the dim light in the car's interior made it difficult to read his expression.

Max said nothing. Why couldn't she be brave enough to ask him how he felt now that he'd seen Brittany again?

***

Dozens of conflicting thoughts filled Max's mind as he drove down the tree-lined road. He wanted to share his feelings with Heather, but fear kept him silent. Would she think he was crazy for having all that anguish over Brittany and then finding it was all for nothing?

The hum of the motor was the only sound filling the otherwise silent car. He glanced over at Heather, but she was staring straight ahead. He should ask her something, but he didn't know what. He wished she would open the conversation. She usually did. Why was she so quiet tonight?

Max wrestled with his thoughts for several minutes. Finally glancing Heather's way, he took a deep breath. "What did Brittany say to you right before we left?"

Heather continued to look straight ahead without answering.

Letting out a harsh breath, he gripped the steering wheel tighter. "Is it none of my business?"

Still she didn't say anything. What could he do to

relieve the tension swirling through the air?

He reached to turn on the radio to fill the quiet, but Heather laid a hand on his arm. "No need for the radio. I'll tell you what she said."

"Okay." He prepared himself for something he didn't want to hear.

"Brittany asked me what was going on between you and me."

"So what did you say?" Holding his breath, he waited for her answer. Heather shrugged and bit her lower lip as he brought the car to a stop at an intersection. She stared at him, and the traffic light showed the uncertainty in her eyes.

"I wasn't sure what to say, because I don't know where we stand with each other. I don't know how you feel about Brittany. I don't know anything." Heather glanced down at the hands she twisted in her lap, her voice trailing off in a whisper.

Max wanted to pull over and have a heart-to-heart conversation with Heather, but this crossroads provided no safe place to stop. Telling her that his affection for Brittany was all in the past was all-important. He didn't want to wait until they arrived at home because he feared he would chicken out when it came to explaining his illogical emotions.

His feelings for Heather scared him. They weren't the thoughts of a sixteen-year-old boy infatuated with the cute cheerleader or the college student who thought he was in love and wanted to get married. Maybe all that time he'd only believed he'd been in love with Brittany. Their relationship had become comfortable, and they were more friends than anything else. He hadn't realized that until tonight. In the end he hadn't been a very good friend either. Could he explain all this to Heather and make sense?

Max didn't want to mess up again. Heather had seen him at his worst, and she still said she was willing to explore their attraction. She'd told him the cancer didn't matter, but she was counting on his recovery. What if that didn't happen?

As he rounded a curve, he spied a gas station ahead, its lights flooding the surrounding area. He turned into the parking lot.

"Does my car need gas?" Heather asked, her eyebrows knit as she stared at him.

"No." Max brought the car to a stop in front of the building and looked over at Heather. "We need to talk and not while I'm driving."

"About what?"

"You and me. And I don't want to wait until we get back to your place."

"Okay." Heather's expression spelled uncertainty.

He rubbed a hand across the back of his neck. He wanted to do this, but he was afraid of doing it wrong. He'd been a fool to hang on to the shreds of a lost love like a toddler carrying around what was left of his baby blanket. It was time to grow up, stand up, and be a man. He swallowed the lump that had formed in his throat and looked Heather in the eye. "I'm not sure where this thing between us will lead, but I want you to know this one thing. My feelings for Brittany are part of my past, and that's where they're going to stay. Seeing her tonight made that completely clear. I realized that in the end Brittany and I had treated each other like brother and sister. I've been a meathead."

A little smile lingered at the corners of Heather's mouth. "Am I allowed to call you a meathead?"

Max chuckled. "If you want."

"So what are you really telling me?"

Max gave her a lopsided grin. "You're not making this easy on me."

"I didn't know I was supposed to."

Did he mean he was in love with Heather? He didn't want to tell her unless he was completely sure. "I want you to know that you're an important part of my life, and I'm moving ahead and not looking back."

Heather's expression brightened. "And you're important to me, too. I'm not sure what to say to Brittany because she insisted that she was going to get an answer from me before she left."

"Tell her the truth. That you hated the sight of me when you walked into that exam room, but my considerable charm won you over against your will. You couldn't resist me."

Heather laughed out loud. "Do you think she'd believe that?"

"Absolutely." Max grinned.

Sighing, Heather shook her head. "How am I going to keep your ego in check?"

"Kiss me." Max unbuckled his seat belt, then

Heather's as he took her hand and pulled her toward him while he leaned across the console.

"Somehow I don't believe that's going to work."

"Sure it is. Give it a try." Max brought her closer until their lips met. All thoughts fled except those about this one woman. She was making him a better man, and he didn't want to make a shamble of things this time. When the kiss ended, Max settled back into the driver's seat. "I believe that worked."

Heather gazed at him, a smile in her eyes. "I've saved you from getting too full of yourself?"

"Definitely." He turned to her with a grin while he maneuvered the car back onto the road. "Let's get out of here before I'm accused of keeping you out too late. Do you think I can steal another kiss when we get back to your place, or will Mrs. Riley be watching?"

Heather laughed. "You can't let Mrs. Riley scare you."

"Is that an invitation for another kiss?"

"It is. Mrs. Riley or no Mrs. Riley."

"I'll take you up on that invitation." Max's heart was lighter than it had been in years, even though he was battling a dreaded disease. Heather had made his world better in so many ways. He prayed for the wisdom to make this relationship work.

CHAPTER SEVENTEEN

Sunshine filtered through the trees in Boston's Public Garden as a breeze rustled the leaves overhead. Heather eased herself onto a bench near the walkway and laid her crutches across her lap as she looked up at Brittany. "I hope you enjoyed your tour of Boston."

Brittany sat beside Heather. "I did, and I'm so glad you managed to get around on your crutches. Thanks for making the effort."

"I love showing people the history in the city. Thankfully, most of the time we were sitting."

Brittany grimaced. "But getting in and out of the Duck Tour vehicle was a little tricky with your cast."

"Yeah, but I couldn't let you come to Boston without doing a Duck Tour."

"Next time I come, I'm going to insist that Parker do some sightseeing instead of spending all his time on business. And we have to bring the kids, too." Brittany fished her phone from her purse. "I'm going to take a picture of the Make Way for Ducklings statues so I can show them to the girls."

"Have they read that book?"

"More times than I care to count." Brittany laughed as she pointed her phone toward the statues just across the walkway.

"The girls will love the photos."

After snapping several pictures, she returned to the bench. "Parker sent a text saying he'd be around to pick us up in about twenty minutes. That gives me some time to ask you about Max."

Heather had been expecting this all afternoon. Although she didn't know what she was going to tell her friend, it would be good to get it out of the way. "What do you want to know?"

"I got the feeling that you two aren't enemies anymore." Brittany gave Heather a speculative glance. "I'm glad you found each other, even though the circumstances aren't ideal. Max needs a friend. Maybe that's all you are—friends?"

How could she explain her complicated relationship with Max? She couldn't tell Brittany about how he lamented over and over about his breakup with her only to discover he'd been holding on to a false idea?

"You seem hesitant to talk about him. So maybe it's none of my business. But when my mom told me that he had cancer, I hurt inside." Brittany placed a hand over her heart. "He's like a brother to me, and I worried about him. I'm so glad you're here to help him."

"Me, too."

"So is that all there is to tell?"

Heather knew she shouldn't have trouble talking to her good friend about her feelings. "It's complicated."

"I'm sure it is. Brittany chuckled. "Are you feeling weird because you told me to end our relationship?"

"Yeah." Heather gave Brittany a wry smile. "I couldn't believe it when I found him in that exam room. He wasted no time in telling me that he didn't appreciate my interference in his life when I convinced you to finally dump him."

"He didn't request a different nurse?"

"No. Surprised me. I have no idea why. Despite our animosity, maybe he needed someone familiar in the strange world of cancer."

"So when did things change?"

"I don't know. Our feelings for each other changed and grew over the past few weeks." Heather shrugged. "He kind of said the same thing you did about the brother and sister bit."

"Are things serious between you?"

"Our relationship is very new. So it's too soon to tell what will happen."

Brittany smiled. "That makes me happy. Even though Max wasn't the right guy for me, I want him to find happiness. And if it's with my good friend, that's even better."

"Thanks."

"I'm glad you found each other."

"Me, too. Max keeps things interesting." Even though Brittany had expressed her happiness about Heather and Max's relationship, Heather still couldn't shake that bit of awkwardness about falling for the guy she'd told her friend was a loser. Heather pushed that thought away. Brittany wasn't bothered, so why should she have worries about it? She shouldn't. But could Brittany give any insight into Max's search for his biological father?

"You look like you're lost in thought. What's creating that faraway look in your eyes?" Brittany asked.

"You know me too well. I could never pull one over on you."

"True." Brittany tilted her head. "Are you worried about Max?"

"Sometimes, I worry that he keeps things bottled up inside."

"That's Max."

Heather wished she knew how to deal with Max's quiet nature. Despite their attraction to each other, would their opposite personalities be a problem in the long run? Would Brittany have any insights?

For a few minutes, they sat in silence as they watched a group of youngsters exclaim over the duckling statues and sit on the mother duck. Finally, Heather glanced Brittany's way. "Did Max ever talk about his biological father with you?"

Curiosity knit a little frown across Brittany's brow. "Where did that question come from?"

"Did you know that Max moved here to find his father's family?"

Brittany shook her head. "Wow. I had no idea."

"Do you know anything about his biological father?"

Brittany let out a heavy sigh. "The only time Max ever mentioned him was the time we watched this movie called *August Rush*. There's a little boy who—"

"Who's looking for his parents."

"Yeah. That's the one. You've seen it?"

"Not exactly. I was going to watch it with Max, but he said he'd already seen it." Heather went on to tell Brittany about the incident, leaving out the part about his laments over the demise of his love life.

"Max had a very despondent reaction to that movie. He told me it was sappy because it had an improbable happy ending. He said he didn't think there were any happy endings for him."

"Really?" Despite her unfavorable perception of Max from the past, Heather had a hard time believing that he had such a negative attitude, even when he'd been talking about his breakup with Brittany. "Although he's dealing with cancer, I haven't seen him that downhearted."

"I think it was that time in his life. It was right after his football injury. The pain meds could have had a part in his dejected tone."

Could Max's reluctance to talk to the Harkins have roots in doubts that his life could have a happy ending? His cancer diagnosis certainly had done nothing to make him think things were going well in his life. But he'd never expressed those doubts to her. Or had he, and she'd missed them or downplayed them because he was trying to put on a happy face for her? She considered talking to Brittany about the Harkins, but would that betray Max? Heather shook the negative thought away. She needed every insight to help him. "Since you know Max so well, I want to ask you something."

"I hope I can help. He was an important part of my life, and I still care what happens to him."

Heather nodded. "That's why I'm hoping you can give me some advice."

"So how can I help you?"

"A few weeks ago I talked with some folks who had also bid on the house we planned to use for the families of cancer patients. I met with them to tell them about our project and hoped they would withdraw their bid after they learned about it."

"Did they?"

"No, I never heard from them again, but it didn't matter because we got the funding we needed before the deadline."

"So what does this all have to do with Max?"

Heather took a deep breath. "Well, in the course of the meeting with Dana Mahoney, I met her brother Rob Harkin."

"Harkin." Brittany's eyes grew wide. "That's the last name of Max's biological father, right?"

"Yeah, and the same first name as the grandfather."

"Did you tell Max?"

"Yeah, but he didn't want to meet with them. Do you have any idea why?" Heather asked.

Brittany frowned. "Did he give you any reason?"

"He told me he didn't want to show up and announce that he might be related to them and chance their rejection."

"That sounds like Max." Brittany nodded. "You know everyone always thought he was this confident, outgoing and fun-loving guy in high school, but I learned over the years that he had a lot of insecurities."

"I've seen the insecure guy, especially right after his cancer diagnosis, but not so much lately until this episode. Do you think I should push him, or will he think I'm still interfering?"

"I wish I could be of more help. You've given him the information, so now I think you have to leave it up to him to act."

"I suppose you're right. Thanks for the input." Heather had wished for a different answer. This was one time when her instinct to intervene came on strong, but her friend was probably right. She should butt out. Max wouldn't appreciate her meddling.

Maybe her patience would pay off in the long run. She wanted to do whatever she could to help Max to see that there could be happy endings. She had no doubt that she wanted to be part of his happy ending.

***

Nearly three weeks had passed since the PMC and the visit from Brittany and Parker. Max had completed his chemotherapy, and he was ready to celebrate with Heather. During the week, he still drove her back and forth to work, to the grocery store and to the House for Families on workdays with the youth group. They spent weekends sharing a takeout meal or grabbing a bite to eat at a few of their favorite restaurants and participating in church activities.

Life was good.

Max breezed into the clinic, ready to hear the good news about his latest PET scan. He didn't see Heather and supposed that she was with a patient. He checked in, and within minutes a nurse escorted him to an exam room. He remembered the time he'd waited for Dr. Vargas to explain the test results. Today he had a much better feeling.

When Dr. Duffey walked into the room, all those positive thoughts evaporated. Even before Dr. Duffey shook Max's hand, the doctor's demeanor told Max that he wasn't going to like the results.

"Hi, Max." Dr. Duffey looked down at the chart he had in his hands. "I've got the results of your test here, and I'm afraid they aren't what I had hoped for."

"What does that mean?"

The doctor pulled up a chair and looked at Max. "After your first PET scan, I could see some shrinkage in the tumor—and not as much as I would've liked. Now this last scan shows none. I'm also seeing active cancer cells."

"So what happens now?" Max summoned all his energy to remain calm and not get up and pound his fist through the wall. Why did this happen to him? He thought he'd be through with the chemo and able to get on with his life—do all the things he wanted to do whenever he wanted to do them.

Dr. Duffey rubbed his chin. "I'm going to recommend four more chemo treatments, and in the meantime, I think we should look into a bone marrow transplant."

Bone marrow transplant. The words rattled around in Max's brain. What did that mean? "Are you saying I need one for sure?"

"Nothing is certain right now." The doctor gave Max a no-nonsense look. "I want you to be prepared for that eventuality. And by that, I mean you need to find a donor. You may not need one, but I want a donor in place if the extra rounds of chemo don't give us the results I'm looking for."

"How do I find a donor?"

"It's best to start with family members, but you can put out the word to all your friends. They'll have to be tested to see who's a good match." Dr. Duffey called in the nurse who'd been working with him since Heather had excused herself from his case.

After the doctor left, the nurse gave Max information on bone marrow transplants and scheduled his next chemo treatment. He tried to absorb everything she was telling him, but he couldn't wrap his mind around this bad news. What was he going to tell Heather? How was he going to tell his mom? He'd been so prepared to celebrate. Now there would be no celebration. Only more chemo.

Max stuffed the information the nurse had given him into his back pocket. He didn't want to read it now. He didn't even want to think about it, but it held his mind captive as he sat in the waiting area. He'd purposely made his appointment late in the day so he would be there to give Heather a ride home.

He glanced at his phone. She should be finished with work in ten minutes. What would she think when he told her the bad news?

Twenty minutes later, he still didn't know how he was going to tell her. When she came into the waiting area, her crutches clomping on the floor, Max's heart thudded.

She smiled at him and held up one hand. "You don't need to say it. I'm late."

Max shrugged. "I wasn't going to say a word. But now that you mention it, I think I'll put this on my calendar so when I'm not on time, I can hold this over your head. Ms. Punctuality was tardy on…"

"Yeah." Heather gave him a smile. "Are you ready to celebrate the end of your chemo?"

Max took a deep breath. "No celebration."

"What?"

"You heard what I said." Max motioned toward the door. "Let's get out of here, and I'll tell you what Dr. Duffey said."

"It's not good news?" Heather's eyes filled with worry.

"Let's wait to talk till we're back at my place. We can order pizza."

"Okay, if that's what you want."

Heather followed him to the parking lot and thankfully didn't press him for answers. After Max helped her into the car, he stowed her crutches in the backseat. As he started the drive home, he asked her to order the pizza so that it would be there when they arrived. When she was finished placing the order, he turned on the radio to keep conversation at a minimum.

They reached his place just as the pizza delivery pulled up in front of the house. He paid for the pizza, then set it on top of the car as he helped Heather with her crutches. Once inside, he got each of them a drink while Heather waited for him on the couch. He'd managed to delay this conversation, but the time had come to face his uncertain future with this woman he'd come to care so much about.

Worry still clouding her expression, she looked up at him as he handed her the glass of cola. "Okay. It's time to tell me what's going on."

Nodding, Max sat down beside her and opened the pizza box. He put a slice on a paper plate and gave it to her, then helped himself. He took a big bite and chewed slowly. Why couldn't he tell her what was happening? She was an oncology nurse. She would understand. But saying it out loud would make it true. He didn't want to believe it, acknowledge it, or even think about it.

"Max, please don't shut me out."

He swallowed hard. "I'm not trying to shut you out. The chemo didn't work. I have to have more."

Heather leaned closer and put a hand on his arm. "Tell me exactly what Dr. Duffey said."

Max blew out a harsh breath as he looked at the ceiling, then lowered his gaze to the floor. He couldn't bring himself to look at Heather while he recounted what the doctor had said. When he finished, he finally looked over at her.

Sadness had replaced her worry. "Oh, Max. I'm so sorry you didn't get better news. But Dr. Duffey has a plan, and it's a good one. You can beat this disease."

"Is this the nurse or the friend talking?"

"Both. I want to be here to help you through this. I'll be the first one to get tested to see if I can be a donor."

Max grabbed Heather's hand and pulled her to him and held her tight. "I don't want you to go through that for me."

Heather extracted herself from his embrace. "But I want to."

"Maybe the extra chemo treatments will work, and I won't even need the transplant."

"True, but Dr. Duffey wants you to be prepared for the worst-case scenario. You have to let your family know. They'll want to help, too." Heather took a deep breath. "And you should talk to Dana Mahoney and Rob Harkin. They could be family who might provide you a match."

Max gritted his teeth as he shook his head. "I'm not going to ask strangers. Asking people I know is bad enough."

Heather sighed. "They won't be strangers if you make the effort to meet them."

Max took another bite of pizza, refusing to argue with her. She was going to meddle in his life. He could feel it in his bones. As he swallowed his pizza, he stared at her. "Promise me you won't interfere."

She stared back, tears filling her eyes. "I can't make that promise. I love you too much, and I can't bear the thought of losing you."

"You love me?" How was that possible when he'd had all those mixed-up feelings about Brittany? "Are you sure you aren't saying that because I've got this terrible disease?"

"I don't know why or how, but I do love you. And I'm sorry if I've ruined things by telling you." The tears spilled over onto her cheeks, and she wiped them away with her hands.

"You didn't ruin anything. I can't believe it after the way I've been since...since forever. I love you, too." Max took her hands, still damp from the tears, and pulled her to him. He held her and drank in the wonder of being loved by this woman. "You've made this miserable day so much better."

"So are you going to contact Dana or Rob?" Heather whispered as he held her.

Max released her and held her at arm's length. "No. Family and friends, but no strangers. Please don't fight me on this."

"Why do you have to be so stubborn?"

"Isn't that one of the things you love about me?"

Heather frowned at him. "This is serious business."

"I know, but sometimes you have to joke to keep

things from falling apart."

"I know you don't want this disease to get you down, but you have to face the facts." Heather looped her arm through his as she snuggled closer. "You have to call your parents."

"Yeah." Max pulled his phone from his pocket and stared at it. Then he turned her way. "Will you help me answer their questions?"

Heather nodded. "Do you want to put the call on speaker so I can hear their questions?"

"Good idea. I'll let them know you're here." Max hoped that his mother wouldn't cry if she knew Heather was listening in on the conversation. He released a loud sigh. "Here goes nothing."

Even though Heather was on the call, his mother cried. Clay was the rock. Heather answered the medical questions and agreed to give Max's grandparents the same information.

When the call ended, Max tossed his phone on the coffee table, then laced his fingers behind his head as he stared off into space. He didn't have the energy anymore. He glanced at Heather. "I can't talk to my grandparents now. I can't deal with people worrying about me and fussing over me."

"Not even me?"

"Not even you." Max put an arm around her shoulders and pulled her close as he planted a kiss on her cheek. "Let's imagine that everything's good."

"You can't ignore reality."

"I don't want people feeling sorry for me or feeling

obligated to get tested." He shook his head. "I just want to be normal again."

"I know you do, but that doesn't mean you can pretend you aren't fighting a terrible disease." Heather sat forward and stared at him. "I'm not going to let you discount the need to talk to people about this. If you don't, I will."

Max only nodded. How had he managed to fall in love with a woman who liked to meddle in his life when he didn't want her to? If she loved him, wouldn't she let him do this in his own time and his own way? But he wasn't going to argue with Heather tonight. They would have to work this out one way or another.

***

In the six weeks that followed Max's bad news, he had four more chemo treatments. Heather prayed more than she'd ever prayed in her life that those treatments would bring the end to Max's cancer. During that time, dozens of family members and friends subjected themselves to testing. Even with all the people who were tested, none of the eligible folks were a good match.

When the additional chemo treatments yielded less than desired results, Dr. Duffey referred Max to a transplant specialist who started the procedure to find a donor for him. During this time, Heather tried again to talk to him about contacting Dana and Rob. Max refused to listen and became angry every time Heather brought up the subject. He made excuses not to see her, or anyone else, claiming he was too tired to socialize. His withdrawal worried her.

After he declined the invitation to the party to celebrate the removal of Heather's cast, she considered talking to his mom. In the end, Heather decided against it, fearing that such a conversation would worry Beth too much. Max didn't need that in addition to everything else he was dealing with. The thought of contacting Dana Mahoney kept crossing Heather's mind until she couldn't ignore it. She called and made an appointment with Dana.

The day of the appointment arrived, and Heather prayed as she drove down the road and took in the leaves displaying their fall colors. When she arrived at Renovations for You, she stared at her reflection in the window and prayed again that this meeting with Dana Mahoney would result in a positive outcome.

After Heather had given up trying to get Max to call this woman who might be related to him, she wondered why she'd fallen in love with such a stubborn man. Would this meeting with Dana alienate Max or unite him with the family he'd never known? At this point, Heather would rather lose his love than have him lose his life.

Straightening her shoulders, she opened the door and walked into the reception area. The receptionist immediately instructed Heather to go back to Dana's office. As Heather walked down the hall, Dana waited in the doorway.

She stepped forward and extended her hand. "Hello, Heather, I was surprised to see you on my appointment list today. How are things going with your House for Families?"

"They're going well. We should be ready to serve the families of cancer patients starting after the first of the year. Thank you for asking." Heather sat in a nearby chair and wondered about Dana's inquiry since she'd made no contact since their initial conversation.

Dana took a seat behind her desk. "How can I help you?"

Heather wished she had a better plan for starting the conversation, but honesty was her best approach. "I'm not sure exactly what to say here, but I have a friend who needs a bone marrow transplant."

"I'm so sorry to hear that, but what does that have to do with me?"

"My friend has been unable to find a compatible donor." Heather said a silent prayer before continuing. "And I believe you may be related to him and could be a potential donor."

Dana wrinkled her brow. "And how would I be related to this person?"

"I think you may be his aunt."

Dana let out a sound of disbelief as skepticism carved the expression on her face. "I know all my nieces and nephews."

Heather licked her lips. "Maybe you don't."

"Would you like to explain that statement?" Dana

leaned back in her chair, suspicion the cornerstone of her stare.

Heather reached into her purse and brought out the photo she'd taken of Max and Brittany back in Montana. Heather fingered the edges of the picture as she held it in her lap and formulated her response. "When you introduced me to Rob, I was struck by his resemblance to my friend Max. You see, he's been looking for the family of his birth father—"

"Are you accusing Rob of having a love child that the rest of us don't know about?" The question spewed from Dana's mouth.

Heather sat back and took a deep breath. Had she started this all wrong? "Not Rob. Scott. Scott Harkin. Did you have a brother named Scott who was killed in a motorcycle accident?"

Dana's complexion paled as she put a hand to her mouth. Unblinking, she stared straight ahead, not meeting Heather's gaze. Her eyes filled with wariness, Dana finally looked Heather's way. "How do you know about Scott, and why didn't you mention this when we met the first time?"

Not wanting to say the wrong thing, Heather didn't speak right away. "So Scott Harkin was your brother, and your family used to live near Cincinnati?"

Dana closed her eyes and lowered her head as she placed a hand to her forehead. She sat like that for a moment as if she was trying to gain control of her emotions. When she finally looked up, her eyes were shiny with unshed tears. She took a shaky breath.

"You didn't answer my question."

"I'm sorry." Heather grimaced. "I didn't feel it was my place to say anything when we met before. The last name and resemblance made me think you and Rob are Max's aunt and uncle. I wanted to talk to Max first before I said anything to you."

"If he's been looking for his family, why isn't he here instead of you?"

How could she answer Dana's question when she didn't know the answer herself? Max *should* be here pleading his own case, but he wasn't, so she would do it for him whether he liked it or not. "I can only guess. I think he's afraid of being wrong—that you aren't his family. He possibly fears your rejection. He didn't want to go to strangers with this request. He's most likely not happy that I'm doing this."

"So he doesn't know you're here?"

Heather nodded. "But I had to take the chance that you could help him."

"Doesn't he have other family who can help?"

"The only close relative who is an eligible donor is his mother, and she's not a good match. His maternal grandparents are too old, and his half brother and half sister are too young."

"How do you know that the Scott Harkin you're talking about was my brother?"

Wishing not to reveal more than she had to, Heather recounted enough of Allen and Sara's story about Beth and Scott so hopefully Dana would believe that Max was her nephew. When Heather finished, she pushed the photo across the desk. "This is a picture of Max that I took several years ago. I wish you'd show it to your family. I hope you'll decide to meet him."

Dana picked up the photo as if it might burn her. She let out a little gasp, then placed a hand over her heart. "I'm not sure what to say. This could be a picture of Scott."

"Does that mean you believe Max could be your nephew?" Heather held her breath as she waited for Dana's response.

"I'm not sure what to think." Dana held up the photo. "You want me to show this to my family?"

"Absolutely."

"Thanks." Dana picked up her purse and placed the picture in the side pocket. "I'll call you after I talk with them."

Heather figured this signaled the end of their conversation. She hoped the promised call would come, unlike that one that hadn't materialized after their discussion about the house. She stood and shook Dana's hand. "Thanks for seeing me and considering my request."

Dana walked Heather to the door. "I don't know what to say. This has been a bit of a shock, and I'm still trying to digest it all."

"I understand. I only want to help Max, so I'll be waiting for that call."

During the drive back to Oakton, Heather replayed Dana's reaction in her mind. Dana clearly thought Max looked like Scott, but what would the other members of the Harkin family think? Would they be willing to accept Max? If they did, would he be brave enough to meet them and accept their help? So many questions and no answers.

Heather worried that she may have done the wrong thing, but she had to accept the consequences of her actions. Good or bad.

CHAPTER EIGHTEEN

A full moon danced in and out of the clouds as Heather made her way across the street. She pulled her jacket closer to ward off the nip in the air or maybe the chill she might expect from this meeting with Max. Dana had called and said her family wanted to meet him. That should be good news, but what would he think? Afraid of his reaction, Heather hadn't told him about her meeting with Dana. Heather didn't want to mention something that might bring no results.

Heather hesitated on the front porch. "Lord, please let Max accept this invitation." With the prayer still on her lips, she rang the bell.

Max smiled as he opened the door. "I ordered Chinese."

"Okay." Heather was happy to see the smile that had been missing for the past few weeks. "I'm glad you're feeling better tonight."

"Only because you're here."

Heather hoped he would feel the same way after she talked to him. Maybe they should eat first even though she wasn't that hungry because her stomach was tied in knots. But it was a good sign that he'd put aside his hermit ways at least for tonight.

"I hope you don't mind eating here." Max motioned to the couch and the parade of little cardboard cartons sitting on the coffee table.

"Works for me." Heather made herself comfortable.

After she sat, Max said a quick prayer of thanksgiving for the food, then handed her a plate. They helped themselves to the almond chicken and beef with broccoli. They ate in silence for several minutes while Heather continued to pray.

Max set down his plate and leaned back on the couch. "I know I've been stubborn and unpleasant to be around. The extra chemo did nothing but make me feel lousy."

"I won't argue with you there, and I'm sorry about the bad results. Do you have any news on the transplant front?"

Max shook his head. "But my mother is going to drive me crazy."

Heather stared at Max. "Why?"

"She has already rented a temporary place for me to stay after I have the transplant. She plans to stay with me for the month of recovery."

"That's not so bad. Why are you so reluctant to let other people help you?"

Max sat there silently brooding. A muscle worked in his jaw as he stared at her. "Do you have any idea how it feels to have someone always asking you how you feel? Or how it feels to be tired, tired, tired? Will

I ever get my old life back?"

"The one without me?" Heather hoped that question would bring a little levity to the situation. She didn't know how to deal with Max anymore. If she was honest, had she ever? When she finally told him about the Harkins, would he wish her out of his life?

A reluctant smile escaped. "Are you trying to put me on the spot?"

"No. Trying to gauge where I stand with you."

"Do you have to ask?"

"Yeah, sometimes, especially when you keep everything to yourself." Heather raised her eyebrows.

Max slid closer on the couch and pulled Heather closer, kissed her, then held her while he whispered in her ear. "I wish I could be better at relationships. You knew I was a bad bet going into this."

Heather extracted herself from his embrace. "What's happening with you and me isn't the same as what happened with Brittany. I love you, and that's all there is to know."

"And I love you, but I can't bring much to this relationship. I feel like half a man."

"You'll get through this."

"I wish I had your faith."

"I brought you something to make you feel better." Heather reached into her purse and plucked out a blue-and-gray stocking cap. "I finally got this made in time for cooler weather."

Max laughed and shoved the cap onto his head.

"Thanks. This is perfect."

"Glad you like it. I've also got something else I want to tell you." Heather took a deep breath and let it out slowly. "Please don't be angry with me."

Max eyed her. "What have you done now?"

"I went to see Dana Mahoney. Her family wants to meet you."

Max got up from the couch and turned his back to Heather, his shoulders stiff. "And you expect me not to be angry?"

"Yes. Maybe one of them will be a perfect match for the transplant."

Max turned, his eyes sparking with anger. "What right did you have to—"

"To do something you're afraid to do?"

Max pounded a fist against his chest. "This is my life. My disease. And I'll handle it the way I want."

Heather closed her eyes to hold back the tears. When she finally had control of her emotions, she opened her eyes. "Why, Max? Why won't you let me or anyone else help you?"

"You didn't ask me. You just went ahead and—"

"You refused to listen. You cut me off every time I brought it up. So don't say I didn't ask."

His eyes narrow slits, Max worked that muscle in his jaw. "What did you tell them?"

"Do you really want to know?"

"Yeah." Max returned to the couch, a contrite expression replacing his earlier anger.

Heather said a silent prayer that Max would listen

with an open mind. Then she described her meeting with Dana and their subsequent phone conversation. After Heather finished, she waited for Max's response, but he sat there, still brooding. "So what do you think?"

Max leaned back on the couch and laced his fingers behind his head as he stared straight ahead. "I think you interfere where you're not wanted."

"So you're going to ignore their invitation?"

"I didn't say that." He turned to look at her. "I said…you butt in where you aren't wanted."

"You still didn't answer my question. Will you meet with them?"

Max let out a harsh breath. "So they can look me over and see if I'm part of the family?"

"What have you got to lose?"

"My dignity." He got up from the couch and started pacing. "Of course, I might as well face it. I've already lost that. Cancer will do that to you."

Heather stared at him, her hands in a prayer-like position in front of her mouth. Even though she'd worked with cancer patients for a good number of years, she'd never been this close to someone with the disease. She'd never seen the day-to-day toll it took. But she wasn't sure all cancer patients acted the way Max did—like a turtle pulling into its shell. Could she accept his decision, whatever it was? "So what are you going to do?"

"I'm not happy about the way you try to orchestrate my life, but I'll go as long as you go with me."

"You can count on me." She put her arms around him and held him close. The emotions she'd been holding in came rushing out as tears overflowed onto her cheeks. She blubbered into his chest. "They'll love you."

Max tightened his arms around her. "I hope so."

Pulling away, Heather smiled through her tears. "You won't regret this. I promise."

Max reached over and wiped away her tears with his thumb. "You're brave to say that."

"Not brave, just confident that God will see you through this." Heather took his hands in hers. "I've been praying a lot about this."

"I should too." He squeezed her hands.

"Let's do that together now."

Max nodded and bowed his head. They took turns praying, and Heather said a silent prayer of thanks that he was willing to put himself out there. She didn't always understand him and couldn't figure out why he would even think about turning down the opportunity to meet the people who might be the family he'd been searching for. But she knew one thing for certain. She loved him.

***

Lights blazed from nearly every window in the massive cedar-sided house on a quiet street in Concord. Max stepped out of Heather's car and shoved his hands into his black leather jacket. Heather had assured him that this dinner was casual, but there was nothing casual looking about this house. It said money all the way from its circular drive made of pavers to the well-manicured lawn and shrubs. What was he going to say to these people who might be family? He prayed that Heather would take the lead.

As he rang the bell, she squeezed his hand and looked up at him. "Smile. They're not going to bite."

"Are you sure?" Max gave her a quick kiss on the cheek. "I think my smile muscles are too nervous to cooperate. I wish they were meeting the real me, not the cancer me."

"You're you no matter what." Heather slipped her arm through his. "It won't be nearly as bad as you're imagining. They're nice people."

Her presence warmed his heart, but it didn't take away his nerves. "Yeah, but you've only met two of them."

"True, but you should look on the positive side of things."

"Am I guilty of doing the opposite?"

"Sometimes." Heather turned her attention to the door as it opened.

Max held his breath as a woman with shoulder-length dark hair greeted Heather, who stepped aside and looked his way. "Dana, I'd like you to meet Max Reynolds."

"Nice to meet you, Dana." Shaking her hand, he wondered whether this woman was his aunt. He managed to produce a smile. What should he say now? Everything he thought of sounded terribly lame.

"Come on in, and I'll introduce you to the rest of the family." Dana waved her hand in the direction of the living room to her right.

Did she mean his family? Was she accepting him as Scott's son and her nephew, or was she only referring to her family? He took a deep breath and cautioned himself to take everything in stride. He had to accept whatever the outcome of this meeting brought. He'd been learning to do that through this whole cancer thing. Sometimes, he was dragged kicking and screaming into reality, but eventually he got there. He glanced over at Heather. She was a big part of how he'd managed, but he still feared this disease would tear them apart.

As they stood in the arched entrance that led into the room, a tall man with hair the same color as Dana's, except the hint of gray at his temples, moved toward them. He extended his hand. "You must be Max. I'm Rob Harkin. Glad you've joined us."

"Thanks." Once again forcing a smile, Max wondered if anyone thought this whole situation was awkward besides him.

As he stood there feeling like a specimen under one of his microscopes, an older man with a trim physique and thick silver-gray hair inserted himself into the conversation. "So you're the young man who claims to be my grandson."

How should he respond to that? Max looked the

man right in the eye. "Yes, sir."

"That remains to be seen, but I like your forthrightness. I'm Robert Harkin." He turned to the woman with the short dark hair. "This is my wife, Nancy."

"Nice to meet you, ma'am." Max tried not to let the older man's intimidation work as he shook hands with Nancy.

Dana stepped forward, an embarrassed smile hovering at the corners of her mouth. "Let me introduce you to everyone else."

"Sure." Max followed. Was he going to meet his cousins? Was everyone reserving judgment like the man who might be his grandfather? Did he want to be related to these people? Why had he agreed to this meeting?

Dana made quick work of introducing him to her husband, Gareth, and their teenage daughters, Ava and Ailene. Then he met Rob's family—his wife, Cindy, and their two college-age sons, Patrick and Ryan, and their daughter, Cara. Finally, Dana turned to her younger sister, Erin, her husband, Jared, and their two children, Jack and Brianna. Max wondered whether he'd be expected to remember all these people.

After a rather stilted few minutes of conversation, the group moved into the huge dining room dominated by a table that was able to accommodate the entire Harkin clan plus their two visitors. Max had never seen anything like it. The Harkins appeared to be a wealthy family. Was Robert Harkin concerned that

Max was after money? He tried not to worry about what the older man was thinking while they ate the four-course meal served by two uniformed servers.

Max listened to the voices swirling around him without contributing to the discussion until the talk turned to football. The young men were all impressed that he had played college football, even though it was for a small school. The whole evening got a little bit better.

He glanced over at Heather, and she smiled at him because she knew he was finally in his element. She'd been talking with the women. He wasn't sure what they'd been discussing, but he hoped she wasn't pushing him on these people. No one had said anything about his conceivable relationship to them since Robert Harkin's opening salvo.

Max wasn't sure what he wanted to happen here. If these people didn't want anything to do with him, he didn't want to make them feel obligated to accept him or help him find a bone marrow donor.

When the evening came to an end, Max and Heather thanked Robert and Nancy for the meal and bid them good-night. Max didn't want to be angry with Heather for putting him through the awkward evening, but he couldn't suppress the irritation. What had it accomplished? Nothing that he could see.

As they reached the car, Dana called after them. "Wait."

Max turned. Now what? He tamped down his unhappiness. "Did we forget something?"

Catching her breath, Dana came to a stop in front of him. "I want to apologize for my dad."

Max wanted to tell her that the man should apologize himself, but that wouldn't be a gracious response. "No need to apologize."

"Yes, there is. He was rude to you." Dana looked up with a rueful expression. "Will you give me a minute to explain?"

"Let me put on my stocking cap." Max opened the car and grabbed the knit cap lying on the seat, then slapped it on his head.

"Sorry about keeping you out here in the cold, but I can't talk to you around my dad."

Max tried to keep the irritation out of his voice. "So what do you want to tell me?"

"Please listen to what I have to say about the man who is most likely your grandfather."

"And why are you convinced of that, when he isn't?" Max asked.

"Besides the photo, I watched you tonight, and I see the little expressions and mannerisms that are so much like the men in our family."

"Like what?"

"I can't exactly explain them. I just knew when I saw them." Dana sighed. "Dad is reluctant to believe it because he is suspicious that you're out to get money."

"What would give him that idea?"

"You weren't supposed to know, but our family foundation supplied the rest of the money for the

House for Families—"

"You did?" Heather blurted.

Dana nodded as she looked over at Heather. "We all agreed after talking to you that it was something we should do, but we wanted it to be anonymous."

Max frowned. "So why are you telling us now?"

"Because I wanted you to understand why my dad's skeptical about your connection to this family. He thinks you somehow discovered the source of the money and want more."

"That's ridiculous." Max shook his head. "What would give him that idea?"

"You have to understand that over the years people have tried to use my father to get to his money. That has made him distrustful."

"So are you saying, despite your father's skepticism, that you believe I'm your nephew?"

Dana nodded. "I've got something for you."

"What?"

"After Mom saw your photo, she was convinced that you're Scott's son." Dana held out an envelope. "We found Scott's baby book and retrieved a couple of his baby teeth from it. I put those and some hair samples from our parents in this. You should have enough here to have a DNA test to determine your relationship to us."

Max stared at the envelope. Was it a key to his past? "Thanks. I don't know what to say."

"Find out the truth and let us know." Dana laid a hand on Max's arm. "Even though Scott's death brought a lot of pain to this family, it also brought us closer to God. Heather explained your circumstances, and we want to help. All of us who are eligible donors are going to be tested to see if one of us can help you."

A lump rose in Max's throat, and he couldn't speak. His emotions had taken a roller coaster ride tonight. How would Robert Harkin react when he held proof positive that he had another grandson? Max swallowed hard. "Thanks for everything. I'll let you know what I discover."

"I'm pretty sure I already know the results." Dana smiled up at him. "Good night."

While Heather drove home, Max let everything that had happened during the evening soak into his brain and his soul. He was still trying to process the event. Thankfully, Heather wasn't peppering him with questions.

What would his mom say when he told her? Her DNA wasn't needed, but it would help. She hadn't been happy about his search. Would she welcome the outcome?

"Care to share your thoughts?" Heather's question made him look her way.

"Wondering what my mom will think."

"I'm wondering what you think about all this."

"I suppose you want to say 'I told you so.'"

She shook her head. "Not really. I'm glad you'll know for sure about your father's family."

"Me, too, but I'm still worried about how my

parents will deal with this information."

"They'll be thrilled if one of the Harkins can be your donor."

"Do you think Mr. Harkin will think I'm using them—not their money, but their bone marrow?"

"So you're worried about what Dana said about him?"

"Yeah, after his initial rather stern greeting, he didn't say much to me the whole evening. Everyone else was friendly and accepting." Max let out a heavy sigh. "I'm not sure he'll acknowledge me as his grandson even after he sees the results of the test."

"You can't let him ruin everything that you will gain."

"But he seems rather intimidating and could make the rest of the family stay away, too."

"He didn't intimidate Dana."

"You're right, but that doesn't mean he still couldn't do it."

"Why not look on the bright side instead of the negative?"

"I should." Max made the statement as much to himself as to Heather, but the negative often overruled the positive. She'd told him as much earlier tonight. Too many times he'd planned for the best and ended up with the worst. Would he reach out to these people and have them reject him in the end? Did he dare hope for a positive outcome? His life was so uncertain—too uncertain to ask Heather to stay with him. She deserved a healthy man, not one whose life was completely complicated.

***

While Max trudged up the stairs to Heather's apartment, he hoped he could make this meeting as painless as possible. She'd been there for the good and bad news. The DNA test had confirmed that Scott Harkin was his biological father. His newfound family had accepted him with open arms, all except his grandfather, who still remained somewhat reluctant to receive a new grandson. Patrick Mahoney, Rob's oldest son, was an excellent match with Max and had agreed to be a donor. But the most surprising element of the last few days was the way the Harkins and his mom had connected.

Dana had assured him that her dad would eventually come around, but Max had his doubts after accidentally hearing an argument between his grandparents. He'd been on his way to the bathroom at Dana's house when he'd overheard them.

"You can't deny the DNA test is ninety-nine percent certain that Max is our grandson. Why can't you accept that?" His grandmother's voice was firm, yet controlled.

"He works in a lab. He could've altered it."

"That's silly. Max looks exactly like Scott." His grandmother's voice raised a pitch.

"I know. Every time I look at him, I think of the way I failed Scott."

"You can't undo the past, but you can move forward and give this young man your support. He needs that."

"I'm not sure I can do that." Robert's voice dripped with worry. "What if this treatment doesn't work? If I get too close, it will be like losing Scott all over again."

"Is that what's worrying you?"

Max didn't hear Robert's response, only Nancy's reply. "We have to pray for Max."

The conversation was still stuck in his mind. He knew he should be grateful that he'd found the family he'd been searching for, but his grandfather's attitude reflected some of what Max was feeling. He'd prayed, but he still had cancer. Whenever he thought about praying, the only thing in his mind was a question. *Why me, God?*

All the final tests and preparation for the transplant were underway, including the talk with the transplant team and his parents. Chaos and uncertainty would claim him for a year or more. That didn't even take into account the possible short- and long-term side effects—damage to the thyroid gland, cataracts, damage to the lungs, bone damage, or development of another cancer years later. After his unsuccessful chemotherapy, he feared the worst.

Heather had made an accurate assessment when she'd pointed out his negativity. She deserved someone with a better physical and emotional outlook, not a pessimist like him. Besides the health issues, he would be dealing with debt that would take years to pay off. The kindest thing he could do was let her go. As much as it might hurt both of them right now, it was the best thing for the future.

He remembered how much he'd worried over Heather's broken leg and how it seemed to crush his heart when he thought she was in a life-threatening situation. Now he faced a trauma of his own. He had no guarantees that the transplant would work. He couldn't make her deal with that kind of uncertainty.

He had weeks of recuperation in isolation. That would give them a clean break. The thought of telling her squashed his heart, but this was the way things had to be.

He rang the bell and hoped he could get through this. Still wearing her work uniform, Heather opened the door and greeted him with a kiss. Max knew that would be the last. He had to make the separation permanent.

"Did your parents get settled in that apartment?" She sat on the couch and looked up at him.

"Yeah."

"That's good." She frowned when he didn't make a move to join her on the couch. "Come sit down."

Max shook his head. "I'm not staying long."

Heather's brow knit in a frown. "Is something wrong?"

"I suppose you could say that." This was it. Max took a deep breath, but he couldn't get the words out.

"What do you mean?"

He couldn't chicken out now. "I don't think we should see each other anymore."

She sat there for a moment with her mouth open, then shook her head. "Why? Are you angry with me for meddling in your life?"

"No. I don't want you to go through this uncertainty for more than a year. Just understand."

"Well, I don't understand. I love you, and I'll deal with whatever life hands you."

"That's what you say now, but my experience has shown me that people change their minds. We'll both be happier if we end this now." He held up his hands as Heather tried to approach him. "I'm not changing my mind."

"Please don't do this." Tears welled in her eyes. "I know you're scared, but—"

"You don't know what I'm feeling. Don't pretend that you do." He walked to the door and put his hand on the knob. "I'm sorry things have to end this way, but you'll thank me later."

"No, I won't." Her words came out in a sob.

His heart breaking, he opened the door and fled down the stairs. He couldn't bear to see her cry, knowing he had caused her tears. She would eventually get over this, and so would he. He didn't know what lay ahead, but he didn't want to drag her through it with him.

CHAPTER NINETEEN

The beauty of a snowy Montana landscape and the decorations on the twelve-foot Christmas tree sitting in front of the massive window did nothing to cheer Heather's heart. Even Christmas with her family didn't ease the pain of breaking up with Max. She'd hoped escaping to Montana for a week would put distance between her and her heartache. She should have known better.

Her folks, siblings, aunts, uncles, and cousins had all gathered at Parker and Brittany's home to celebrate the holiday. Brittany had asked about Max, but Heather had only mentioned his marvelous recovery progress. Talking about the end of her relationship with Max was too upsetting. She only wanted to forget, but she couldn't.

"Hey." Brittany joined Heather as the full moon illuminated the nearby mountain range. "You ready to talk about you and Max yet?"

"I don't know. I feel like such an idiot because I fell for the guy I advised you to break up with. Now he's dumped me, and I'm an emotional mess."

"That's why you need to talk to me." Brittany motioned toward the empty den. "Everyone else is downstairs watching a movie, and the baby's sleeping soundly. This is a perfect time to talk. We'll have some hot chocolate and conversation."

Heather looked at her friend, who glowed with happiness, despite being a little sleep-deprived. Joseph Parker Watson had made his appearance just days before Thanksgiving. Even the newborn's name reminded Heather of Max. She'd become an oncology nurse because her Grandpa Joe had died from cancer. Now he had a new namesake in Brittany and Parker's son. "You sure you want to listen to me whine?"

Brittany chuckled. "I'd say it's time that I gave you some advice."

"Probably." Heather sighed. "So what do you think?"

Brittany made some hot chocolate in the microwave, then led the way into the den and flicked the switch that turned on the gas fireplace. Flames bobbed and weaved behind the glass screen as Heather found a seat on the tan sofa, mug in hand.

Brittany sat beside her. "First, tell me what's happening with Max."

"What do you know?"

"My mom's passed along some information because she's friends with Beth. So I know he found his birth father's family and a cousin was the donor for the transplant."

"Yeah. They probably think I'm a terrible person because I've never been to visit him."

Brittany shook her head. "But that's what he

wanted, right?"

"That's what he told me." Heather nodded, hoping she wouldn't cry. "He never once hinted that he was thinking about kicking me out of his life until he sprang it on me two days before the transplant at the end of October. He was in isolation in the hospital for about three weeks. Now he has limited visitation while he lives in the apartment his parents rented near the transplant unit where they monitor his progress."

"My mom said Beth took a leave of absence from her teaching job to take care of Max."

Nodding, Heather thought about the heartrending conversation she'd had with Beth right after Max left the hospital. "I wanted to help her, but he told Beth he didn't want to see me. I wanted to march over there and tell him he couldn't continue to push me away."

"Why didn't you?"

Heather took a sip of her hot chocolate. She wasn't sure she knew the answer. Had she been afraid of further rejection? "I let Beth convince me that I should wait until Max had made steady progress in his recovery. She didn't want my presence to upset him."

"She actually said that to you?"

"Not in those exact words." Heather sighed. "I read between the lines."

Brittany eyed Heather. "Beth's always been very protective of Max—like a mama bear protecting her cub."

Heather smiled at the image. She'd thought the same thing when she first met Beth. "Yeah, but my own fears kept me from acting. I know from my experience with patients like Max that a transplant can take an emotional toll on everyone involved. He had the support he needed, and my interference wasn't going to help him."

"So where do things stand now?" Brittany asked, her eyebrows raised.

"Since things are going well for him, I want to tell him that I still love him."

"Do you have a plan?"

Heather shook her head. "I'm afraid if I go over there, he'll refuse to see me."

"Yeah, he's stubborn that way." Brittany smiled wryly. "He wouldn't appreciate having you tell him he was wrong."

"So where does that leave me?"

"Do you still talk to Amanda?" Brittany took a long drink from her mug.

"I haven't lately." Heather grimaced. "She's probably seen Max while I haven't."

"Maybe Amanda can help you."

"You mean I should go with her to visit, and he wouldn't be able to ignore me?" Heather wasn't sure that was such a good idea. "If he really doesn't want me around, I can't force myself on him."

Brittany looked at Heather over the top of the mug. "That doesn't sound like the Heather I've always known. You go after what you want."

Heather set her mug on the coffee table and crossed her arms. "Yeah, but I don't know how to change Max's mind."

"Doesn't he have some kind of milestone coming up soon?"

"Yeah. It'll be one hundred days since the transplant on February eighth."

"Right around Valentine's Day. Perfect." Brittany grinned.

Narrowing her gaze, Heather shook her head. "Not from where I'm sitting."

"Why not?" Brittany shifted in her seat.

"That'll make it even worse if I try to barge in where I'm not wanted." Heather let out a harsh breath.

"Max has always been a glass half-empty kind of guy, but you've always been an optimist. Has he rubbed off on you?"

"No." Or had he? Heather looked at the flames licking at the glass in the fireplace. When it came to Max, nothing was clear. "Maybe. I don't know, but I do know the emotional impact of a transplant on the patient. I don't want to do anything to add to Max's burden."

"Then talk to Amanda, and see if she knows his state of mind. Maybe the two of you can plan something with his family."

"You mean with Beth and Clay?"

"Yeah, and the Harkins. Make it a celebration of his one-hundred-day anniversary as well as Valentine's Day. With all those other people around, he's not going to make you leave." Brittany grinned again. "And you have six weeks to plan the best celebration ever."

Heather leaned over and hugged Brittany. "Thanks for being such a good friend."

Brittany sat back, a smile curving her mouth. "It's my privilege to be your friend. Do you see how God has led us to be in the right place at the right time?"

"Thanks for that reminder, too." Heather hugged Brittany again. "Max and I didn't wind up in Massachusetts at the same time for nothing. He's going to know that I won't give up on our relationship."

"Now that's the Heather Watson I know." Brittany squeezed Heather's arm. "I'm going to be praying about this. In fact, let's pray about it now."

Heather nodded as Brittany held out her hands, and Heather grasped them. While Brittany prayed for Max's complete recovery and a smooth transition back to his normal life, peace enveloped Heather's heart. She wouldn't shrink from helping Max find a renewal of spirit and their love right along with the healing of his body. She prayed for wisdom to make the right choices, and she was confident that God would be with her all the way.

***

Max stared at himself in the mirror. For weeks he'd very seldom looked in a mirror because he knew he wouldn't like what he saw. Now he had hair, and he could comb it. It was several shades lighter, but it was there. That was a good thing. He almost looked normal. His face was still thin but better than the puffy one he'd had during the first couple of weeks after the transplant. He actually had to shave. He was beginning to feel like a man again instead of a pincushion.

During the transplant and time in the hospital, he'd withdrawn from everyone emotionally. Talking and interacting with people required too much energy— energy he didn't have then. Talking on the phone and reading email or a book took too much out of him. He felt as though he was walking through a long, long tunnel, and it was an effort to put one foot in front of the other. Some days, the only thing that helped him to cope was his mother's presence. He would never again think of her as trying to interfere in his life. She'd given up so much for him, and he could never repay her.

He'd come a long way from what the transplant team called the "basement period" when his white blood cell counts were so low that the medical team couldn't detect them. During that four-day period in the hospital, he'd been weak, tired, and sometimes nauseated. Even the smallest tasks, like eating or taking a shower, took a major effort and required a lot of rest immediately after. He'd dealt with the mouth sores, bloating, intestinal problems and loss of appetite because everything tasted like cardboard. He was finally getting his taste buds back, but he still had to be careful to eat small quantities and do it slowly.

The threat of infection made him wary about having visitors, but his mom screened them, as well as the nurses at the hospital. The transplant process and recovery was a strange combination of having someone constantly monitoring his existence while at the same time keeping him from having the everyday interactions he'd become used to. Now that he'd passed one hundred days since the transplant, his life was looking more normal again. Once he started to feel better, he realized the isolation had taught him that he actually liked being around other people rather than the solitary life he thought he preferred.

Best of all, he hadn't suffered with the graft-versus-host disease that many transplant patients had. He thanked God every day that his body had accepted the transplanted cells, not without difficulty but in a much better way than many. Sometimes he wanted to run down the street with his hands in the air as he shouted praise to the Lord. He couldn't do that now because he couldn't overexert himself, but someday he would do just that. With each passing day, he got stronger, and the fears he'd experienced about the whole process were gradually receding.

But mostly he missed Heather. His life didn't feel normal without her. He missed her more than he'd ever imagined. Could he undo the boneheaded move he'd made when he'd broken up with her?

Had he done it again—sabotaged his love life? Was there any chance that he could mend his relationship with Heather? Could she forgive him?

The questions crashed through his mind as he turned from the mirror and looked out the apartment window to the snow-covered streets below.

His mom would be returning soon from the airport where she was picking up her parents, Clay, Abby, and Alex. He'd seen them briefly at Christmas, but the visit had been strange because his mom had served as the germ gestapo. She made sure everyone constantly washed hands and took off shoes when entering the apartment. Everyone was on pins and needles, afraid he would get some kind of germ or infection. He'd almost been glad when the holiday was over.

This visit promised to be much better. He would make one of his infrequent ventures into the world outside of this apartment. He'd been looking forward to his hundred-day anniversary since his mom had told him about the plans for the party right after the beginning of the year. This was going to be his New Year's, Valentine's, and hundred-day anniversary celebration all rolled into one. All the people he cared about were going to be there.

Everyone except Heather.

He should have called her, but he was a coward. He couldn't forget how she'd once told her friend to dump him. Then he'd rejected her love. What reason did she have for giving him a second chance?

His phone sat on the nearby end table. He picked it up and stared at it. Heather's number was on speed dial. He could call her with one swift motion. Taking a deep breath, he punched the *H* at the top of the screen. His heart pounded as he put the phone to his ear.

Ring. Ring. Ring. Voice mail. Should he leave a message? Silly question. She would know he called.

"Hey, Heather. This is Max. I know you might be surprised to hear from me. I'm asking you to consider coming to my hundred-day anniversary party at my grandparents' house tomorrow. I know this is short notice, but I hope you can make it. You have the address." Max swallowed hard. "I've missed you. I...I hope to see you there."

Releasing a harsh breath, Max ended the call. He'd almost said he loved her. That was the truth, but that was something he should tell her when they were face to face, not over the phone. He didn't deserve her love, but he somehow hoped he could win her back.

Before he could return his phone to the table, the door burst open. Abby and Alex raced into the room, but they stopped short in front of him.

Abby tilted her head as she looked up at him, her eyes wide. "We forgot to take off our shoes and wash our hands."

Max laughed as he looked over their heads to where his mother stood in the doorway. "Yeah, you'd better do that before the germ police get you."

His mom tried to hide a smile behind her frown. "You'll say thank you some day."

"I already do." Max plopped onto the couch. "I'll sit here until you decontaminate everyone."

Abby scrunched up her little face. "What's

decontamit?"

"Decontaminate. Listen to what Mom says, and you'll be fine."

Within minutes, Abby and Alex were deemed safe to interact with Max. He gave each of them a big hug. When his parents and grandparents returned from putting away the suitcases, Max hugged them, too. He would never take hugs for granted again.

Clay stepped back. "You look a good bit better than the last time I saw you."

Max smiled. "I feel a lot better, too."

"Are you ready for the big party?" Clay asked.

"I can hardly wait." Max knew Heather's presence there would make it the best party ever. Could he hope she would show? He would definitely put hugging Heather at the top of his list. He hoped that wasn't an impossible wish.

***

The snowy yard sparkled under the moonlight as Max approached his grandparents' house. He remembered his first visit here and how Heather had held his hand and told him everything would be all right. She'd been his lifeline, and he'd severed it. If he could only go back and redo everything, but he couldn't. He prayed she would be here so he could begin to make things right.

When the door swung open, greetings and cheers filled the air. He stepped inside, and everyone moved aside to let Max pass. He glanced around at the smiling faces of his grandparents, aunts, uncles, cousins, and friends. "Thanks, everyone. I know you're used to my mom greeting you with her Dustbuster and alcohol swabs, but I'm ready for handshakes and hugs."

"Not to worry. Grandma Harkin already swabbed us down." Patrick grabbed Max in a big bear hug. "You're lookin' good. Must be those fabulous Patrick cells you're sporting."

A collective chuckle rolled through the room as Max nodded and hugged his cousin back. "I've said it before, but I'll say it again. I can't thank you enough for being my donor."

Patrick gave Max a lopsided grin. "I was happy to do it."

Max greeted more people as he fought back overpowering emotions. He'd climbed the mountain, and now he was on the easier downhill journey. These folks were here to help him reach the finish line, but there was one person missing.

Heather.

Had he been a fool to think she would come? Her absence was his fault. He'd chased her away, then waited too late to issue the invitation. He reminded himself that tonight was a night for celebration, not recrimination. He had a lot to be thankful for and a lot of people to be happy with, even if Heather wasn't here.

Max marveled at the number of people who had

come to celebrate this milestone with him. Many had been praying for him, and that meant a lot. He found his way over to Grandpa Harkin, who'd made peace with having an additional grandson. Max was thankful for two sets of grandparents who had found common ground in the Lord.

"Hey, Grandpa Harkin. Thanks for the party." Max hugged the older man.

"We're so excited to do this, and we've got a little entertainment to start out the evening." Robert put an arm around Max's shoulders, then motioned to everyone in the room. "Please find a seat. The youngsters can sit on the floor."

As folks found seats in the room filled with a tan sofa and several beige chairs, Max craned his neck to see what was happening. His heart thudded against his ribs when Heather walked into the room with Amanda, Cara, and Ava. Amanda and Cara carried guitars. He couldn't take his eyes off Heather. She didn't look his way, but at least she was here.

Amanda stepped to the front of the group. "We're all glad you've come to celebrate with Max." She glanced at the others, then back at the crowd. "Our little group of musicians has been practicing for a few weeks so we could entertain him on his big day."

Applause filled the room as the girls took their places. His uncle Rob pushed a big plush chair to the center of the room. "Your chair, Max."

While he made himself comfortable, the quartet hummed a few bars and then sang several silly songs that had the crowd laughing and applauding. He listened to the performance and wondered whether Heather had planned to come to the party all along, even before his invitation. He had to find time to talk to her tonight.

After they finished singing, Robert came to the front of the room. "Thanks, ladies. Now we've got a great buffet in the dining room for you to enjoy. I just want to say a few words before we eat." He looked over at Max. "Max, I'm glad you're a part of our family. I know I've already told you, but I wanted to tell you one more time. And we thank God that you've made such good progress."

Max stood and hugged his grandfather again. "Thanks, Grandpa. I'm glad to be part of this family, too, and I appreciate everyone's prayers."

Max knew his grandfather's words weren't just empty platitudes. Robert and Nancy had stayed in their Massachusetts home during the winter rather than escaping the cold by going to their second home in Florida. They'd wanted to be there for Max and Patrick during the transplant procedure and the days following.

Robert smiled. "Let's give thanks for this food and for Max's recovery."

The folks in the room bowed their heads, and Robert prayed. Max let the words of the prayer weave their way into his mind and heart. He had so much to be thankful for. God had showed him what it meant to trust in Him through a difficult time, and He had put a lot of wonderful people in his path along the hard journey. Max realized he could face anything as long as he put his trust in God.

When the prayer ended, Max searched the room for Heather. She stood near the fireplace as she talked with his cousin Cara. Amanda had said they had practiced for weeks. He had to talk to Heather.

While most of the guests made their way toward the buffet line, Max maneuvered his way across the room toward her. His heart was in his throat, and he wasn't sure what he would say. She looked his way, and a smile spread across her face. He swallowed hard as she drew nearer.

Max took a deep breath, hoping to calm his nerves. "Hi, I'm glad you came. Thanks for the songs."

"I wouldn't have missed this, even if you hadn't called."

There was so much he wanted to say to her, but how could he do it in a crowded room? She seemed friendly but guarded. What could he expect after their last conversation? "Sorry I didn't call sooner."

"No problem. Sounds like everything's going well. I'm happy for you." She gave him an uncomfortable smile. "Are you going back to work soon?"

Max shook his head. "Not at the lab. It's still too soon for me to be exposed to the viruses and things that come in there. I'm actually going to be doing some work for Parker. I talked with him a few weeks ago, and he has a lot of new clients and can use the help. That way I can work from home."

"Wow! That's fantastic. You might like that work so much you won't go back to the lab."

"I'll wait and see."

"Well, it's been good talking to you." Heather gave him another forced smile. "Now I'm going to get some of that good food."

"Sure." He tried not to let her dismissal hurt. Obviously she wasn't interested in spending more time with him. Had she moved on—found someone else? The thought had never occurred to him until just this moment. His stomach sank. Sometime before the night was over, he had to find out whether he still had a chance to renew their relationship. He'd faced cancer. He could face anything—even a rejection from the woman he loved.

***

Max bid good-bye to the last of the guests while his parents helped with the cleanup. He sat in a chair near the fireplace in the living room and stared at the flames that flickered behind the screen. He'd failed to find another moment to talk with Heather alone. He should've known with so many people here that any chance to have a meaningful conversation with her was doomed.

He couldn't shake the thought that she had purposely avoided him, giving him no chance to speak with her about anything important. Had he still seen hurt in her eyes—hurt he had caused? He straightened in the chair. Negativity wasn't going to win. Tonight had been a new beginning, and it wasn't going to stop with this party.

"Max." Abby bounded into the room, a book in her hand. "Will you read this to me?"

Max took the book. "Where'd you get this?"

"From your grandma."

Max helped Abby onto his lap. As he opened to the first page of *The Berenstain Bears and the Big Road Race* by Stan and Jan Berenstain, Alex joined them. While Max read the story, he remembered how Aunt Violet used to read this same book to him when he was young. The lessons about not giving up were something he continued to learn. It was a reminder that he shouldn't lose heart when it came to Heather. As Max read the last page, he gave Abby and Alex a hug.

"Okay, kids. Time to head back to the apartment. It's late, and I see two sleepy children. Maybe three," Beth said, eyeing him.

"Not me. I've got places to go and people to see." Max stood as Alex and Abby hopped off his lap.

"Max, you can't be serious." Beth frowned. "It's kind of late to be going out, and you know you have to be careful about being in crowds."

Max put a hand on Beth's shoulder. "Mom, I'm going to visit a friend. I promise I won't be in any crowds or stay out late. I'm a grown man, and I know my limitations. I'm not going to jeopardize my health."

Skepticism painted Beth's face. "You don't have a car."

Max smiled. "I already asked Grandpa Harkin if I could use his, and he said I could."

"I hope I'm not in trouble." Robert grimaced as he glanced at Beth.

"No, I just want him to be careful."

Max held up his hand. "I promise. I will be."

Abby tugged on Max's arm. "Can I go with you?"

He hunkered down beside her. "Not tonight, sweetie. Another time."

As he stood, his mother eyed him again. "I suppose there's no point in asking you where you're going."

"You've got that right." Max jiggled the keys in his pocket. He wasn't about to tell his mom he was trying to make up with Heather. "I've got to get going so I can keep that promise not to stay out late."

Max gave everyone a hug and expressed his thanks again before he headed to the garage and a chance to drive his grandfather's sports car. Heather would be surprised when he showed up in the fancy car. She'd be surprised when he showed up, period. He prayed that she would let him in and give him a chance to ask for her forgiveness.

After Max parked in front of Heather's place, he sat in the car for a few minutes and stared up at her window. Her light was still on. A good thing. He tried to formulate his speech, but he couldn't focus his thoughts. Finally, saying a prayer that Heather would give him a hearing, he slowly climbed the stairs to her apartment.

He stood in front of her door for a few moments as he gathered his courage. He reminded himself that she had come to the celebration, spent weeks practicing to entertain him and kindly greeted him at the party. Those things should signal some encouragement. So why was he standing here afraid to knock?

He took a deep breath and rapped his knuckles against the door. Footsteps sounded on the other side. Locks turned, and the door opened a crack, the safety chain still in place. "We don't want any."

"I'm not selling anything." But maybe he was. Himself. "It's Max."

Heather undid the chain and opened the door a little wider, a puzzled expression on her face. "What are you doing here?"

Max tried to smile even though she didn't sound happy to see him. Oh well. He could plead his case and hope for the best. "I'd like to talk to you. May I come in?"

"I suppose." She stepped aside so he could come in. "It's kind of late for you to be out."

"You sound like my mother."

Heather smiled. "I believe you've accused me of that before, but I'll remind you that I'm not your mother."

"I know that very well." Max chuckled, feeling better already as they reprised some of their old conversations. "Is it okay if I sit down?"

"Sure." Heather motioned toward her brownish-gray sofa that sported a mountain of decorative pillows. Max took a seat, but Heather remained standing as she stared down at him. "Is there a special reason why you've come to see me?"

Max patted the spot next to him on the sofa. "Sit with me?"

Heather shook her head. "I think I'll stand right here for the time being."

"Okay." He felt like the kid who'd been kept after school. She wasn't going to make this simple. "It would be easier to have a conversation if you were sitting here instead of standing there."

"That's probably so, but the last time we talked in this room you were the one who stood there and gave me a declaration that ended our relationship." Heather crossed her arms as she eyed him. "What's changed?"

Max swallowed hard. "Me. I was mistaken. I thought I was doing both of us a favor. I've learned that's not so."

"So you're telling me that you want to get back together?" She still didn't look happy.

Max squirmed in his seat. This was not going well. Was she going to send him packing? He couldn't blame her. She'd seen the worst of him, and yet she'd loved him. But he had pushed that love away. He looked down at the floor, afraid to see her closed expression. "I'm sorry I let my fears about the future steer me in the wrong direction. I thought I was sparing you all the things that might go awry."

"Do you think just because you removed me from

your life that I wasn't going to think about you, worry about you, pray for you?" Anger simmered just beneath the surface of her calmly stated question.

"I know I don't deserve a second chance, but I'm asking for one." He looked up at her, ready to face her anger. "My life isn't ever going to be exactly what it was before, but there's one thing I don't want to change—your presence in it. Can you forgive me for the wrongheaded decision I made? I promise I won't do that again."

She let out a half laugh, half cry. "You expect me to believe you won't ever make any wrongheaded decisions again?"

He deserved her incredulity. Letting out a heavy sigh, he sank back against the sofa. "I didn't mean I won't ever make another bad decision. I'm just saying that I won't push you away again. That's a promise."

"I still haven't heard what I need to hear."

Max searched his brain. He'd apologized. He'd promised not to push her away. He'd asked for forgiveness. What else could there be? Realization hit him. He smiled wryly as he stood and stepped toward her. "You're right. I forgot one very important thing." He gently unfolded her arms, thankful she didn't resist. He put his arms around her waist. "I love you, Heather Watson. You're the most important person in my life, and I want you to stay there. I don't know what's going to happen in the future, but I want you to be there with me when I face whatever I have to face. Can we start over?"

"I love you, too." Tears sparkled in her eyes as she nodded.

"Thank you for giving me another chance. I promise you won't be sorry. I love you more than words can say."

She looked up at him. "Are you allowed to kiss me?"

"Allowed or not allowed. It doesn't matter. I'm going to kiss you." He pulled her closer. Their lips met as she melted into his arms. He would fight to keep his promises and make her happy. No matter what the future brought, he had found the love of his life and his happy ending.

Dear Readers,

Thank you for reading *A Love to Call Mine*. I hope you enjoyed Max and Heather's journey to love and cheered for Max as he battled cancer and the problems from his past. Relying on God when things don't seem to be going your way is sometimes difficult. Max and Heather learn to trust in God and recognize that His plans are the best plans in the long run.

I would love for you to write a review and let other readers know what you think about *A Love to Call Mine*.

I've had so much fun writing the books in the Front Porch Promises series. If you haven't read the other books, I hope you'll look for them. Although each book can be read without having read the others, I enjoy connecting the books through characters and settings. Please check out the other books in the Front Porch Promises series, *A Match to Call Ours, A Place to Call Home, A Family to Call Ours, A Song to Call Ours, A Baby to Call Ours, and A Place to Find Love*. If you would like to get information on my current and upcoming books, please sign up for my newsletter by visiting my website at www.merrilleewhren.com. I love to hear from readers, and you can write to me by using the contact button on my website.

Blessings,

Merrillee Whren

ABOUT THE AUTHOR

Merrillee Whren is an award-winning and a *USA Today* bestselling author who writes inspirational romance. She is the winner of the 2003 Golden Heart Award for best inspirational romance manuscript presented by Romance Writers of America. She has also been the recipient of the RT Reviewers' Choice Award and the Maggie Award for Excellence. She is married to her own personal hero, her husband of forty plus years, and has two grown daughters. She has lived in Atlanta, Boston, Dallas, Chicago and Florida but now makes her home in the Arizona desert. She spends her free time playing tennis or walking while she does the plotting for her novels. Please visit her website, www.merrilleewhren.com or connect with her on social media, https://twitter.com/MerrilleeWhren
https://www.facebook.com/MerrilleeWhren.Author/

OTHER BOOKS by
MERRILLEE WHREN

Dalton Brothers Series
Four Little Blessings
Country Blessings
Homecoming Blessings

Kellersburg Series
Hometown Promise
Hometown Proposal
Hometown Dad
Hometown Cowboy

Front Porch Promises Series
A Match to Call Ours
A Place to Call Home
A Love to Call Mine
A Family to Call Ours
A Song to Call Ours
A Baby to Call Ours
A Place to Find Love

Pinecrest
Second Chance Love
Second Chance Gift
Second Chance Forgiveness

Novellas
Puppy Love and Mistletoe

Puppy Love and Jingle Bells
Puppy Love and Christmas Cookies

Other Books
Miracle Baby
Second Chance Christmas

Village of Hope
Annie's Hope
Kirsten's Mission
Melanie's Resolve